Arden

ALSO BY MELODY ANNE

Undercover Billionaire

Kian

Billionaire Aviators

Turbulent Intentions
Turbulent Desires
Turbulent Waters
Turbulent Intrigue

Arden

AN **UNDERCOVER BILLIONAIRE** NOVEL

MELODY ANNE

This is a work of fiction. Names, characters, organizations, places, events, and incidents are either products of the author's imagination or are used fictitiously.

Published by Montlake Romance, Seattle

www.apub.com

ISBN-13: 9781503902817
ISBN-10: 1503902811

Cover design by Letitia Hasser

Printed in the United States of America

This book is dedicated to my son, Johnathan, who I've enjoyed watching turn from a boy into a young man. What a joy that is to do. I love you.

Prologue

A crash sounded outside Arden Forbes's door before a curse loud enough to wake everyone within a three-mile radius echoed through his nearly empty hallways. Arden turned, ready to take action, when the voice became clearer.

"Dammit, stop!" the voice shouted on the other side of Arden's oversize front door.

The tension left Arden when he realized it was Declan, his oldest brother—and the man didn't appear to be in a good mood. Arden was tempted to stand there for a while to see how irritated his brother might become, but his curiosity about all the noise won out over his desire to torture his oldest sibling.

Swinging open his front door, Arden looked around in confusion. The flowerpot his mother had given him as a housewarming gift was now shattered across his porch. Declan wore a scowl as his fingers held tightly to a leash—attached to a very large German shepherd, who gazed up at Arden with perfectly innocent chocolate eyes.

"Find a new friend?" Arden asked with a chuckle.

Declan grumbled as he stepped forward. Arden could either get out of his brother's way or the two of them were going to crash into each other with the force of a sonic boom. Sometimes that was fun—but tonight, Arden was tired. He'd been grading papers for the past few hours, and that was after a daily double of football practice.

Though he and Declan were about the same height and build, both of them standing at about six foot three with shoulders made for tackle football, and had features that were too similar to make them anything other than brothers, that's where their similarities stopped.

Arden was the most laid-back of all his brothers, not easily rattled. Hell, as a schoolteacher, it was necessary for him to have a calm demeanor. Otherwise, he wouldn't have lasted a single year, let alone ten.

While Arden was the most relaxed of the siblings, the same certainly couldn't be said about Declan. Since the time they'd been teenagers, there had been a dangerous glint in Declan's eyes that tended to make people steer clear of him. Arden wasn't even sure if his brother was aware of it.

"He's not mine," Declan said as he tugged on the leash and the dog obediently followed him inside.

"Looks like yours," Arden pointed out.

"He's yours," he said.

Arden was perfectly aware his brother was a man of few words, but he waited a moment for Declan to continue. When he didn't, Arden decided he'd better nip this in the bud real quick.

"Thanks, but no thanks," Arden said as he led his brother into his oversize gourmet kitchen. What had he been thinking, buying a six-thousand-square-foot house? Maybe it was the urge to start a family, or maybe he was just insane. Hell if he really knew. It was probably his other brother's fault. Kian had made the idea of a big house and family seem pretty damn appealing. "Most people just bring a toaster or something as a housewarming present," he said as he moved to his fancy new espresso maker and pushed a few buttons, inhaling as the scent of dark roast invaded his senses.

"It's eight at night. A bit late for caffeine, isn't it?" Declan asked.

"Nah, it's never too late for coffee," Arden assured him. He finished making his java, throwing in a generous dose of sweet cream, his guilty pleasure, before he moved over to the kitchen island and sat on a stool. "Really—what's up with the dog?"

Declan sighed before moving to the refrigerator and pulling out a bottle of beer, twisting off the top as he sidled over to the island and sat across from Arden. He took a long swallow before he looked up.

"You have a problem at your school," Declan declared.

"Yeah, don't all schools?" Arden said. "I don't know what that has to do with the dog."

"We have intel there's a drug ring going on there," Declan told him. The fire in his brother's eyes most likely matched his own at that moment.

"No way," Arden said. "There's no damn way."

"We don't have hard proof, and we don't know who's running it, but we need info and we need it fast," Declan told him. "We need someone on the inside."

"Where did you come up with the information?" Arden asked.

"You know there are things I can't tell you," Declan said.

Arden let out a frustrated breath. "You want me to help you, but you won't give me anything to go off of," he pointed out.

"I shouldn't even be involving you in this, but I trust you implicitly, and I know you'll want answers, as will the entire town," Declan said.

They stared each other down for several moments, seeing who would blink first. Finally Arden sighed, though he wasn't happy about it.

"I'll see what I can find out," Arden assured his brother.

He'd been a history teacher at Edmonds High School for the past ten years, and he loved his job. He didn't *have* to work for barely any money; he did it because the kids mattered to him—his community mattered. There was no way he was letting some twisted drug lord screw with his school . . . in his town.

"And now you have Max to help you," Declan said.

"Explain," Arden told him. He knew Declan had a plan, and since it involved his school, he was a lot more willing to listen.

"Max is officially retired. He was injured in a drug raid last year and isn't moving as quickly as he used to. He's served his community well and deserves to live out his golden years, or whatever the hell that Jeannette—the lady I got him from—said," Declan explained. "But he's not ready to be off the job yet. He's brilliant and can smell drugs from a mile away. He's also loyal. His handler got killed the same time Max was injured last year."

"Oh man, I'm sorry," Arden said, now understanding that lost look in the dog's eyes. His partner and best friend was gone. That sucked.

"Jeannette told me she hadn't seen him respond in such a positive way since the accident until the day I walked in. I think he was meant to be in our family," Declan said, oddly mushy for his tough-as-nails brother.

"So what does this have to do with me?" Arden asked.

"He's yours now. You take him to school, keep him with you at all times. He'll solve this case without the kids having to be aware of what's going on," Declan told him.

Arden looked at the dog. Max stared back. There was almost a challenge in the canine's expressive eyes. He was taunting Arden, maybe even assessing him. Suddenly Arden felt as if he were in a job interview—and coming up short.

"I give him back when this is done?" Arden asked.

Declan smiled, knowing he'd gotten his way. "We'll talk about it then."

"Declan . . ." Arden's voice trailed off as he glared at his brother.

"I'll get Max's stuff. You and him need bonding time before school on Monday."

With that, his brother walked from the house. Arden would normally follow his brother and give a hand, but instead he found himself locking eyes with Max.

"This is going to be fun, isn't it?" he complained.

Arden would have sworn on a stack of Bibles the damn dog's lip quirked up and he winked at him. The gauntlet was being thrown down. If it hadn't been for the very real possibility drugs were being sifted through his school, Arden might have felt like laughing at the dog. But tonight, mirth was the furthest thing from his mind.

He and this dog appeared to have a crisis to solve, whether Arden wanted to be a part of it or not. Max continued staring at him, and Arden was finally the one to break, looking away as Declan came back into the room.

"You *will* take the mutt when this is over," Arden said, hearing what sounded like a grumble coming from the otherwise quiet dog.

"Yeah, yeah," Declan said. "Gotta run. We'll talk more tomorrow."

And with that, Arden's traitorous brother left.

This was going to be a long weekend. He refused to look at the dog again as he set up his food and water bowls. Those eyes were far too knowing for him. Kids he could handle, but apparently animals were out of his comfort zone.

Chapter One

Keera Thompson stopped midstride when she turned the corner and saw her office door ajar. School had been out for hours, and this was the one room in the building the janitorial staff didn't go into unless she was right there with them. The confidentiality of her students mattered to her, and too many times private information got leaked because principals and/or teachers were lax about who was allowed near important documents.

Though she tried telling herself she must've left the door open when she'd gone for a stroll to the soda machine, a sense of unease was causing her spine to tingle. Even if she thought she'd only be gone for a couple of minutes, she always shut that door. Sometimes what was supposed to be a quick stroll ended up turning into a long walk to clear her brain.

Moving quietly, Keera stepped forward, her ears on high alert as she listened for anything suspicious. There wasn't so much as the sound of a ticking clock, which was eerie in its own sense, but even with no unusual noises, her heart was thudding too hard to ease her sense of dread. Cautiously, she pushed her door open with her booted foot. Blackness greeted her.

After a few tense seconds, she began to realize she was being foolish, so she moved through the doorway and was reaching for the light switch when a cold chill washed through her. Looking up, she noticed a shadow behind her desk—and it was moving.

Her pupils dilated as her eyes adjusted to the darkness, and she realized a man was standing there, barely visible in his black clothes. Before she had even a second to process what was happening, the man began moving toward her, which brought him into clearer focus. Not a trace of skin showed; even his head was obscured by a black mask.

Fight or flight kicked in with a vengeance—and she was definitely fleeing.

Flight. It was time to get out of Dodge. It was late and she was utterly alone, her janitorial staff currently working in the gym and all of her teachers long gone. Before she was able to flee, the man shot at her like a bullet. Keera didn't even have time to let out a warning cry, just in case someone happened along.

Moving at lightning speed, the intruder's body slammed into hers, sending her flying sideways, straight into the filing cabinets she'd been so worried about protecting. Her neck jerked to the left, and bright dots flashed before her eyes as her head cracked against the unforgiving metal.

Pain ripped through her as she fought not to lose consciousness. Dizziness made it difficult to remain on her feet, but she didn't know where the man was, or if he was coming for her again.

The sound of a door shutting barely registered in her brain, and somewhere inside, she knew that meant she wasn't alone, but it was taking her longer to process things than it should have. But then her office door hit the wall as the man fled her office, and she heard the blessed sound of footsteps fading as he got farther away. She should go after the person, but there wasn't a chance of that.

The first step away from the cabinet nearly undid her, the throb in her head so intense it made her nauseous. She gripped the wall as she flicked on the light and squinted around her office. She'd only been gone ten minutes, so the intruder couldn't have been there long.

What in the world was going on? Things like this didn't happen in Edmonds, Washington. She'd taken this job as school principal less than a month earlier *because* she'd wanted out of the city. She'd needed to get away from the fear of coming to work, wondering if this was the day she was going to be attacked.

Had she made a mistake coming to this town?

No. She wouldn't allow one scary incident to skew her opinion of an otherwise peaceful place where the sidewalks were clean, the merchants friendly, and her students happy and eager to learn.

Sure, there were problems. Of course there were. No place was without them, but overall, Edmonds was a haven compared to other places in the world. Shaking her head, Keera looked around her office, but she didn't move. It was officially a crime scene, and she didn't want to erase evidence the criminal might have left behind.

Her desk drawers had been opened, the contents spilled across the floor. Her computer monitor was tipped over, and she hoped not broken. The one picture she kept on the corner of the desk was halfway across the room, as if he'd swept his arm across the desktop with no regard to noise or destruction.

She was more upset over the picture being thrown than her desk being gone through. She didn't keep anything in there that would be of value to anyone but her. She might have thought the person was a student, but his size assured her he couldn't be.

The school wasn't that big, and she'd have an inkling of who'd plowed into her if she had any future NFL players wandering her halls. She needed to call the police, but she was having a difficult time tearing herself away from her visual perusal of the room.

She spent more time in this office, in this school, than she did in her small apartment. Work had become her main focus in life, and to have someone so carelessly come into her sanctuary and treat it with such disregard made her feel violated.

Her shoulders stiffening, Keera stopped her mind from traveling down that path. She refused to act the victim or pity herself. She'd make sure the person was caught; then she'd have answers as to why he'd been in her school.

Pulling her cell phone from her back pocket, Keera dialed the Edmonds Police Department. As school principal, she'd memorized that number the day she moved into the sleepy town. She'd always hoped she wouldn't have to use it, but she knew being prepared was necessary.

The call was answered on the third ring by a very perky woman. "Edmonds PD. How may I help you?"

"This is Principal Thompson at Edmonds High School. I've had a break-in," Keera said, hating the slight quaver in her voice. She told herself it was only because her head was pounding and the adrenaline was still surging through her.

"Is anyone hurt?" the woman asked, her voice going from perky to alert in an instant.

"No. I'm the only person in this part of the building," Keera answered.

"Is the perp still present?" the woman asked.

"I don't think so. He ran from my office, and I heard his steps heading toward the door."

"Was he armed?" was the next question.

"I . . . uh . . . I don't know. My office was dark, and as soon as he spotted me, he lunged for the doorway," Keera said. She'd tell the whole story when the police showed up.

"One moment," the woman told her.

Keera heard her speaking to someone, or possibly into a dispatch radio.

"Okay, there's a unit nearby. They'll be there shortly. I want you to step into your office and lock your door just in case the perp didn't flee the building," the woman said.

"I'll check if he's still here," Keera told her, moving into the hallway, doing the exact opposite of what the woman had told her.

"Ma'am, please wait for the officers," the woman said, her voice firm.

Keera was shaking, but she'd already let her fears get in the way once. She couldn't keep hiding away when her school was in danger. "This is my school, and I need to do this. I should've done it already."

The woman continued telling her to go to her office, but Keera just thanked her and hung up the phone. She made it to the large double doors at the end of the hallway, which were closed. Using her key, she unlocked the right side so the alarm wouldn't sound, then pushed it open, her heart thundering as she looked out into the semi-lit parking lot that was nearly empty.

There wasn't a sign of life anywhere. When she stepped back inside, leaving the door unlocked so the officers could get in, she closed her eyes and listened for any unusual noises.

All was quiet.

Her school was safe. She knew she'd feel something if she were somehow still in danger. If she hadn't been so lost in her own thoughts as she'd made her way back toward her office, she was sure she'd have felt something was out of place sooner than the moment she'd spotted her open door.

She leaned against the wall and waited for the officers to arrive. It was less than a minute later when she heard footsteps rushing down the back hallway, heading in her direction. Keera's heart began pounding so loud it drowned out the sound of whoever was in such a hurry to get to her.

Before she had time to decide what to do, a person turned the corner, his face lit up as he gazed at his cell phone and continued forward.

"Ethan," Keera called.

The man stumbled a step, always a bit klutzy, and looked up at her in confusion as his hand lifted and he pushed his ever-sliding glasses back up his nose so he could see her more clearly.

"Keera? What are you still doing here?" he asked as he took a good look at her. Confusion vanished as concern lit his eyes.

"I'm here this late just about every night," she said with a wry smile, feeling safer in his presence. It wasn't that she felt he could protect her, though she'd never say that thought out loud. The hallways just felt a lot less ominous with two people versus one.

Ethan Dower was her vice principal and had been at the school for twenty years. He was a good man, at least to her. What she appreciated most about him was that anything she needed done, he was the person she could go to. He'd spent countless hours familiarizing her with the building. He liked to brag he'd once been a student in the very halls he now walked as staff.

Keera knew she'd rather walk over hot coals than be a principal at the school she'd attended, but some people took comfort in staying in one place their entire life. Maybe if she'd had a different experience when she was younger, she'd feel how Ethan did.

Ethan had never been married, and though he wasn't the largest of men, he had beautiful green eyes that were hidden behind his bifocals. He rarely ever smiled, and she'd quickly learned he was a no-nonsense kind of man, but still, she'd managed to grow attached to him, as she spent more time with him than any other person in the town.

He was somewhere in his midforties, though with his receding hairline he seemed a little older. He had told her that keeping the kids in line was a full-time job, and if the students didn't respect him, they wouldn't do what needed to be done. So the fact that he was losing his hair worked to his advantage, as he didn't want to look like *a damn high school kid*—his exact words.

And though it appeared Ethan was always quick to leave when the day was over, he normally was the first person there each morning, making sure everything was good to go for a new school day. Though he was certainly respected, the one thing Keera didn't love about Ethan was how he viewed the majority of the students.

It was almost as if he was just waiting for them to fail. Though Keera had wanted to get away from a large city school, she had always held the belief that the majority of people were good. She refused to allow a few bad apples to change her view of the world. Ethan seemed to think his view was the only correct one.

"Keera, what's going on?" Ethan asked, pulling her back into the here and now.

She shook away the cobwebs before speaking. "Someone broke into my office. They got away."

His eyes widened, and he looked around as if he was afraid the intruder was going to jump out of one of the lockers and attack. Then his eyes flashed back to her face before he scanned her from head to toe.

"He didn't touch you, did he?" he said, a protective edge entering his voice that, surprisingly, caused her to grin. Ethan certainly wasn't old enough to be her father, but his demeanor made her think he would've been a pretty good dad, and maybe that would have made him a lot less grumpy.

"Yes, I'm good. He ran into me as he rushed from the room, and I got a decent smack on the head when it connected with the file cabinet, but I'm okay," she told him.

"Let me check." He stepped forward, his fingers instantly twining in her hair. She was so shocked, she stood there for a moment as he felt for injuries. Then she pulled away. He was just concerned for her, but he'd never invaded her personal bubble like that before, and she wasn't comfortable with it.

"I promise I'm okay," she said with a smile she hoped would ease the look of rejection in his gaze. He'd just been acting as a friend, and she'd pushed him away, like she did with everyone.

"Think it was a student?" he asked, now refusing to look her in the eyes.

"No. The guy was too big. He was dressed in black from head to toe, so I really don't have much to give the police," she said on a sigh of frustration.

"Pity," he said as he began pacing the hallway.

Lights flashed through the glass doors she'd unlocked, and Keera let out a sigh of relief she hadn't realized she'd been holding in. The police had arrived.

Chapter Two

The sound of the glass door knocking into the doorstop made Keera jump even though she was well aware of the officers' arrival. She turned from Ethan and listened to the sound of several pairs of shoes rushing across her clean hallway floors.

When she saw a pair of dark brown eyes about three feet from the ground, it took her a moment to realize there was a large German shepherd attached to a leash heading her way. This night had already been odd, and now, along with several officers, there was also an animal in her school.

Her eyes trailed up the leash to the hand gripping it, then to the concerned eyes of Arden Forbes, her history teacher. What was he doing there? And why was a dog with him?

The intensity of Arden's gaze made her unable to maintain eye contact with him, and she found her gaze straying back to the dog that was quickly approaching. The animal was pretty adorable—so was the man holding the leash.

That was a thought Keera *absolutely* didn't want to have. She'd been at the school a short time but already knew *all* about Arden and his sexy siblings—and the fact that the town considered them to be its most eligible bachelors. All of them except for Kian, who was now a happily married man.

As soon as she'd caught wind of how this small town worked, and the many ways of gossip within it, Keera had avoided Arden as if he were an infectious disease. She was in no way in a place to date anyone, let alone someone like him. She was much too broken, and she certainly didn't have a whole lot of faith in the opposite sex.

But Keera would have to be blind, deaf, and have no sense of smell for her not to notice Arden. Not only was he a teacher at her school, but he also coached the football team—and apparently worked out with them at each practice, as his body was certainly sexy as hell.

She appreciated how he filled out a pair of jeans, and how his wide shoulders tapered down into a perfect waist. He wore his dark locks just a tad too long and seemed to have a permanent five-o'clock shadow that also increased his sex appeal. Add to all of that his crystal-blue eyes, and she could see why the female teachers, both young and old, stopped in their tracks just to look at him.

Though his eyes always seemed to be filled with humor, there was also a presence about him that spoke of power. He was confident in himself, and that quality had always been appealing to her. And not a lot could shake Keera after the life she'd lived, but she had to admit, at least to herself, that Arden Forbes terrified her. It wasn't that she was afraid of the man himself, but more afraid of what he made her feel.

Behind Arden walked a couple of police officers carrying what she assumed were crime-scene kits. *Wow.* Just the sight of Arden along with his new companion had made her temporarily forget about the intruder in her office.

Stupid. Her reaction was just plain stupid.

"Ms. Thompson?" an officer asked.

"Yes, I'm Keera Thompson, the high school principal," she replied, taking her eyes away from Arden as he and the dog stood back and watched her speak with the officers.

"I'm Officer Miller. This is my partner, Officer Jayden. If you want to show us the area the intruder was in and tell us what happened, we can sweep the scene."

"Thank you for your quick response," Keera said. She knew this was a small town where everyone knew everyone—*and* all their business. But she was an outsider here, so she wanted to impress them, wanted to fit in.

She went over the details with the officers, who then took their kits and went inside her office to look for fingerprints and anything else that might lead them to the discovery of who'd been in there.

"Do you have any idea of who was here or what they wanted?" The question startled her. Arden and his dog had approached without her being aware of it. For a man and animal who were both so large, it was even more intimidating how stealthily they could come up on someone. Of course, she was a little flustered at the moment, making it that much easier.

"No. His head was completely covered, and I don't know why he'd be in my office," she said after a long pause. Before he could say anything else or she could add more, Ethan stepped back up to her side and sent a less-than-accommodating look Arden's way.

"Why are you here so late, and what's up with the dog?" Ethan asked.

"I heard the call come in over the scanner, and since I teach here, and this school matters to me, I wanted to make sure everything was okay," Arden said, his tone implying he had just as little love for her vice principal as it appeared the man had for him.

"We have it under control," Ethan told him, puffing out his chest the slightest bit. Keera seemed to have been forgotten in their macho posturing. She didn't mind.

"Obviously, things aren't under control," Arden said as he pointedly shifted his eyes toward Keera's office, where the officers were doing their job.

"Just because we've had one little break-in doesn't mean the school needs to have a SWAT team here," Ethan said with a wave of his hand.

"Thanks for the compliment, but last I checked, I wasn't on a SWAT team," Arden said with a laugh that stiffened Ethan's shoulders even more.

"What's up with the dog?" Ethan repeated. Keera had noticed Arden hadn't said anything about the mutt that was currently turning his big brown eyes to look between Ethan and Arden. The dog turned and looked at her, and Keera felt her lips twitch. It was almost as if she could read the dog's thoughts, and he was asking her for some popcorn to watch the show.

"He's my new pet," Arden said, though Keera wondered what the story was behind that, because he didn't appear to be happy with his new friend. "He's a retired police dog, and I thought it was a good idea to have him here, with what's happening."

"A break-in?" Ethan asked, seeming a little hostile and confused at the same time.

"The break-in is the tip of the iceberg. I'm talking about the drug problem going on in our school."

"What are you talking about? There aren't drugs in this school," she said. She wasn't going to sit by while her school's reputation was on the line. Yes, Arden had been a teacher there far longer than she'd been principal, but she was in charge of this place now, and she cared what was being said about it.

"I've heard differently," Arden said, the full intensity of his gaze locked on her.

Keera felt as if she was being interrogated—and it wasn't coming up favorably for her. She said nothing, holding his gaze, though it wasn't easy to do. The dog nudged her leg, and she was able to finally break eye contact.

"This is bullshit," Ethan said. "You won't find anything."

"Good, then none of us have to worry," Arden said. "But I think Max and I are gonna do a sweep of the place."

"And what gives you the authority?" Ethan challenged.

"I work here," Arden said. His shoulders seemed to widen a couple of more inches as he towered over Ethan. Keera almost felt sorry for her vice principal. But she wasn't too worried, because the man didn't seem the type to back down.

"Or you just think your family money gives you the right to do whatever you want," Ethan grumbled.

Anger leaped into Arden's eyes, and Keera felt herself take a retreating step. He might seem easygoing, but there was fire underneath his relaxed attitude. That was something she was definitely taking note of.

"I don't need anyone giving me the right to do anything," Arden said in a low growl. Ethan seemed to realize he'd gone too far because he looked away from Arden.

"I've got to go. Let me know if the cops find anything," Ethan said to Keera before he turned toward the front doors and walked away.

Keera wanted to call out to the man that he was a traitor for leaving her with the now-seething schoolteacher—who still seemed uncomfortable with his new pet. She felt a little bad for the dog, too.

But right now she was more concerned about her school. She'd become a principal in the first place to protect students because of what had happened in her past—and because of how she'd lost her brother. If there were drugs in her school, she'd find out the cause, and the perps would be harshly dealt with. If she could save others the way she hadn't been able to save her brother, then she could call her life a success, no matter how messed up she was on the inside.

"Do you know if anything was stolen?" Arden asked, pulling her from her thoughts.

"I didn't have time to look. It happened very quickly, but it didn't seem as if he had time to get away with anything," she answered.

"Do you think it was random?" he pushed.

"I don't know," she said, feeling frustration building again. "Has this happened at the school before?"

"Not since I've been teaching here. We've had random acts of mischief, and students up to no good, but the building hasn't been broken into before," he told her. "Could it have anything to do with you personally?"

That thought put a shiver of dread straight down her spine. She wanted to give Arden an emphatic *no*, but she couldn't do that. She did have ghosts in her past that could rise up to haunt her. She wasn't going to tell this man about her personal life, though.

"I . . . I don't know," she answered, deciding an outright lie was unacceptable.

He stepped closer, making her incredibly aware of his body temperature, giving her a false sense of safety as his scent engulfed her in what felt like a protective cocoon. It rattled her even more than she'd already been. She could see herself leaning into him, seeking comfort from him—and almost did just that before she looked up, thankfully stopping herself.

His eyes narrowed as he regarded her, looking as if he was trying to read her mind. She looked down at the dog again, whose head was tilted. The soulful brown eyes seemed to be seeing right through her, reminding Keera why she kept herself isolated.

She didn't want to share her secrets with the world, and she didn't want to be judged for things beyond her control. She just wanted to live her life the best way she could and never put herself in a position where she could be hurt again.

What had the intruder been after? And was it personal? Keera honestly didn't know. But she did know for sure she wasn't going to play the victim. She'd get to the bottom of this. And she'd keep her school safe. Even if that put her life in danger. Even if that meant that the secrets of her past she so desperately wanted to keep buried rose to the surface.

Chapter Three

Arden had been both relieved and disappointed when Max found nothing at the school. He was glad because maybe—just maybe—that meant his brother was wrong, and he could breathe easier. He was disappointed because that meant he was going to have the frustrating dog awhile longer.

As if the mutt in question knew he was thinking ill thoughts of him, Max stopped and sat, nearly making Arden trip as he continued walking while the leash suddenly went taut. Looking back at the dog, he could have sworn the damn thing wore a triumphant grin.

"Come on, Fido, it's time to go," Arden grumbled.

The dog's eyes seemed to narrow. That made Arden smile for the first time since the night before, when he'd been roaming the halls of his school with his very sexy principal walking at his side.

"He's a prestigious dog, not some mutt named Fido," Declan told him.

"He's a pain in the ass and didn't prove very useful last night," Arden pointed out.

"Give it some time. Something else has to be frustrating you more than the dog," Declan said.

Arden could try to hide it, but what was the point? "The dang principal is driving me insane. I think she wears the same perfume daily, just to send me over the edge. Of course, considering she avoids me most of the time, that might be my ego speaking instead of my brain," he admitted.

"So you got some alone time with her last night . . . in the dark hallways?" Declan asked with a smug turning of his lips.

Arden sighed. Brothers were a pain in the ass. "I might have been a bit aware of her with just the two of us walking down the abandoned hallways. But I decided long ago not to date complicated women. I have a fulfilling life, a great career, a family most envy, and I'm secure in myself."

"So you don't like women?" Declan asked.

"Hell no, that's not what I'm saying. I like women, hell, *love* them. I just refuse to be one of those guys who fall into the dating games so many people like to play," he said.

"What makes you think she likes to play games?" Declan asked.

"I figured out within the first ten minutes of meeting Keera Thompson that she was far too complicated for me. She's guarded, has secrets, and is mysterious, and not necessarily in the good way. I've tried staying away from her, but I'm failing on that front."

"Just avoid her when you're not dealing with this investigation," Declan suggested.

"That's easier said than done. Just walking down the hallway, I can feel her before I even see her," Arden admitted.

"Maybe you should just give up and find out if complicated is exactly what you need in your life," Declan said.

"Keera is trouble with a big, fat capital *T*," Arden said.

"Yeah, but hasn't trouble always led to the best adventures in life?" Declan asked.

"Who are you? Aren't you the suspicious one?" Arden asked.

"Yeah, but I also love seeing you so twitchy," Declan said.

"I seem to recall most of my trouble involved you and my other siblings," Arden said. "No matter what mess we got into, we had a hell of a good time while we did it."

"That's my point," Declan told him.

"Yeah, following the rules can be a little boring if we get into too much of a rut," Arden told him.

"You'll figure it out," Declan said. "Now, get your dog in line. Let's go to my office."

"Max, it's time to move," Arden commanded as he tugged on the leash. The dog still refused to move. He wanted to kick his brother's ass for this brilliant idea of man's best friend. What had Declan been thinking?

Taking a deep breath before speaking again, he calmed his voice. "Max, can we go?" Now he was asking the dog's permission to leave? What in the hell was the world coming to?

The dog seemed to smirk at him again as he rose, aligning himself next to Arden. *Seriously! The dog was now demanding respect?* Arden had never been an animal lover, and now he knew why.

"Do you actually listen to my tone?" he asked the dog, not finding it foolish at all to be speaking to him. "You obviously know your name, and seem to not listen worth crap."

The dog looked at him with that smug expression Arden was growing used to, and if he wouldn't have been accused of going insane, he'd swear the dog nodded at him, as if not only understanding Arden's tone, but the question he'd asked. Maybe Arden needed more sleep.

"Fine. But just know I'm not buying you any bones," Arden grumbled.

A soft noise came from the dog's throat, definitely sounding like a scoff. Arden knew he was starting off his day in a bad way when a dog was mocking him.

Declan moved to the back of the room and sat behind his massive desk, picking up a thick folder filled with notes and images. He looked up after a few seconds, not giving away what he was thinking about.

"Anything in those folders, since you seem to have all the answers?" Arden asked. Declan gave the closest thing he ever gave to a smile as he smirked at his brother.

"I know what goes on in this town, as should you," Declan said.

"Yeah, you know way too much," Arden said with a relaxed tone. "This chair is great. I might need to take it from you."

"Get your own," Declan told him.

"It's more fun to take yours."

"So you didn't find anything last night?" Declan pushed, getting right back to business.

"You're no fun anymore," Arden told him. Declan just gazed at him with that no-nonsense look. With a sigh, Arden decided he'd ribbed his brother enough. "We don't have a heck of a lot of info. There was a broken window in the back of the school, so we know a man got in and was in Keera's office rifling around, but he didn't seem to get away with anything. Max and I investigated the building for a couple of hours, finding nothing. I don't know if you think this break-in and the suspected drugs have anything to do with each other, but the cops didn't seem all that concerned."

Declan sat back as he took his time processing what Arden had just told him. That was another thing about his brother—he wasn't impulsive. Arden looked forward to the day when some tornado of a woman came into his brother's life and swept Declan right off the ground. He'd pay money to watch that storm.

"I think the two are definitely connected. I've told you before I don't believe in coincidence. I also don't ever trust anyone," he added.

"Including family?" Arden asked with a raised brow. He wasn't worried.

"That's a stupid question. I'd die for family," Declan said as he waved his hand in the air. He was so nonchalant about it, but the reality was, they'd all take a bullet for each other. There was no doubt there was trust and love between them.

"And what do you really think of Keera, all kidding aside?" Arden asked.

Declan sat back as he studied his brother. Arden suddenly felt as if he were under a microscope, and he fought the urge to shift in his seat. That was just stupid.

"I'm just processing more what *you* think of the principal," Declan said.

"What I think doesn't really matter," Arden told him. "You've always had a good instinct about people, so it matters more what you think."

Arden was shocked by how much he wanted his brother to tell him there was nothing fishy going on with Keera. She couldn't be a bad guy. She definitely had secrets, and she was complicated, but she wasn't a villain—or at least he hoped not.

"I don't trust anyone," Declan said again, and Arden felt disappointment run through him.

"Do you know something I should know?" Arden asked.

Declan again gave nothing away. "Nothing I need to share," his brother said noncommittally. Arden tensed. There was something his brother wasn't telling him. He knew there was no way he'd get it out of Declan until his brother was ready to talk, which made it that much worse. Declan sighed and Arden waited. "I won't rule Keera out . . . but I don't necessarily think she's involved."

The relief flowing through Arden was a bit ridiculous. Just because his brother felt a certain way didn't make it the truth. Maybe there were drugs in the school, and maybe Keera was involved. Most likely, that wasn't the case, but Declan believing or not believing it to be the case shouldn't influence what Arden felt about it. But of course, it did.

"How long do you think I'll be keeping this mutt?" Arden asked. He didn't want to talk about Keera or her possible role in the underworld of drugs anymore. It was too confusing for his muddled brain.

"As long as it takes," Declan told him.

"He's a pain in my ass," Arden said, glancing at the dog out of the corner of his eye. He felt a little guilty talking bad about him while he was listening.

"Be a better pet owner," Declan said.

"Max isn't a pet. He's a working animal," Arden pointed out.

"He's one hell of a worker, but he's also a dog, who needs attention," Declan said. Then his eyes narrowed. "And he's definitely earned respect."

"Like you'd give either attention or respect to an animal," Arden grumbled. He couldn't look at Max now, because he felt even more disloyal.

"Hell, I like animals a lot more than people," Declan said.

"Yeah, I get your point," Arden told him. "But I'm *not* getting attached to this dog. I don't want any animals, much less this old thing."

"Good luck with that," Declan said with his version of a chuckle.

Arden's phone rang, and he glanced down at the screen to see a blocked number. He thought about letting it go to voice mail, but somehow he was a little jumpy as he gazed at the ringing phone. He answered.

"Your principal's at the school, and she's in trouble," the male voice said.

Arden's eyes narrowed, and he didn't miss how his brother tensed as he gazed at Arden, unable to hear the other person, but knowing from his brother's reaction that the call wasn't good.

"Explain," Arden said in a crisp voice.

The phone call ended, and Arden looked over at his brother.

"What was that about?" Declan asked.

"I didn't recognize the voice, but the caller said Keera was in trouble," Arden told him. He was already on his feet and moving over to Max, who seemed to be on instant alert just from Arden's body language.

"I'll come with you," Declan said, rising as he tucked a sidearm in his holster.

"No. It might be nothing," Arden told him.

"What's she doing at the school on a Saturday, anyway?" Declan asked. It was more than obvious how guilty this was making Keera look. She might just be the bad guy at the end of the day. Arden might have to face that.

"Like you don't already know where she is and why she's there," Arden pointed out.

"Just seeing if you knew," his brother commented.

"Yeah, most principals don't come in on the weekends for the kids, but I like the program she's running. Instead of detention, she has classes they can take, like art, music, woodworking, and community service. She's gotten a lot of people from town to volunteer."

"She doesn't seem to be such a bad person," Declan said.

"You confuse me," Arden admitted.

"I told you, I don't trust anyone, but I also follow the clues. Just . . ." Declan stopped as he looked down. "Just be aware," he finished.

"Of what?" Arden asked, his voice rising loud enough to make Max tense.

"All in good time," Declan said.

Arden wanted to punch a wall.

"Whatever," he snapped. "She might be doing all of this as a show of smoke and mirrors, or she might be who she says she is, but you obviously know something, and since you won't share it, I'm going to see if the caller was another distraction or if the woman is actually in trouble."

"You aren't moving very fast for a worried man," Declan said.

"I'm going," Arden told him, feeling guilty about his brother pointing that out.

"Let me know if you need me," Declan said as Arden began walking from Declan's office.

"You know I will," Arden called back as he picked up his pace. Taking his time was no longer an option.

Though he tried telling himself there was nothing to worry about, that the call had most likely been someone's idea of a joke, Arden couldn't erase the sense of unease he felt.

Someone *had* broken into Keera's office the night before, and his brother wasn't a man to take rumors and run with them. There might be drugs going through Arden's school, and *if* there were, and *if* the principal *wasn't* involved, then she might be in the way of some very bad people.

It was time to get some answers.

Chapter Four

Arden climbed into his truck and hit the gas pedal as soon as the engine was running. He needed to get to Keera, see her with his own eyes, and know she was okay. Then he was sure he'd feel foolish about taking the bait from some kid who'd managed to disguise his voice and scare his teacher. Hell, Arden had pulled many pranks on his teachers in his youth.

Of course, he'd never threatened any of them.

There were several cars in the school parking lot when Arden pulled up. He climbed from the truck, Max at his side, as he held the leash and moved forward. He had his keys pulled out and was heading toward the front door when Max looked over at the side of the building, his body tense.

Without a second thought, Arden changed direction, moving toward the employee entrance at the back of the school. Before he could turn the corner, he heard the sound of rising voices. Max let out a low growl that would, and should, scare anyone the sound was aimed at.

"Let's find out what's happening," Arden whispered to Max, whose gaze was focused ahead of them.

"This isn't funny and needs to stop now," Keera said. There was determination in her tone, but he could hear the faint trace of fear underlining her words. The thought of whoever was scaring her, holding her hostage, truly pissed Arden off.

He quickly moved forward as a male voice spoke words that made Arden want to shoot the guy.

"Can't we all just get along? We can have a nice chat and all be friends, can't we?" The voice was anything other than friendly.

Keera was in trouble, but not nearly the trouble this punk was in. Arden was going to do some major damage to the guy if he so much as laid one finger on her. He stepped around the corner, determined to be this woman's white knight.

There were three thugs, definitely not high school students. He had to adjust his approach, because dealing with kids was one thing, dealing with street thugs was another. He should've taken this a lot more seriously from the moment he'd gotten the call.

"You absolutely don't want to do this," Keera said. She was one hell of a strong woman. It was obvious she was nervous, but he was impressed, and somewhat irritated, to find her shoulders stiff as she took a step closer to the one who seemed to be the ringleader of this rough-looking group. "Now get off my property."

Arden was in fight mode as soon as he noticed the knife the one confronting Keera was wielding. She might not realize the danger she was in, but Arden knew how quickly a situation like this could escalate.

"I don't feel like going anywhere," the guy said. Arden didn't want to startle the punk and have him grab Keera. He had to be smart.

"I don't care what you want," Keera said. The guy's eyes narrowed as he stepped closer to her. The foolish woman didn't try to run, just squared her shoulders. Arden knew it was time to announce himself.

"You need to drop your weapon and step away from Ms. Thompson," Arden said, his Glock in hand. He normally didn't carry it at school, though he had his concealed carry license. He hadn't felt the need to until yesterday. He was damn glad he had it on him now.

Max growled at his side, assuring the men they were serious. The two punks who'd been hanging back, leering at Keera, whipped their heads around, their eyes going wide—most likely from Max's snarling mouth, versus the gun aimed their way.

They didn't hesitate a moment longer before they turned and ran away. Max's body trembled from his need to pursue them, but Arden was focused on the one with the knife and wanted Max by his side. The others would be found quickly enough.

"I said, back away from Ms. Thompson," Arden told the guy. His tone assured the punk he wasn't going to repeat his words again.

The man finally took a step back, but he didn't release his blade. With Keera a little less in danger, Arden slowly moved forward. He didn't want to shoot anyone, would much rather take the thug down and have his ass thrown in jail. Maybe Arden should've brought his brother. He should have called the cops the second he'd arrived. There was a lot he should've done.

"You aren't that different from your brother, you know," the guy said, and Keera's head whipped back to him.

"What does that mean?" she demanded. "How do you know my brother? Is that why you're here?" She stepped toward the thug, making Arden clench his teeth.

"Yeah, I knew him, just like I know you. He wasn't a good guy, and you aren't any better. You can put on airs all day long, but there are some of us who know the truth about you," the punk said as he backed away a few more steps, keeping Arden and his very irritated dog in his line of sight.

"You need to drop the weapon and surrender," Arden said as he drew closer to Keera.

"Kiss my ass," the guy said. Arden wanted to teach him a few things about manners.

Keera stared at Arden with almost a death glare before facing the guy again, no longer looking frightened. She seemed more determined than ever before.

"Are you the one who was in my office?" Keera demanded. "What do you want with me? And what does it have to do with my brother?"

"Some of it you'll find out," the guy sneered. "The rest doesn't matter 'cause your brother's dead."

"If there's anything you know, you damn well better tell me." Keera took another step toward the punk, and Arden was ready to strangle her. She definitely had no regard for her safety.

"Keera, back up," Arden told her.

She ignored Arden as she had a stare-down with the knife-wielding punk.

"We'll be in touch," the guy said before he sent one more worried glance in Arden's direction. Then he turned and sprinted away. Max tugged against his leash again, and Arden thought about releasing him. But the guy had a knife, and Arden didn't want to take a chance on Max getting injured. Keera took a step in the kid's direction as if she was planning on chasing him down. Arden stepped into her path.

"Don't even think about it," he said, his voice a low growl. Max looked up and let out a warning sound, as if echoing Arden. He was liking the mutt a little bit more by the moment.

"But . . ." Keera stopped trying to explain herself as she looked into Arden's eyes. It was more than obvious he wasn't going to allow this to happen. "You don't understand," she said, her shoulders sagging.

He stepped closer to her. This woman was drawing him in; she was in danger, and everything within him wanted to protect her, keep the rest of the world away from her. It was an odd feeling for him. She was practically vibrating with raw emotion.

"He might have been able to tell us something," she said, her composure barely in place.

"I have no doubt this isn't finished. Right now, I just want you safe," he said, stepping closer to her, feeling comforted by the heat emanating from her body, letting him know she was uninjured.

"What does it have to do with my brother? How is this all connected?" she asked, looking at him with such vulnerability he couldn't help but reach up and brush her hair away from her face.

She was either lost in emotion, or maybe trusting him a little more, but either way, she didn't push him away. And he didn't press his luck. He wanted to pull her into his arms, but he knew it would take time.

"I don't want you to get yourself killed," he told her, his voice quiet.

"But if he knows something, it's worth the risk," she said.

"Hold that thought." Arden pulled out his phone and dialed the police, letting them know what was happening. He hung up, then focused on Keera again. "What do you think he could give you?"

"You heard as much as I did," she said in frustration.

"How did you end up out here with them?" Arden asked.

He reached out to touch her again, and she scooted back. There was something in her eyes telling him she wanted to accept his touch, but something was holding her back. They were at a standstill.

"I was just taking a walk, getting some air, and they appeared. I don't know why they're after me," she said. Arden knew she wasn't telling him the entire truth. There was a hint of guilt in her eyes.

"What are you hiding from me?" he asked.

Her eyes connected with his and, for just a moment, time stood still. She looked vulnerable, and it took everything in him not to pull her close. He'd been right about her from the moment he'd met her. She was trouble. But it appeared as if it was a trouble he didn't want to back away from.

She shook her head, and just that quickly, her eyes narrowed. "Why are you interrogating me? I'm *your* boss," she pointed out.

"Really, Keera?" he challenged, looking down at the dog, who appeared quite amused by their interaction. Max was looking at Keera as if she could do no wrong. Just as soon as he thought he might like the dog, the mutt pissed him off again. "You don't have to treat me like the enemy. I'm here, and I'm trying to help."

"Because you're protecting the school, not me," she said.

"I can protect both you *and* the school," he told her.

She was quiet for a moment, then gave him a slight smile. "That is, if I'm worthy of protecting?" she finally asked. "That's what you aren't adding."

"That's not true," he insisted.

"It doesn't matter," she told him with a wave of her hand. "We all have things in our past we want to keep buried."

"Is your past that bad?" he asked. He felt tense.

She took a deep breath. When she spoke, he wasn't expecting what she had to say. "My brother was killed a few years ago, and the case was never solved, and now thugs are after me who apparently know him. I'm just wondering what the connection is."

Arden felt a deep tug inside him. He couldn't imagine what would happen to him if one of his brothers, or his baby sister, was taken from this world.

"I'm sorry, Keera."

"I'm sick of people being sorry," she snapped, her eyes shining with tears. "I want someone to do something about it."

Arden nearly smiled. He could understand how she felt. Of course, he hadn't ever experienced that type of loss before, but he knew beyond a doubt that if he had, there would be nothing stopping him from seeking revenge, from finding out what had happened, and from doing whatever it took to obtain justice.

"And you think what's happening at the school has to do with your brother?" he asked. "How could it?"

"I don't know," she said, her voice rising again. "But sitting around thinking I'm doing something to harm this school isn't solving anything."

Arden felt like an ass as he gazed at the hurt and frustration in her eyes. Obviously, she was used to people letting her down. Maybe it was time someone didn't disappoint her. He smiled at her.

"You're absolutely right. Let's do something about it," Arden told her.

Her head snapped up as she looked at him with watery eyes and a shaking mouth. Finally she nodded, respect and maybe a hint of trust showing in her eyes.

He hadn't wanted to get involved with this woman, had known from the beginning she was too complicated. But it didn't matter what he wanted, because he was now involved, whether he wanted to be or not. Maybe it was time he learned exactly what complicated was like.

Chapter Five

Keera was incredibly aware of Arden following closely behind her as the two of them made their way into the back entrance of the school. Trust wasn't easy for Keera. As a matter of fact, it was impossible for her to trust in a person's word, but even with that conviction, she wanted to believe in Arden.

This whole situation was an utter mess, and there wasn't a whole lot she could do about it. That wasn't going to keep her from trying, especially with the offer of help from Arden. If anyone could find answers, it would be him.

They reached the back hallway where the gym was located, and after sniffing around for a few moments, Max lost interest and lay down, his leash dangling as he looked at Keera with bored eyes. He'd been ready to eat the kids alive. They were damn lucky Arden hadn't let go of the dog's leash. She was grateful she was an animal lover or the dog would be downright intimidating.

"What information do you have about your brother's case?" Arden asked after a couple of minutes of silence.

She could feel his eyes burning into her, willing her to look at him. His gaze was so captivating, it was hard for her to keep eye contact too long. It was much safer to gaze over his shoulder.

"I know he got involved with drugs. He began hanging around with a bad crowd, and before I could stop it, he was dead," she said. It was a very simple explanation for an incredibly complicated issue.

"You might not ever get to the bottom of his case," Arden warned. "You won't know the whys and hows, but you can possibly get the who, especially if this is connected with this school."

"It never should have happened. If I'd been more aware, taken more interest in his life . . ." She trailed off. "My brother was eight years younger than me, only eighteen when he died. It was too soon. It was much too soon."

"It's always too soon," he told her, reaching out and putting his hand on her shoulder. She knew he was trying to comfort her, but the feel of his fingers against the thin material of her shirt nearly scorched her. Arden Forbes was far too powerful for her liking, and the feelings he inspired in her scared her to the very depths of her soul.

She stepped back, trying not to make it appear too obvious. Them being alone in this hallway was far too intimate for her liking, especially with how raw her emotions were. She didn't want to accept his compassion—that would make her weak.

"My brother, Dean, was a good kid. He was always an honor-roll student, involved in sports and active in clubs. Then something happened the summer before his senior year of high school. He clammed up, wouldn't talk to my mom or me about it. I don't know what it was, probably will never know. I just know that I can't leave things the way they are," she admitted. She was sharing more with Arden than she'd shared with anyone, and she didn't know why.

"I want to help you," he said.

This time Keera looked up at him. There was sympathy and determination in his eyes. She wanted to tell him he could take back the offer. She didn't want to depend on anyone, but especially not on this man. She had no doubt it would be dangerous to her peace of mind.

Needing to do anything other than stand there in front of Arden sharing her innermost thoughts, Keera took another step away from him and looked down at Max, who seemed to be in no hurry to do anything.

"What are you doing here on a Saturday, anyway?" she asked.

"I got a phone call that you were in trouble," he told her.

"What? From who?"

"I have no idea, but it appears someone is either your guardian angel, or out to get you. Maybe both," he told her.

A shiver traveled down her spine. She feared he was right. There were too many events happening in her life to call them coincidence. Were the same people who'd messed in Dean's life coming after her now? What exactly had her brother gotten himself into? She honestly couldn't imagine—didn't want to imagine.

"We definitely need to add a security detail to the school," she said with a sigh. "I'm just afraid the budget won't allow it."

"I agree, and we'll make it work. I don't like how much time you spend here alone," he said.

"I've never felt threatened being alone. It's why I wanted a smaller school in the first place."

"Your safety matters, and you should be more conscious of it," he told her.

"I hate people telling me what to do or how to feel. It drives me insane," she said.

"You might want to learn that, in a community such as Edmonds, we care about each other. If you're in trouble, you won't be alone." The words sounded a bit like a warning to her, but that might have been her paranoia instead of her rational brain.

"I thought this school, this town, would be a new start, a safe place," she said.

"It is. It just appears some trouble might have followed you to town."

His words instantly made her back stiffen. "So you think this supposed drug problem at the school involves me, or that I brought it here?"

"There's someone stalking you, and we have rumors of drugs running through the school, rumors we've never had before," he told her. "What am I supposed to think?"

"You're supposed to not make assumptions. A person is innocent until proven guilty," she pointed out.

"I agree," he assured her. His head tilted as he analyzed her. "How did you learn about the job here, anyway?"

"Why does that matter?" she asked.

"Come on, Keera, there's no need to be defensive about every little thing I ask," he said with a sigh.

"A friend e-mailed me about the position," she told him. "There's nothing wrong with that."

"Had you heard of Edmonds before that?" he asked.

"Yeah, I've lived in the Seattle area most of my life," she said. "Edmonds isn't on the other side of the planet."

"It just seems odd that someone from your past is popping up a month after you take a job you were led to," he said.

"Or it's just all a giant mess, and a huge coincidence," she told him. "I'm not a part of this!"

He held up a hand as if to fend her off. "I'm not implying you are. I'm just saying we need to follow all possible leads. Obviously, something's going on, and it's foolish for us to ignore the facts."

She crossed her arms and glared at him for a moment. How was she going to work with this man? He drove her crazy—in both good and bad ways.

"Then, let's search the school again. We can see how useful your dog is," she said in a clipped tone.

He gazed at her for a moment, then nodded. "Let's sweep the school," he agreed.

Unease filled Keera. What if they did find something? What if Arden thought she really was involved? She shouldn't care what he thought, but for some reason she did.

The two of them were silent as they began walking through the gym. A dozen kids were playing a fierce game of basketball, their voices echoing through the mostly empty area. This was the reason Keera loved what she did. These were good kids choosing to spend their Saturday together, being active and involved. If her brother had made that same choice, he'd still be alive, and she wouldn't feel so lost.

"This doesn't look like any after-school detention I attended," Arden told her, leaning too close into her personal bubble. The scent of his cologne tickled her senses, making goose bumps appear on her arms. She prayed he wouldn't notice. But the man always smelled like wood and spice, an oddly erotic combination that hit her low in her belly whenever she got a whiff.

"There's only a few kids here working off their detention. The rest *want* to be here, and I like having a safe place for them to go on the weekends, where they can stay out of trouble. I also believe that just because they've done something wrong and they have to pay the price for that, it doesn't have to be miserable. If I show them a more positive experience, then I think they'll learn more than if I lock them in a small room and make them write stupid sentences one hundred times in a row."

"I agree. Our last principal didn't," he said.

"I've seen much better responses from getting kids involved in activities that interest them than by doing it the old way. If we don't continue to learn, then we shouldn't be in the education system," she said.

"I wish more people felt the same as you," Arden said. Keera was so used to people arguing with her that she didn't know how to respond to his positive words.

As they continued on, leaving the gym, Max was busy sniffing the ground, the walls, and the lockers as his eagle eyes took in everything around him. A bug couldn't squirm up a wall without him tracking it.

She was growing more impressed by Arden's dog the more she was around him. She might even miss seeing him at the school when he was done with this job.

"Are there any particular areas you want to take your pup through?" Keera asked.

"Let's just walk the halls," Arden suggested.

The school was old but well maintained. Though the rumors hadn't been confirmed, she'd heard it was Arden's family's donations that kept everything in the place top-of-the-line, right down to the vending machines. She wanted to ask him about it, but it wasn't a conversation she was comfortable beginning.

They rounded a corner and ran into Ethan, who appeared startled to find them there. From the stiffening of his shoulders, she was guessing he hadn't thawed any toward Arden.

"I don't have you on the volunteer roster today," Keera said. Ethan's eyes softened slightly when he turned toward Keera.

"I don't have to be a volunteer to take pride in being at *my* school," he said.

"That's true. I guess I'm here more often than not, as well," Keera said with a false chuckle she figured no one was buying.

"I see the dog is back. Is he going to be a permanent fixture?" Ethan asked. Max's upper lip lifted as he met Ethan's gaze, as if he was begging the man to make a move. It was almost comical how much personality this dog had. Ethan didn't appear amused as he took a step back. If the dog had been gazing at her that way, she'd have probably done the same.

"For now," she told Ethan, who sighed with disgust.

Before anyone could say anything more, Max's attention strayed as his body stiffened. His alert eyes focused on the set of lockers across the hall from them. He then began tugging against his leash.

When Arden didn't move quickly enough for his liking, he turned his head and looked with exasperation at the man holding on to him.

"What is it?" Arden asked. The dog almost seemed to sigh, which made Keera's own lips twitch.

"I think he wants you to follow him," Keera said.

Arden shrugged and allowed Max to lead him to the lockers. Max sniffed at them for a moment, then sat, his paw lifting as he scratched at number 213. Arden looked at her as if unsure what to do next.

"I think he wants in that locker," Keera said, feeling a sense of foreboding. She turned to Ethan. "Do you have the register so we can see who it belongs to?"

Ethan glared at Max and Arden before turning and moving back to his office. He returned a few minutes later, holding a paper.

"It doesn't belong to anyone," he grumbled. Before she or Arden could respond, they heard the voices of students as they rounded a corner. The three girls stopped, looking unsure of whether to keep moving. The somber faces of their principal, vice principal, and history teacher caused instant worry to appear in their expressions.

"Everything's okay," Keera quickly informed the students. "Why don't you get back to your projects?" She tried keeping her voice cheery. The girls looked at each other and then back to the group of adults, not buying her tone.

"Why is that dog pawing at the locker?" the leader of the small group asked.

"We aren't sure yet, Kimberly," Keera told her.

The kids knew something was going on, and though they stepped back a couple of paces, it was obvious they weren't interested in going anywhere.

"You'd better open the locker, Ethan," Arden told him.

Though Ethan grumbled, especially at having a teacher tell him what to do, he stepped up to the locker and entered the lock code that was on his paper. The door popped open, and Max let out a whine as the contents were revealed.

Keera gasped, and Ethan stumbled back as if afraid of getting contaminated by the contents inside. This couldn't be happening—not in her school.

"Is that coke?" Kimberly asked. The students had crept closer to see what was happening.

"We aren't sure," Arden said as he pulled out his phone. It was obvious by the look he sent Keera's way that he was pretty sure it was drugs. But he was keeping calm because of the students standing by.

"Whoa, that's a lot," a boy named Daniel said. The group of kids had grown as students held their phones, texting as fast as their fingers allowed.

"Let's not make assumptions," Arden said.

Though his voice remained calm, Keera could see the rage in his eyes. There were drugs in his school, and he wasn't happy. Some of the trust she'd seen in his expression earlier had evaporated as he looked at her with a bit of suspicion that nearly broke her heart.

"Arden . . ." She didn't know how to finish the sentence.

"School's out for the day," Arden said, his voice harder than she'd ever heard before. He then stepped away as he picked up his phone again. Her fingers trembled as she gazed back at the contents in the locker. There were far too many drugs for them to be one student's stash.

Someone was dealing out of her school. Her heart broke because she feared this was more about her than the school. Her past was following her, and it seemed the ghosts weren't going to be satisfied until she was destroyed—personally, physically, mentally, and professionally.

The demons of her old life might just win.

Chapter Six

There was no way to express the anger Arden was feeling. He'd been teaching at Edmonds High School for ten years, and in that time, nothing like this had happened before.

Sure, kids had been caught with bags of weed, and those students had been expelled. The staff took an incredibly hard stance on drugs. He was even harsher with his football team. If a player was caught with drugs or alcohol, they were off the team—no second chances.

He knew that was a road too hard to make a U-turn on, and he wanted to be harsh to prevent them from starting down that path. Now, coincidentally, after they got a new principal, they also got a drug ring associated with their school. Declan had been right. Dammit!

He called his brother, giving only a few curt words. Declan said he'd notify the authorities and they'd be there quickly. Arden hung up without bothering with a goodbye. Neither of them was in the mood for pleasantries.

Keera was doing her best to answer the kids' questions and calm their fears. He studied her pale face, the disappointment she was trying to hide, the tense set of her shoulders. Everything within him said there was no way she was involved—at least not of her own free will.

He'd learned long ago to trust the voice within. But this was his school, and he was just as responsible for these kids as she was. Therefore, he had to keep his eyes wide open and not let his attraction toward the principal skew his investigation. His brother might have begun this, but he was now involved.

Keera hadn't tried to keep him from the locker area, hadn't tried to steer him away. That didn't speak of guilt. Him thinking of her as innocent wasn't because of his attraction. He could afford to believe in her innocence without compromising his integrity.

Max hadn't moved from the locker, guarding his find. He looked from Arden to Keera, then Ethan, who was standing by in shock. The dog really didn't like the vice principal. Arden didn't blame him. The smarmy VP had never been a favorite of Arden's, but he tried to give the guy the benefit of the doubt.

Right now he didn't see Ethan as being very helpful, which was making it much more difficult for Arden to be gracious. The man just stood there while Keera did all the damage control with the students.

"You did good, Max," Arden said. Max looked at him as if he was already bored with the scenario. "Take the praise like a real dog," Arden grumbled. He would've sworn on a Bible that the dog had rolled his eyes. He turned away before he got into a fight with the mutt. That would certainly be on YouTube within minutes with the number of cell phones around him. Damn dog.

Footsteps could be heard coming down the hall, and Arden turned to see an eager student leading Declan and a couple of crime-scene techs their way. The girl then went and joined the other kids as they waited to see what would happen next. This was a pretty exciting Saturday for them.

"Wow, we've never been called here twice in the same weekend," Joe said with a grin.

"I'm sorry," Keera told the tech.

"Hey, I like a mystery. Wish it wasn't at a school, but we'll get to the bottom of it," Joe assured her.

Arden noticed how men acted around Keera. They puffed out their chests and had extrawide grins for her. The vice principal did it—hell, half the students did, too. He also noticed that she was seemingly oblivious to it.

"Please figure it out," Keera told the tech while placing her hand on his shoulder and squeezing. Pink infused Joe's cheeks, and he turned, catching Arden's gaze. There must have been some sort of ominous look on Arden's face because the young man turned away and scurried over to the locker. Arden needed to cool it.

"Max did good," Declan said as he gazed over Joe's shoulder at the plastic-wrapped white powder.

"Yeah, the mutt's been useful," Arden admitted.

"I'm not happy about this," Declan said.

"I know you aren't. I was just hoping you were wrong," Arden admitted.

"I was hoping the same thing," Declan told him.

Joe had taken a sample from one of the bags, putting the powder into a vial and swirling it. He turned around, and Arden knew there was no doubt. Of course there wasn't. If it hadn't been drugs, Max wouldn't have bothered with the locker.

"Yeah, it's coke," Joe said. He turned back to the locker, and he and his partner carefully inventoried the drugs and the few other items in there before taking their time swabbing the area, getting every trace of evidence they could find. The techs were thorough.

Declan hovered over them, making Joe sweat a little more than he normally did. There was just something so damn commanding about his brother, it tended to make anyone around him a little jumpy.

The kids were chattering with each other as they did their best to share this latest bit of gossip with the entire town of Edmonds. It wouldn't do them any good to try to keep this contained. But, then again, Arden didn't want to do that. The more people talking about this, the more likely they'd find whoever was responsible. In a small town, secrets tended to be unwrapped rather quickly.

Keera began questioning the kids, her shoulders more set now that the initial shock had worn off. She was firm as she looked them in the eyes and began asking some hard questions.

"Have any of you seen anything suspicious around this locker?" she asked. Arden noted how she looked the students in the eyes, never being the first one to break contact. A few kids squirmed as if they might want to talk, and that made both Arden and Declan step closer to the group, which only appeared to make them more nervous.

Good. They should be afraid. Enough dope had been found in their school to OD half the students. It wasn't something to be taken lightly. All it would take was one student stepping forward, and they could end this.

Most of the kids looked clueless, but there were a couple who might have information. Both he and Declan seemed to zoom in on them, and those kids were inspecting their shoes an awful lot.

"Come on, you guys. This is *your* school. Take pride in it. You won't be in trouble for sharing information," Keera pleaded with them.

Ethan had disappeared into his office and hadn't emerged again. He was a coward who should've been out there dealing with the situation instead of hiding. Some people preferred to live in the shadows while others couldn't help but seek the light. Arden respected Keera for being a light-seeker, and he found himself drawing closer to her.

They'd get to the bottom of this, and they'd get Keera answers about her brother, as well. When he made a promise to another person, he delivered on his word. It was a code of conduct that had been instilled in him from the time he could barely walk.

His ego took a surge when Keera leaned a bit closer to him. Whether she'd done it intentionally or not, she needed him. He just hoped neither of them let the other down. He had no doubt she'd been disappointed too many times already in her life, and he was determined to show her what faith in another person looked like.

Chapter Seven

Keera's nerves were frayed as she watched Arden and his brother huddle together away from the group of kids. What were they discussing? Did he still think she had anything to do with this?

She'd been so confident nothing amiss was happening, and just that quickly she'd been proven wrong. Had the drugs been brought in since the night before? She couldn't remember if she and Arden had walked this path with his dog the previous night. She'd been incredibly shaken, though, so she could definitely give herself a break for not remembering all the details.

She'd come to this town for a fresh start—to become a new person. But it seemed her past wasn't something she could outrun. For now, she had to keep her fears and worries locked tightly away. There were kids who needed reassurance, and cops who needed answers. And it would be great if they didn't think she was the guilty party in all this. She could see how they'd believe that, since she was so new—and since she did have a past.

One of the kids looked up, determination in her eyes as she faced Keera. "I noticed Jeff Engel hanging in this area even though his locker's around the corner," Deanna said.

Only a few tense moments had passed since Keera had pleaded with the kids for any kind of information that would lead to who was behind this, but it seemed a lifetime with how frayed Keera's nerves were.

"That's just gossip, Deanna," another of the students growled, glaring at the girl. "Jeff's been getting his shit together."

"Let her speak, Mitch," Keera sternly told him. She'd speak to all the kids one-on-one, if need be, but for now she needed to figure out who knew anything that might help the case. All of the students were obviously afraid to rock the boat.

"I just saw him in this area," Deanna insisted, though her voice had lowered, and she was now looking at the floor. The shy girl didn't normally step up, and Keera was proud of her.

"Yeah, well, I hang around areas my locker isn't at, too. Does that mean I'm dealing dope?" Mitch snapped.

Deanna seemed to sink within herself as she took a step back. Keera wanted to pull Mitch aside and tell him to keep his mouth shut, but instead, she studied him. Maybe he knew more than he was letting on. When he noticed her full attention had turned to him, he stood his ground and glared at her. He was an angry boy to begin with, and having any adult try to put him in his place infuriated the teen.

"Do you know something you aren't sharing, Mitch?" Keera questioned. "All we want is to ensure the safety of the school," she added. He obviously came in on weekends, so this place was a refuge to him as well as the others. She figured none of them would want to mess with that.

"I don't think it's a student at all. It's not like people can't come and go as they please," Mitch said.

"What do you mean by that?" she asked.

"There's always a door open. If a person looks long enough, they'll get in, whether there's anyone else in here or not," he said.

Keera's eyes narrowed. This wasn't good news—and certainly not what she wanted to hear. Was more going on in her school than she'd realized?

"We lock up every day," Keera told him.

"The gym door is hardly ever locked. The coaches are constantly running extra classes, doing weight lifting and stuff, and I think they just figure someone is always here," another girl said. She was on the volleyball team, and Keera knew they were required to lift weights twice a week.

"We always lock up when we leave," Arden said from behind her.

"Not all the coaches are as thorough as you," Mitch said with a grin.

"And how are you so aware of this?" Arden questioned the kid. "You aren't on any of the teams and shouldn't be going through that door."

The boy tried to keep his composure, but it wasn't as easy to do with Arden as it apparently had been with her. She hated the lack of respect she sometimes got from the students. But because she was small, and young, they tended to seek out the older, male staff members more than her. That would one day change, she assured herself.

"Come on, Mr. Forbes, it's not like I have information that everyone here doesn't have," Mitch said, not seeming quite so tough now as he realized the hot water he was in.

Declan stepped forward and eyed the boy, and Mitch shifted on his feet, clearly wanting to be anywhere but where he was.

"Do you have anything useful for us?" Declan asked. Even the way Arden's brother spoke was enough to send shivers down their spines. He was a man of power, and there was no denying it.

"No. I'm sorry," Mitch said. "Can I go? I promised my mom I'd be home by now."

Declan paused for several moments, and the boy shifted again. All of the students were looking at the ground now. Even if they hadn't done anything wrong, with the way Declan was studying them, it probably made them feel as if they had.

"You're all dismissed," Declan said, and there was a visible sigh of relief until he spoke his next words. "For now."

Mitch and the remaining students practically ran from the scene, all of them knowing they could be questioned again. They were probably regretting hanging around to see what was happening. In this case, out of sight, out of mind seemed a much better option.

"I'm going to check on things. I'll see you in a few," Declan said before he left.

Keera watched the intimidating man walk away and felt herself wanting to flee with the rest of the kids. That seemed to be preferable right now. Arden was quiet for a few moments before he spoke.

"My brother would like us to come down to his office," Arden said.

"I can't leave," Keera told him. The police were still working, and she had to make sure the school was cleared out—and locked.

"I can take care of everything here," Ethan said, finally deciding to make another appearance.

"You need to come in, too," Arden said, making Ethan's eyes narrow.

"Why?" the vice principal asked. "I have no information."

"You're here as much as I am, Ethan. You might have info you're not even aware of until someone asks the right question," she said, hoping to appease the irritated man. "You've been at this school for a long time."

"Maybe I've been here too long," Ethan grumbled. "It seems the kids are getting worse the more the years go on. Drugs used to not be such a big deal. Sure, the occasional hit of pot would happen, or someone would find it funny to slip a mushroom into their soup, but this hard stuff, this new day and age . . ." He stopped talking as he shook his head. "I don't get it."

Keera didn't know what to say. Had he been doing this job too long? Would she feel the same as he did after running a school for ten or fifteen years? She certainly hoped not. She loved her job and wanted to continue feeling that way. She loved her students and doubted that would ever change. One bad apple shouldn't ruin it for everyone else.

"Let's get the school closed up and make sure the kids are out. Then we can go speak to the authorities. The sooner this problem gets solved, the sooner it will go back to normal," Keera said to both Ethan and Arden.

"We're finished here," the techs said as the locker was shut. The evidence was fully contained, and they had plenty of it to analyze. If anything turned up from it, then they were on their way to solving this mystery.

Arden thanked them, and they walked to the front doors. Keera and Ethan began clearing the school. Not many students were left, and it didn't take them long to get the building locked up. Ethan took off out the back with a grumbled promise to meet her.

Keera stepped outside, finding Arden leaning against his car, Max sitting at his heels. She wanted to walk past him, suddenly feeling more tired than she had in a long while.

"Why don't we ride together?" Arden asked as he opened his passenger door.

"I'm good. I have my car," she told him.

"Let's save fuel, and we can discuss what I missed while you were speaking to the kids," he said, placing his hand on her lower back and steering her inside the vehicle.

She either had to crawl in or have his body pressed against her back. She decided to jump into the seat. Yeah, it was going to play hell on her senses to sit next to him, but it wasn't a long ride, and she was a bit too shaky to be driving, anyway.

Arden shut her door, then let Max into the back seat. She could feel Max's hot breath on the back of her neck as she pulled her seat belt over her with shaky fingers. Whether or not Arden felt as if she was an outsider unfit to run his school, she had been hired for the job, and she intended to keep it.

Keera didn't know what to think. All she knew for sure was there was a problem, and the sooner they got to the bottom of it, the sooner everything could get back to normal—whatever normal was.

Though his excuse to give her a ride had been for them to talk, the drive was ominously quiet as they made their way through town to one of the older government buildings. Keera hadn't seen Declan leave the school, but she had no doubt he'd beat them there. Arden's brother was intense—and that was putting it mildly.

Arden parked the car, and Keera felt as if she were being led down the green mile as he walked next to her into the dark building, passing several people who nodded at them but didn't say anything.

"How's your brother involved in this?" Keera asked. She didn't know much about the Forbes family, to tell the truth, just what was said through the gossip channels. She knew they put a lot into the community, and knew they were ridiculously wealthy, but from what she'd heard, they also seemed to lead normal lives.

Of course, could you really call it a normal life when they owned private jets and took off to another country for a weekend picnic? Sure, they might work what most would call regular jobs, but they had big toys, as well. She'd grown up with wealth, and she knew exactly what that could do, and often did, to a family.

"Declan's FBI, but he doesn't share much about what he does," Arden said with a chuckle.

"He doesn't share with his own family?" she questioned.

"Top secret," Arden said with a wink.

"So this is a federal office?" Keera asked, feeling like the walls were closing in on her.

"Not officially," Arden said.

Keera had nothing to hide—not really. But her past was coming back to haunt her, and she felt a deep-rooted fear that she was going to be hauled away to some secret chamber, never to be seen again.

Arden led Keera into a small room with windows up high and an old table with rickety-looking chairs sitting on both sides of it. She was cold as she fought the urge to run from the room. Ethan was sitting at the table, looking completely put out. She knew exactly how he felt.

Declan Forbes stood in the corner of the room where he could view the doorway and the table—where he was making it clear he was in control. His hands were clasped behind his back as if he was trying to give the appearance of being at ease, but the intense look in his eyes told her he was a man who never let down his guard.

She moved a little closer to Arden, wanting some of his natural light to infuse her. As much as she was trying to keep her distance from Arden, she was also finding herself wanting to lean on him. That made her uneasy.

"Please get comfortable," Declan told them, though his gaze was boring into her. Another shiver racked her body. There was no way she wanted to make herself comfortable. The moment this was over, she was out of there.

With reluctance, Keera sat on the edge of her seat, her back ramrod straight, her gaze focused on the scratches in the table. She didn't want to look at anyone. She knew that was a sign of guilt in any interrogation, but she didn't even care right now. There was too much stress and fear running through her to try to hide it.

"Do either of you have any idea how the drugs got into your school?" Declan asked. He didn't come to the table, didn't try to make them feel as if they were all friends. No. This was an interrogation, and he was letting them know they were suspects.

"I didn't know we had a problem," Keera answered. "I'd like to know how you got wind of it before I did."

When Declan didn't answer, she looked up. His gaze was on Ethan, but it switched to her as if he knew she was looking at him.

"I don't give out sources," Declan said, making her feel as if he'd slapped her.

"There's no need to be rude," Arden reprimanded his brother.

"I've found in my line of work it's better to be honest and to the point," Declan said. He turned his attention back to Ethan, who hadn't spoken.

"There's no way of knowing how the damn drugs got into the school. Hell, half the students are up to no good. I wouldn't put it past some of the staff members, either. There's a bunch of small-minded townies who don't have a lot of ethics in this community," Ethan said, not trying to hide his disdain for the place he'd grown up.

"That's not true," Keera defended. "People in general are good at heart. This one incident shouldn't condemn our entire school."

"What do you really know? You haven't been here that long," Ethan said. He'd never been so rude to her, and she didn't know how to take it.

Keera's back stiffened even more, though she didn't know how that was possible. It was this room, and it was the feeling of being judged. Her fear was beginning to diminish as anger took its place.

"I might be new to this town, but I've committed myself to this school, and especially to these students. I won't stop until I get to the bottom of this mess, and I will ensure this doesn't happen again," she said, making sure she looked all three of the men in the eyes so they'd take her seriously. "Is there just a drug problem at the school, or are they running rampant through the town?" she pushed.

It looked as if there was a hint of respect in the expressions of both Arden and Declan. Ethan grumbled something as if he wasn't hearing her. He was so bitter, and she didn't understand it.

"We're focused on the school right now," Declan said, not answering her question.

"If you want my help, then I need all the information," she pushed.

"You'll get the info you need," Declan said. Though the words were harsh, the tone wasn't. She sat back and stared him down.

"I will solve the problems at my school. Why don't you focus on the town?" she challenged him. It almost appeared as if he smiled before the expression was wiped from his face.

"How do you think you can stop anything at your school when you didn't even realize there was a problem?" Declan asked. His tone had calmed, but she still felt judged by him.

"I'll talk to the school board about security measures. I'll also speak to the students as a group about the dangers of drugs, and one-on-one for those I think need it," she said. The more she sat there, the more plans formed.

"We could frisk the kids as they enter the school," Ethan volunteered, glee in his expression at the thought.

"No," Keera said, her voice rising. "School should be a safe haven for these students. I won't make them feel as if they're criminals."

"I agree," Declan said, surprising her. "I don't believe students are responsible for this."

"You obviously don't know who in the hell is responsible," Ethan snarled. "Or you wouldn't be wasting our time."

Declan's eyes narrowed, and though Ethan was annoying her, Keera felt sorry for the man. She certainly wouldn't want to be getting that icy-cold glare from the huge man who obviously held a lot of power.

"Max will be a fixture at the school until this matter is solved. I don't want any complaints," Declan said. He again looked at both her and Ethan, but his gaze stayed on Ethan far longer than on her.

"I'll have to check the books to make sure that's okay," Ethan said, not willing to cede any of his vice principal power.

"I just told you it's okay, so it is," Declan said.

Ethan mumbled under his breath, but Keera didn't hear what he said. She was sure it wasn't anything friendly aimed at the FBI agent—or the entire Forbes family, for that matter.

"If you hear of anything pertaining to the matter, you need to notify me immediately," Declan told them.

"Yes, of course," Keera readily agreed.

"Yeah, I'll get right on that," Ethan said with sarcasm.

"I think that should be all for now," Declan said, obviously having had enough of Ethan.

"Really? That's all?" Ethan asked. "You just wanted to bring us down here for a smoke show, to exert your power?" he added. He stood up so quickly his chair flew backward. "Next time don't bother."

With that he stomped from the room, probably proud he'd seemingly gotten the last word. Maybe it made him feel as if he was better than the brothers, and Keera wondered if he had a history with them.

"That was entertaining," Arden said as he rose.

Though Keera's knees were a bit shaky, she stood as well, almost grateful when Max nudged a little closer to her as if making sure he'd be there if she fell. She reached out and petted his head, looking down at his shining eyes.

"I like Max being at the school. He's a good boy," she said.

"Yeah, with you," Arden grumbled.

A sound almost like laughter escaped Declan's throat, and Keera looked at him in shock. He was gazing at the dog, a look of amusement shining in his eyes. It transformed the man's face into something she might even call handsome if the guy didn't intimidate her so damn much.

"Is the dog giving you trouble, little brother?" Declan asked.

"Not at all," Arden said, tugging on Max's leash. The dog didn't budge from his position where Keera was still petting him.

"Hmm, okay," Declan said, his eyes still shining.

"Let's go," Arden said to Keera. The moment she began walking, Max stood and trailed after them. Arden grumbled something about women and power, but she didn't catch all of it.

She let out her first breath of relief when they exited the building. She wouldn't breathe easy again until this was completely over. She hoped it was much sooner rather than later. And she hoped her past didn't cast a shadow over the real criminals, because if they focused on her, this would never be solved. She was innocent—but someone out there obviously wasn't.

Chapter Eight

Max lay beneath the water table, his eyes shut, a breeze blowing over him, looking as if he were in heaven. He'd been well received by Arden's football team, the kids deciding they wanted the mutt to be their mascot. The dang dog had seemed to understand their praise and had pranced around with his head held high, maybe trying to prove to Arden how valuable he was.

Then the kids went to do their warm-ups, and he found a nice, cool place to rest for a while. Arden was a little jealous. It had only been a week since the school had been broken into and drugs had been found in the locker. They still didn't have answers.

The dog was becoming a permanent fixture in the school, and Arden was becoming an even more permanent fixture in Keera's life. He hated having her too far away from him. There was just so much going on, and his nerves were on edge. Arden didn't appreciate it.

He wasn't a guy who caved in to stress, and his motto in life was to live each day to the fullest. If something didn't work out the way you thought it would the first time around, then you picked it up again the next day. If it wasn't meant to be, then it wasn't going to happen.

But for some reason, he couldn't feel his normal sense of ease in the current situation. He had classes to run, papers to grade, and football practices to keep him occupied, and every other minute of the day was consumed with trying to find out what was happening in his town.

Arden had no doubt his brother knew more than he was letting on. That was frustrating. But Declan always had been a person to keep to himself. He loved his family—Arden had no doubt about that—but getting anything out of Declan that his brother didn't want to reveal was an impossible task.

The kids finished their warm-ups and rushed over to Arden. He was damn proud of his kids. There was no way he was allowing what was happening at his school to taint how he felt about any of the students. They were great kids.

"We have our first game in two weeks, and I know we're ready," Arden said. The boys smiled, always eager to hear words of encouragement. "But that doesn't mean it's time to slack off. The next couple of weeks are going to be intense," he warned.

There were a couple of good-natured groans from the crowd, but more smiles. These boys would not only work their hardest for each other, and him, but they thrived on being pushed past limits they thought were impossible.

"We're gonna kill at the first game," his star quarterback, Devin, said.

"Hell ya, we are," his running back, Nathan, agreed. The two fist-bumped, and the rest of the team gave a loud "Boo-ya."

"Just remember we aren't playing flag football here. We need to be tackling and blocking, and protecting that arm of Devin's," Arden told them.

"Dang straight. I got sacked fourteen times last year," Devin grumbled.

"Maybe you shouldn't hold on to the ball for so long," Nathan teased. Arden was pretty sure Nathan had been bitten by a radioactive spider and had webs he could shoot from his wrists, because the boy could catch balls that any other person would surely miss. Arden knew he'd one day see him starring in an NFL game, hopefully his beloved Seahawks.

"We don't throw the ball to just throw it. We have to know our plays and work together as a team," Arden told them. "And if that means we need to give Devin a little longer to make the right pass, then that's exactly what we do."

"It's all about the magic when that ball releases," Devin said with a toothy grin.

"Yeah, and your humility," piped in Sean, a six-foot-one, 210-pound blocker.

"It's hard to be humble when you're great," Devin told the team, who laughed.

Yeah, the boy had confidence in spades, and he might come across as cocky to strangers, but Arden knew better. He knew the kid's mom had cerebral palsy and that Devin went home every night to take care of her and his younger siblings. He also knew that Devin tutored middle school kids during the week to earn extra money, and that he did it for free for a couple of kids who couldn't afford to pay. Devin was that one-in-a-million type of teenager who a parent could be proud of, who a coach wanted to do everything for. Devin would go far in life.

"Save the boasting for your weekends out," Arden told them with a laugh. His kids might joke around, and they might rib each other nonstop, but the second they put on their uniforms and stepped onto that sacred field, they were the epitome of class. Arden wouldn't have it any other way.

There were no brawls in his football games, and there was never trash talk from his kids to another team. They were known for their good attitude, positive influence on other teams, and willingness to set an example. They were state champions and were worthy of hero worship from the younger generation. Arden was proud of that as well.

"Okay, we're going to continue daily doubles, but it's going to look a lot different," Arden said, coming out of his thoughts and getting back to the matter at hand. "I want to take you all to the peak and beyond. You're ready for it."

"Hell yeah," the team called.

"Pick up the schedule on the way out, and I don't want any complaints or missed practices," Arden said. "You'll also see that on Saturday we have one practice because we're going by the senior center again."

"Sweet," said Eddie, a small freshman, who was gearing up to be one hell of a running back himself. His grandma lived there, and the entire team felt as if she were their grandma, too.

"Nice, Coach," Jeremy, his tight end, said.

Part of being on his team required ten hours a month of volunteer work. But his boys normally doubled that time without being asked. They were truly valuable members of the community.

"Let's quit chatting and get to it," Arden said.

"Boo-ya," the team called, and took off. Arden's assistant coaches began their training as his brothers, Kian and Owen, walked across the field.

"Not that it isn't great to see you two, but what are you doing here?" Arden asked as he grabbed his water bottle and chugged. For Washington, it was a pretty hot day.

"We should be able to check in on our brother now and then," Owen informed him.

"You're only in town a week. I'd think you'd have more important things to do than hang out at a high school like a washed-up jock," Arden teased.

"There's nothing washed up about this," Owen said, lifting his shirt and running his fingers across his six-pack abs. Both Arden and Kian rolled their eyes.

"You know Declan is harassing all of us to keep an eye on things," Kian admitted.

"Our big brother worries too much. We're going to get to the bottom of this. Just look at the kids out there. It's a great school, and we won't allow anything to taint it," Arden assured them.

"We have no doubt about it. But until this mess is straightened out, you might be seeing a lot more of us," Owen said.

"That's going to be hard to do from New York," Arden pointed out.

Owen was a firefighter, and had taken off ten years ago to the other side of the country. Their mother had been sad, though she'd never made him feel guilty. And to be fair, Owen came home for visits quite often. But it always felt as if something was missing when his brother was gone.

"I might be coming back home," Owen said. The way he spoke the words, Arden had no doubt there was a story to be told.

"Is everything okay?" Arden asked.

"Now's not the time," Owen told him. Arden knew he could push his brother, but they had more respect for each other than to do that. When Owen was ready to share, he'd come to his brothers first.

"I'm here anytime," Arden assured him.

"I have no doubt about it," Owen said.

"Where's Roxie?" Arden asked Kian.

His brother had married his high school sweetheart after years of separation, and the two of them were now raising Kian's daughter, Roxie's niece—yeah, that was a long story—together. And they were so in love it was a little disgusting, to be honest. But seeing them together made Arden think the whole marriage thing wasn't such a bad gig.

"She's with Mom and Lily at the mall," Kian said with a shudder. A trip to the mall was the ultimate punishment in all of their eyes. They didn't understand how anyone could spend hours locked away in a building going from store to store. If a person needed something in this day and age, the best thing they could do was order it online. No hassle, no crowds, and no pushy salespeople.

"Ah, so the truth comes out. You told them you had to check on the security of your town so you could get out of carrying bags," Arden said with a laugh. Kian grinned big-time.

"Damn straight." Kian was anything but a slacker. As a well-respected surgeon, his brother worked hard, played hard, and more important, loved hard. Arden was proud of his siblings.

"Is everyone on for Sunday dinner?" Arden asked.

"Yep, even Dakota is coming with Ace and the kiddo," Owen said.

"Good. It's been a few weeks since I saw her. That's too long. My nieces are growing up too fast," Arden said.

"Yeah, I agree," Kian grumbled. His brother had lost out on the first few years of his daughter's life because he hadn't known about her. But he was more than making up for lost time. The entire family was.

One of the coaches called out to Arden, and he had to say goodbye to his brothers. For at least an hour, he was going to let his mind empty of any worries and focus strictly on his team.

He'd be able to do that a hell of a lot easier if a certain sexy school principal wasn't flashing through his brain more often than not. Maybe he should be running drills with the guys. If he was exhausted, his brain would have no choice but to shut down, right? He somehow doubted it.

He had his doubts about a lot of things right now. One thing he was more than sure of, though, was that he was going to have to do something about his attraction to Keera Thompson. The two of them might combust if he didn't.

That thought made him smile before he focused on his team once more. He couldn't be thinking of Keera in that way when he was coaching. It would lead to an incredibly embarrassing moment for him.

"Let's do this," Arden said.

The kids were rapt as he dove back into coach mode. Damn, he was a blessed man.

Chapter Nine

Keera was a football junkie. Yes, she knew it was going against the grain for such a bookworm kind of girl to be so into not just any sport, but the grueling sport of football. It was something she didn't share with the world. But she truly loved the game—loved everything about it.

There was something magical at that moment when the Friday-night lights came on, illuminating that beautiful field where dreams were both made and broken. The noise on the field, and in the stands, made her heart accelerate. The smell of blood, sweat, tears, popcorn, and hot dogs heightened her senses.

She even loved the cold fall nights, the games when rain was pouring down. The dirtier the game, the better. Yes, she loved football. Season tickets were her one indulgence each year, and she didn't mind being in the nosebleed section. Though, to be honest, oftentimes she'd sneak down to a lower section. It was easier to tantalize her senses the closer she was to the field.

Because of this, it was no surprise that she often snuck to the far corner of the school where she could watch Edmonds's very own sexy football coach run his practices like a professional. She was more than pleased her school had a great team. In fact, throughout her career she had heard words of praise from parents because of her support for the games.

They thought she was dragging herself to them under duress to support her students. It hadn't taken her last school long to see it wasn't a hardship for her to be there. Containing her enthusiasm during a particularly close game wasn't something that was easy for her to do.

Keera wasn't pleased with how much Arden Forbes was on her mind. She'd done so well her first month as the new principal at being professional, yet distant. That was all out the window now. On this day of all days, Keera was even more bothered than usual due to the very erotic dream she'd woken up from in a sweat, staring at one very nude football coach.

She watched him finish his practice. Then, as if he could feel her staring at him, he turned, and his gaze bored right through the double pane window, straight into her eyes. Keera's breath halted as her pulse pounded out of control.

Though they were separated by space and a building, she felt as if he were standing right next to her, the heat radiating from his solid body scorching her oversensitive skin. Finally, a painful gasp of air made its way down her throat, and Keera was able to rip herself away from the intensity of his stare.

"Remember why you can't do anything about this," Keera whispered to herself as she stiffly walked down the long hallway. She passed by her office, not at all interested in shutting herself in there.

Maybe the answer wasn't to isolate herself to the point that the first sexy man she'd been around in a while was making her come undone. Maybe some casual fling with someone she'd never see again was the direction she should go.

Apparently, her body thought it needed sex.

Just as soon as she had that thought, she pushed it from her mind. She'd never been a casual kind of woman, and she didn't think it was going to be possible to begin that sort of lifestyle at the age of twenty-eight. Maybe if her life had been different, she wouldn't have so many hang-ups, but something she knew beyond a shadow of a doubt was that you either cried over things that were beyond your control, or you stiffened your shoulders and set a new path for yourself.

Though life hadn't been an easy road for Keera, she knew who she was, admired the strength in herself, and knew the only path was one of her own choosing. Long ago, she'd decided no one but her could determine her destiny, no matter how many roadblocks were tossed in her way.

Without realizing where she'd been going, Keera found herself in the school gym. The cleaning staff was amazing, keeping the floors polished to a shine and the bleachers nearly unblemished, but if she closed her eyes, she could still smell a hint of sweat and attitude.

Keera might love football beyond all other sports, but she enjoyed the rest of them, too. An aggressive game of basketball, a stout round of baseball, a bloody hockey match, or a thrilling volleyball tournament were all good. The only sport she couldn't get into was golf.

She didn't understand how so many people enjoyed watching a game where hardly anything happened. There was no chance of a bloody nose or a rumble between the teams. There were no exciting last-minute rushes to a goal. It was just one person hitting a tiny little ball that sailed through the air.

She'd shot a few rounds herself and had been bored to pieces by the ninth hole. Of course, she'd been determined to change her mind on the sport and had made herself do it a few times. The last time she'd played, she'd admitted defeat and walked off on the seventh hole. That had been two years ago.

"Hi, Ms. Thompson." The perky female voice pulled Keera from her thoughts of sports, and she looked over to find a group of sophomore girls huddled on the bleachers with their books open in their laps. That was a pleasant sight.

One of Keera's conditions for taking this job had been for her to run the school hours how she pleased. As long as sports practices were going on and she could ensure proper staff supervision, she allowed students to use the school after-hours to do homework or meet with their clubs. It pleased her to see how many took advantage of this safe haven to meet up. She hoped the school GPA climbed with how she ran things. It wasn't a bad number as it was, but Keera liked to be the best, not just adequate.

"Good evening, Tara. How are you girls?" Keera asked.

"Great. We're getting our bio project done, then heading over to the café for burgers," Tara replied.

"Perfect," Keera said.

"This is also a good spot to watch the football players leave after practice," Misty said, which made the girls giggle.

"Ah, I see," Keera said with a smile. It wasn't a bad spot to see the football coach, either, she thought without wanting to. Maybe it was time to scoot out of there so she didn't appear like a blushing teenager waiting to catch a glimpse of the football jock.

She was turning when she heard Arden's deep voice.

"Hurry up, Max. You'll see the boys again in a couple of days," he said. She could either look in his direction where he was coming out of the men's locker room, or she could pretend she hadn't heard him and bolt for the exit.

"Keera," he called before she could make up her mind. There was no way she could pretend she hadn't heard him. His voice echoed through the gym, making the girls in the bleachers snicker. She faced them and watched as they sighed.

She knew how they felt. She turned in his direction and gazed at Max instead of him. That was safer. The large German shepherd had spotted her, and his tail wagged as he picked up his pace and made a beeline in her direction.

"Hi, boy," she said as she knelt down and gave him a good neck scratching. He sat and looked at her with a sparkle in his eyes. She wouldn't be surprised if he leaned over and plopped to the ground. He was obviously enjoying retirement because, for the most part, he simply seemed like a sweet puppy, instead of a deadly police dog.

"Must be nice to get so much attention," Arden said with a chuckle. Max's nose came up in the air the slightest bit as if to acknowledge Arden's words, but since that seemed to take too much effort, he leaned more fully into Keera, and she continued scratching him while her eyes trailed up Arden's muscular thighs, over his tight T-shirt that molded to his washboard abs, and finally to his shining eyes.

A little sweat beaded on his brow, and his dark hair was slicked back, telling her he'd been out there practicing with his boys. Arden wasn't one of those coaches who was happy to yell from the sidelines. No. He showed the boys how to do maneuvers, and he worked even harder than they did, to show them everything was possible.

Her respect for the man continued to grow the more she got to know him. Her desire for him was also growing in ways she wanted nothing to do with. Him in a pair of shorts and an indecently tight black shirt was making her sweat as she heated in all the areas she didn't want to.

"Max says he has no complaints," Keera said, hating the slight rasp in her voice.

She heard another giggle from the girls behind her, grateful to be reminded they had an audience. Not that anything would happen if they didn't, she assured herself. There was just such a beautiful presence about this man that drew out things in her she wasn't even aware she felt.

"That's because Max is lazy," Arden told her, and it took her a moment to remember what had been said last. Yes, they were talking about the dog and him liking to get attention.

"He's not lazy. He just knows better than to pass up a good rub-down," she said with a laugh.

Arden's smile faded as he gazed at her, making her realize the words she'd so carelessly used. Dang, she wasn't normally around people where she felt she had to use caution with word *usage*.

"Don't we all," he said, and he didn't even try to act as if he were teasing.

Somehow Keera managed to rip her gaze away from Arden's intense gaze as she rose to her feet and took a few steps back.

"I'm gonna lock up the school if practice is over. I'm the last one here tonight, and besides the girls here, we're all clear," she said, hating the shake in her voice.

"I'll help you, and then we can grab a bite to eat. I'm starving," he said.

It took a moment for Keera to realize he'd just sort of asked her on a date. Or was that what he was doing? She was confused and about to refuse him when she realized they probably should talk. They hadn't spoken in a few days, and she was sure he wanted to be filled in on anything new that might be happening.

"Um, nothing has happened the last couple of days, so there's no need to eat," she said, wanting to kick herself for how pathetic her words sounded.

Arden chuckled, making her look his way again. He was currently lifting the hem of his tight shirt and stretching it up to wipe away the sweat from his brow, giving her a spectacular view of his solid, rippling, tanned abs.

She felt her heart pound and a chill run down her body. When she felt her mouth water, she sealed her lips tightly closed and wondered if she'd just had a mild heart attack. It was possible.

When he put the shirt back down, she was still gazing at his magnificent abs, making her have to bite her tongue to keep from letting the sigh of disappointment at him covering himself escape her parched throat.

"Like what you see?" he asked, making her head snap up in time to notice the obvious twinkle in his eyes.

"Eh," she replied, proud of herself. He laughed, most likely knowing she was full of it.

"First of all, we need food to survive," he said with his megawatt grin fully in place. "And secondly, I want to go over some things with you, and I've worked up an appetite, so let's do two things at once."

The gravel in his voice as his tone lowered at the end of his words made the knots in her stomach tighten painfully. The man was very aware of his charisma. She'd absolutely love to knock him down from the highest rungs on the ladder where he seemed to live, but apparently it wasn't happening right now.

"Goodbye, Ms. Thompson, Mr. Forbes," the group of girls called out as they made their way off the bleachers and rushed from the gym. Keera realized she and Arden had been there long enough for the football team to clear out.

They both threw out half-hearted goodbyes, and Keera turned to follow the girls. "I have to lock up," she repeated.

"I'll help, then we can go," Arden told her.

Keera didn't want to make this more of a big deal than it was, so she left him so she could go to one side of the school to ensure it was secure, while he did the other. She was more than a little pleased when Max stayed with her instead of going with Arden. It seemed the dog was just as fond of her as she was of him. It was either that, or maybe that the dog was just as suspicious of her as Arden's brother Declan was. She preferred to think the pup liked her.

They met up by the front office, and Keera was happy to see her door was shut. Ever since the break-in, she was nervous to enter her office at night. It frustrated her that someone had given her that fear—had taken a piece of her empowerment from her. She'd worked for too long, and far too hard, to allow anyone to do that.

Some water in front of her door nearly made her fall on her ass. Arden was right there at her side, instantly wrapping his strong arm around her, making her knees turn to jelly.

"Careful. Looks like the floors haven't been finished," he said, his voice low and husky.

"Sorry about that," she said, her voice barely above a whisper. Dang it, she was in trouble.

She took only a moment to inhale the man who, even sweaty, was sweet and tangy, making her think of all the areas of him she wouldn't mind tasting. If she kept having thoughts like that, she wasn't going to be fit to be around.

Pulling back from him, but not moving far, Keera was once again captured by his intense gaze. She had no doubt her sexual frustration could end in an instant with the smallest of gestures. He could take her right there on her desk if she asked him to. The knowledge of that was worse than thinking he didn't want her. Knowing she could at least temporarily end this torment, and doing nothing about it, was so much worse than knowing it wasn't an option.

"Let me get my purse," she said.

He licked his lips, and her own tongue mimicked his, making his eyes flare.

"Keera . . . ," he began, his voice dark and sexy. He stepped closer, and she thought for about half a second of allowing it to happen.

But her logical brain kicked in before he could wrap his arms around her, and Keera turned away, feeling his hot breath on the back of her neck, making goose bumps pop out on her skin.

"Food," she said, as if that was the single most important thing in the world.

He sighed behind her, and she could definitely feel his disappointment since she was feeling the exact same emotion. If it weren't for pesky things like emotions and morality, a person could be quite happy with doing whatever the heck they wanted.

"Food it is," he said with a chuckle that surprised her. She didn't dare turn to see him. She pushed open her door, then nearly slipped again when she stepped on an envelope someone had slid beneath it.

She picked it up without thinking twice and opened the unsealed flap, pulling out a single piece of paper. The alarm bells didn't start ringing until she saw the bold font. Then her heated body turned instantly cold.

Her fingers tightened around the paper, crumpling it in her hand as she gasped, her skin tingling. She had no doubt she looked as if she'd just seen a ghost. She felt as if she had—as if the ghosts of her past were coming back to haunt her.

"What is that, Keera?" Arden asked, his amusement gone as he turned her cold body around so he could see the paper she was destroying.

She couldn't speak past the lump in her throat, but she somehow managed to hand over the paper, barely aware of Max, who was letting out a low growl as he cautiously stepped into her office, sniffing the floor.

She barely registered that the next growl had come from Arden. He must have read the note—and he obviously didn't find it to his liking.

YOU WILL GO BACK TO WHERE YOU BELONG IF YOU KNOW WHAT'S BEST FOR YOU . . .

Chapter Ten

Arden lost his appetite as he read the note someone had left Keera. He didn't understand it. His town wasn't a scary place. His school had always been a haven. Was someone out to get Keera? What did he truly know about this woman?

He had no idea of her past, but he was thinking it might be time to figure it out. No, he didn't suspect her of being involved with the drugs, but even if she wasn't dealing, or didn't approve of the dealing, he was more than aware that she was somehow involved, even if it was unwittingly.

He called his brother and told him the latest, and Declan said he'd send people over, hoping whoever was doing this would make a mistake. Criminals were brash and got stupider as time went on. If the person didn't screw it up this time, then Arden didn't doubt they eventually would. He just prayed it wouldn't be at Keera's expense.

Keera was quiet as they waited for the team to come in, and then she said very few words before they got started on combing through her office again. He couldn't tell if she was embarrassed, angry, or scared.

"You aren't in this alone, Keera," he told her.

She shook her head as sadness filled her eyes. "If someone's after me, I can't be at this school. I'm putting the kids in jeopardy," she said as if a piece of her soul was being ripped out.

There were two sorts of people who worked in the school district—those who did it because it was their passion and they wanted to help shape the younger generation into assets of society, and those who were there for a paycheck because they'd gotten themselves stuck with a degree they didn't want. Keera was definitely one of those who was there for the right reason.

"You aren't putting anyone in jeopardy. Whoever is playing this sick game is doing that," he assured her. "And this school, as well as this community, will stand behind you the entire way."

"You don't need to hang around. I know you're hungry," she told him, not replying to his words. He wasn't sure if she didn't believe them, or if it was difficult for her to accept help. She was going to learn that the people in his community, including him, didn't walk away when there was trouble.

"I'll wait. We'll get food together," he told her.

She shook her head, but before she could respond, one of the techs came and took her statement and sealed up the letter. They'd both touched it, and Arden hoped they hadn't wiped away valuable evidence.

"All done," the other tech said with a reassuring smile at Keera. "We'll get this figured out. Just give us time," he added. And then Arden was alone with Keera again.

"I should get home," she told him. She wanted to put distance between them.

He knew it was because she was in shock, but also because she was scared as hell at what was happening between them. Arden wasn't even sure exactly what that was, but he knew he could barely stand to not touch her.

There was something about this woman that was piquing his interest unlike anything he'd ever been through before. Yes, he wanted to have her crying out beneath him, but even more than that, he wanted to hold her in his arms and not let go. She was consuming him in a way that had the potential to burn them both until there was nothing left but ashes.

"Let's get food," he said, placing his hand on the small of her back. She stiffened for the briefest of moments, and then she gave in, allowing him to walk her from the school. He made sure it was locked tight and then took her to his car.

She only lived about a mile from the school, and he knew she often walked instead of driving. He didn't see her vehicle in the parking lot, and he frowned. Normally, he'd have zero problem with the exercise, but with someone threatening her, and the fact of her staying late at the building, he didn't like that she was then walking home in the dark.

They made their way downtown. It was by no means a huge place, but it was filled with character and had some great dining options. The streets were well maintained, and the shop owners took pride in how it appeared. He loved being a part of this community, loved that he was getting to show it to Keera.

"Does Italian sound good?" he asked.

"Sure," she told him. He'd completely understand if she didn't taste a thing, but if he could awaken her senses, it would be at Bianchi's diner. They had the best Chicken Parmesan in the entire state of Washington.

The best part of the restaurant was that they had outside seating, so he could bring Max with them. Of course, he was still considered to be a working dog, even if Max was retired, so it wasn't as if anyone would stop him from bringing the mutt inside, but Arden liked sitting outdoors. Once the rain started, it might be a while before it let up again.

Keera followed him to the hostess station, and they were led to a corner table where heat from a gas fire kept the area nice and cozy. Large potted trees were strategically placed throughout the small sitting area to give the illusion of intimacy. It wasn't a bad place for their first date even if the timing was off. Of course, Keera wasn't aware he was looking at this as a date.

But Arden had decided he needed to help Keera. Beyond that, though, he had to get to know this woman more. And the only way he was going to be able to do that was to spend time with her. It was too bad their night out had started on such a solemn note.

The server was there within a minute, and much to Max's delight, she had a bowl of water for him, and took a moment to scratch him behind the ears. Arden could swear the dog sighed. Spoiled mutt.

"How you doing, Arden?" she asked. Cammy was a sweet girl, in her second year of college and coming home every chance she could to help out her mom at the restaurant. She'd been a top student of his.

"Really good. How's college life treating you?" he asked.

"I love it," she exclaimed. "I might be one of those forever students. At least that's what my dad fears," she added with a laugh.

"You were always a good student, so I say go for it," he told her. He wouldn't be surprised if she got her PhD.

"And you are still my favorite teacher," she said with a big smile.

"Love to hear it," he told her.

She took their drink and appetizer order, promising a short wait since the main dinner crowd had already cleared out. Arden assured her any wait was worth it with her mother's cooking being so dang good.

After they perused the menu, Cammy came back and finished their order, then left them on their own. Arden wanted to try to get Keera to share what she was feeling or even what she was thinking.

Their appetizers arrived, and Keera picked up her fork, dangling it in her fingers. "You're going to want to savor this. It's heaven," Arden assured her.

She finally looked at him, and he was pleased to see color returning to her cheeks. There was also a new glint in her eyes. Instead of seeming defeated, she appeared angry. *Good.* He'd much rather she was ticked off, than scared or sad.

"Thank you. I can't remember when I last ate," she said, her brow wrinkling as she tried to recall her last meal.

"That's not good," he said, pointing down at the antipasto platter with his own fork. He stabbed an olive and enjoyed the tartness of it on his tongue. He was happy when Keera munched on a piece of salami and cheese on a hot piece of bread. She sighed.

"Oh, this is good," she told him.

"Cammy's mom is full Italian, and her cooking is unique. She makes all the bread and pasta from scratch. If they run out, the place closes down early. She tries to make sure that doesn't happen, so she hires high school kids to help in the kitchen. She says there are no egos but hers allowed in there, so that's why she prefers to teach the younger ones than hire other chefs."

"She sounds like a woman I'd like to know," Keera said, making him beam with pride.

"I'm sure she'll come out and say hi. She often does," he told her.

"That's something I like about small towns," she admitted, giving him a little piece of herself as she relaxed.

She sipped the wine he'd ordered, and he topped off her glass, not trying to get her drunk, but hoping a bit of red wine would help her relax. He wanted her to trust him. He'd never had to try so hard to get someone to do exactly that.

Arden didn't think he was the best guy in the world, but he considered himself pretty dang close to perfect. People were generally drawn to him, and it fascinated him that Keera was doing her best to keep him away. There was obvious attraction between the two of them, so that made it all the more puzzling. He wasn't going to be satisfied until he figured out this woman. That was something he knew for sure.

"What else made you decide to come here?" he asked as he dipped a piece of bread in vinegar and oil.

Keera paused with an olive dangling before her lips. He felt himself harden when her tongue swept out and she licked away the seasoning before popping it in her mouth. Damn, she made eating downright sexual without even trying.

He shifted in his seat as he tried to get comfortable. He might as well give up because he had a feeling he was going to be hard until the two of them ripped each other's clothes away. Needing a distraction, he grabbed a piece of salami and tossed it down to Max, who eyed him for a moment before he carefully picked it up and ate it. Arden was almost surprised when the mutt didn't demand a plate and fork. He hadn't been aware a dog could have such a big personality, but Max was the exception to the rule when it came to pets.

"You know you can feed it to him. Would you like to eat off the ground?" Keera asked as she held out a piece of meat, which Max took gently as he scooted closer to her, his head on his paws as he patiently waited for the next morsel.

"He's a dog. They like to eat things off the ground," Arden assured her.

"Max is far from an ordinary pet," she told him in her sternest tone. He could totally see her giving kids a good talking-to. The teens would probably be shaking in their boots. "He has more class," she added.

Max gave a murmur of agreement as his eyes slanted at Arden in a mocking manner. Arden wasn't normally a man prone to violence, but he wanted to give the mutt a swift kick in the hind end. Since he didn't abuse people or animals, he grabbed another piece of salami and savored it as the dog looked on.

Now he was taunting an animal. Arden realized he might have issues. He assured himself it all stemmed from sexual frustration. It was either that or he was slowly losing his mind.

"Well, he likes you a lot more than he likes me," Arden told her as Max laid his head on her shoe and closed his eyes. It appeared he was done with eating for now, but he wanted to stay close to her.

"That just shows he has taste," Keera said, her lips turning up in a smile that was quite the beautiful sight.

Their plates were cleared, new silverware was brought out, and their wine glasses were topped off. Salad was brought out next, and Arden kept their conversation light as he watched Keera relax. He couldn't actually remember the last time he'd enjoyed someone's company as much as he was enjoying hers. Other than family, of course.

By the time they finished the meal, Arden was stuffed to the gills and still not in a hurry to go anywhere.

"Do you want dessert?" Cammy asked.

"Definitely," Keera said. "What's the best you have?"

Cammy smiled in delight. She liked customers who trusted her. It was her mama's place, and the girl would know what the best of the best was.

"We have one big slice of the pumpkin-gingersnap tiramisu left that's so delicious you'll cry when it's gone. But I have to say, Mom's secret trifle recipe is particularly delicious tonight, as well. Unfortunately, I had both and will have to run ten miles tonight to work off the calories. I refuse to gain the freshman, sophomore, or junior fifteen," she said with a chuckle as she ran her hand across her stomach.

"You've left me no choice. I'll have to get both," Keera said.

"How about we share?" Arden asked. He laughed out loud when her brow wrinkled as if she wanted to turn him down. "I've had the desserts before, and trust me, they aren't small cuts. Each piece is definitely enough for two or three people," he promised.

"Is he being truthful?" Keera asked, making Arden laugh again. He couldn't remember anyone not taking him at his word.

"For sure," Cammy said. Reluctantly, Keera agreed.

The moment Cammy came back with both desserts, and a plate with some chocolates and cookies on it, Arden felt a stab through his gut at the pure ecstasy on Keera's face. If she got this excited over sugar, he imagined she was going to soar when he got his hands on her naked flesh.

A woman who could appreciate a good meal was a woman who liked to be satisfied. And Arden was up to the task of making sure that happened. When she took her first bite of the tiramisu, she let out a groan that nearly had him coming in his pants—something he hadn't done in at least twenty years.

This woman was definitely going to be the death of him. He realized he didn't care—that the end would be so damn pleasurable he'd die wearing a smile. He took a bite of the dessert and let out his own sound of pleasure. Their eyes connected, and he wondered how it was they weren't bursting into flames.

Chapter Eleven

There was no possible way Keera would be able to get even one more bite of food into her overstuffed belly. She squirmed in her seat as she took a sip of water, hoping it would help the food digest a bit faster. She should have gone straight to the dessert menu and ordered one of everything. Her sweet tooth was fully intact.

Greta Bianchi came out and visited with them for a few minutes, and Keera enjoyed the woman. She fell in love with Greta when the lady handed her a sack of goodies for later, welcoming her to Edmonds and insisting she come back soon.

Keera assured her she would. Arden insisted on paying the tab and wouldn't tell her how much it was. But the two of them didn't make it outside the gate before Cammy ran up to them and gave Arden a hug and thank-you, so the tip must have been slightly insane.

"That was pretty sweet of you," Keera told him as they moved down the sidewalk to his car.

"She's a good kid, was one of my favorite students," he said, shaking it off as no big deal. She was pleasantly surprised by the blush in his cheeks. It seemed he didn't want her to know he'd left the girl a large tip. She was glad he hadn't done it to impress her, even if the gesture certainly had done exactly that.

Keera wasn't at all surprised when she didn't have to tell Arden where she lived. Not only was it a small community, but she had a feeling with all that was going on, the community members would want to know exactly who she was.

She wondered if they'd unburied her past. She was too afraid the answer was *yes* for her to ask. She'd hoped to have a fresh start here, to be somewhere her name didn't carry the burden with it that it had carried for so long.

Maybe it was time for her to realize her past had shaped her into who she was, and it was better for her to face it, maybe even embrace it—the good and the bad—and to stop letting it freeze her. If it were that simple, though, maybe she would have done just that by now.

Keera knew Arden wasn't a man to drop her at the curb and take off, so she didn't try to argue when he fell into step with her as she entered her apartment building. It had been so long since someone had escorted her home that she had to admit it felt sort of nice, especially since she was a little jumpy.

"I'm taking the stairs. I have to burn a few of these calories," she said. "You don't have to walk up with me."

Arden didn't even bother with a response, just smiled as he opened the door to the staircase and signaled for her to go on through. She smiled back and stepped into the dim stairwell.

Arden walked at her side up the three flights, with Max leading the way. The dog was so well behaved he didn't have to be on his leash the majority of the time. That gave Keera a sense of security. If there was someone out to get her, she had no doubt they wouldn't make it past Max.

When they reached her floor, they stepped into the hall, and Keera was feeling pretty dang good—that was, until they reached her door. Then she felt that sense of unease again as she gazed down at her doorknob.

Max immediately stood at attention as his head swiveled both ways. She wasn't sure if he knew something was out of place, or if the dog was just picking up on her tension. Arden stepped behind her, keeping her back protected as he scanned the area.

"What's the matter, Keera?" he asked quietly.

"You pick up on things fast, don't you?" she said. "It's a little disconcerting how well you read people—including me," she added with a nervous chuckle. "And that's without really knowing me." She should shut up now, but she was nervous and tended to speak too much when she was. She couldn't imagine what it would be like if they did get to know each other. She was beginning to forget why that was such a bad idea.

"I like to think I read people and situations well," he said. "Now, tell me what's bothering you."

"Someone's been here," she said.

Arden looked at her knob, seeing the scratches around the lock.

"Can you tell if they got the door open?" he asked.

"I don't think so. Someone could have scared them off," she said. "Or at least I hope that's the case. Or that maybe I'm just jumpy and overreacting."

"I want to make sure," he told her. He held out his hand for the key.

Keera didn't want to be a helpless victim, but she allowed herself the luxury of letting him take over, at least this once. Too much had happened in one day, heck, for the past week, and it didn't make her a weak person to lean on someone now and then, especially when that someone had shoulders wide enough to carry the burden of ten people.

Arden carefully unlocked her door, then told Max to stay with Keera as he stepped inside her place. Max didn't budge from his spot at her side, his head resting against her waist as he continued monitoring the hallway.

Keera let out a breath of relief even though Arden hadn't returned yet. She had no doubt no one was in her place. If they were, there was no way Max would obediently stay at her side. The dog would be charging in to protect his owner. Arden and Max might not be on the best of terms at all times, but she knew a loyal animal when she saw one, and Max was that dog who would gladly give his life.

"We're all clear," Arden said about ten seconds later—a very nerve-racking ten seconds. "Let's call the police."

"Are you sure? They didn't make it inside," Keera said. She couldn't stand the thought of the police thinking this was something she was bringing on herself. "This is getting awkward, and they have to be getting irritated I'm monopolizing so much of their time."

"There might be evidence," Arden told her. He didn't continue to argue, just pulled out his phone and dialed. He called his brother next, and Keera could hear Declan swearing through the speaker of the phone. She wasn't sure what was being said, but she could feel tension radiating as the two brothers spoke.

It was oddly anticlimactic as they left her door open and waited for the techs, who came quickly. They were in and out fast, again telling her they were going to solve this problem even if they had to work twenty-four-seven to do it.

Keera felt the sincerity of their words and had to fight desperately not to shed a tear at the loyalty from these people who didn't know a thing about her. It appeared all they needed to know was that she was now a citizen of their community, and that was good enough for them.

"We need to replace your door lock," Arden told her as he looked at the worn piece of metal. "And why didn't you have the dead bolt secured?"

"The dead bolt doesn't work. I told maintenance, but they haven't gotten to it yet," she said. It was important for her to make sure he knew she wasn't some foolish girl who didn't think about her own safety.

"Let's go get new locks. We'll let management know later," he told her.

"I can take care of this, Arden. It's been a long day for you with school, practice, and babysitting me," she told him.

"Do you honestly believe I'd feel okay with myself if I left you to deal with this on your own?" he asked, looking far more puzzled than annoyed. "I wouldn't sleep, knowing someone could easily get into your place at any time with how rickety these ancient locks are."

Keera certainly didn't have a hero complex where she needed to save the day, but she had to agree with the man. If she were walking a student home and came upon the same sort of situation, especially if that student had been stalked recently, she wouldn't leave, either, until she knew the problem had been taken care of.

"Thanks, Arden. You truly are going above and beyond for someone you barely know," she said.

Keera hadn't really thought much about the fact that she didn't have long-lasting relationships in her life. She just figured she was one of those people who had been scarred too much from an early age to allow people in enough for them to form close bonds of friendship.

But as she moved down the staircase with Arden, she realized she didn't want to be that person anymore. She didn't want to live such an isolated life. No, her scars hadn't disappeared, but maybe if she got help, sought out the advice of a counselor, then she'd be able to trust herself enough to trust other people to stay in her life.

Ironically, she'd rather be alone as she was having these breakthrough thoughts. But there was something nice about having Arden walking on one side of her and Max on the other. She felt like she was in a pocket of safety, and it sent a warmth through her that no blanket on this earth could give.

It took a lot of willpower for her not to reach out and touch the strong man beside her. Instead of doing just that, she laid her hand on top of Max's soft fur and gently caressed the overgrown mutt.

Keera had always been able to love animals unconditionally. She thought that was a step in the right direction. But it was rare for an animal to reject a person, and once a bond had formed between a pet and its owner, there was no chance of that bond failing, at least never that she'd seen.

"Max sure eats up the attention you've been giving him," Arden said with a laugh. Max looked at him out of the corner of his eye with what appeared to be a warning. That almost made Keera laugh. She gave him an extra scratch.

"That's because I think I'm in love with him," she said, feeling oddly light considering how dark her evening had been. "Animals love without conditions. It's just something that draws me to them," she admitted.

"People can love that way, too," he told her.

She shrugged, trying not to show too much of what she was feeling. "Sadly enough, I've seen animals abused before, and then watched with a broken heart as the poor baby crawled back to the one who had hurt them, pleading with that person to forgive them, to love them in spite of what they thought they'd done wrong." She had to stop and take a deep breath as she fought not to cry.

"I think a person capable of animal abuse should get punished in the same way they torment their animals," Arden said, his voice a deep growl.

"You haven't seemed like much of an animal lover," she told him.

"I might not be the best pet owner, but that doesn't mean I don't appreciate animals, even love them," he said. "And abuse is abuse, whether of another person, an animal, or yourself." He paused for a moment. "But there's a special place in hell for those who hurt the young, the old, or the furry."

It took all of Keera's willpower not to reach out and caress this man at her side.

"Yeah, I agree with you," she said, finding herself sliding over a little closer to him. "I've always wondered, if an animal can love unconditionally, why is it so hard for us humans to do it," she added. "I honestly don't have an answer to that."

The three of them stepped outside, and Max seemed to grumble when Arden attached the leash back to his collar.

"We're in public. You need the leash," Arden told Max, who turned away from him and stared ahead, obviously pouting.

"There's a store just a couple blocks down if you want to walk," he offered.

"I'd love to walk. It will clear my head and hopefully help my food settle so I can have more." She suddenly smiled, and then chuckled, at Arden's shocked expression.

With all the soul-searching she was doing, she found she didn't want to be afraid or upset. That was giving the people trying to scare her the power they desperately wanted. She wasn't going to let them win that way.

"I just found the pot at the end of the rainbow," she told him.

"I'm a little afraid to ask you what you're talking about," Arden said as he continued walking forward, Max leading the way.

"I have more dessert waiting for me. Maybe we can stop at the store, get what we need, and take the long way back to the apartment," she suggested.

Arden gazed at her as if he were truly concerned she'd lost her mind, but then finally gave her a lopsided grin. "I have to say, I've always been a glass-half-full kind of guy. I'll make a deal with you," he offered.

She was immediately suspicious. "I'm listening," she said, though there was hesitation. She was beginning to learn that any deal Arden put on the table would surely benefit him the most.

"If you share that dessert, we can go on a longer walk," he began, and she was already not liking his deal. "And I'll even put the new locks on."

Hmm. He wasn't being unreasonable. But Keera wasn't too sure she wanted to give up even the smallest morsel of her goodies. She wasn't sure what Greta had sent home, but after one meal at the woman's place, she had no doubt it would be scrumptious.

"Come on. The place opens at eleven tomorrow. You can get more," he said, his voice so pathetic she decided to cave.

"You have a deal, then," she said. The smile he gave her made her lose her step, nearly causing her to face-plant right there in the middle of the sidewalk. She quickly caught herself and turned away from him.

Damn, the man was magnetic, and she was opening up to him more by the minute—hell, by the second, if she was being completely honest with herself. Yes, she had just decided it was time to let people into her life, but Keera would be a fool if she thought Arden would be a good first person to try to do that with.

She realized as they walked side by side to the hardware store, she might not get much of a choice in the matter. Whether she liked it or not, the man was becoming indispensable to her. Now the question was, could she let go enough to accept the offer in his eyes?

Chapter Twelve

Arden didn't understand why he felt like a teenager on his first date as he and Keera sat at her small kitchen table. The lights were dim, and it felt as if the rest of the world had fallen away. Why was he so comfortable with this woman? With everything happening, he should be more on alert, should be more suspicious.

But instead of that, all he seemed to want to do was pull her next to him, close the distance between them, and taste her sweet lips. He had a feeling they tasted like honey. Yeah, he had a strong sex drive, but it was getting a little ridiculous how much he wanted this woman.

Looking up, his eyes connected with Keera's, and Arden quit resisting the urge to touch her. He reached across the small table and let his fingers sift through her silky strands, her tresses flowing over his skin.

"What are you doing?" she asked nervously.

"I love long hair," he told her. "You should wear it down more."

"I try to keep it as professional as possible. It isn't easy being a high school principal when you're as young as I am. It's hard to earn the students' respect," she told him.

"You seem to be doing a good job on that front," he said. He did notice how she backed away from him, though, so he dropped his hand and grabbed his fork instead, taking a bite of pie, the taste not nearly as satisfying as her lips would be.

"Don't you notice how the kids always seem to turn to a male teacher, or even Ethan? It's annoying sometimes," she told him.

"I didn't even think about it," he admitted.

"You wouldn't have to. Not only have you grown up in this town, earning instant trust and respect, but you are indeed a male," she said. He enjoyed the sigh in her voice. She might be fighting him, but she was definitely attracted. He just had to get her to trust what she was feeling.

"I guess I'll have to pay more attention to that," he said.

"Are you saying that to appease me?" she asked with a smile. Damn, when this woman smiled, her face lit up, making her even more beautiful than she was already.

"Not at all," he assured her. "What made you want to be a principal in the first place?" he asked.

"I don't know. I just knew I needed to do something that would make a difference to children," she told him.

"Why not social work, then?" he asked.

"I think I went into school having no idea what I wanted to do, and then it just sort of happened. Why don't you tell me why a billionaire would decide to be a high school teacher, earning a pittance of a paycheck and working long hours? That has to be a much better story than mine."

He laughed. "I've been asked that a lot," he said. "And I think it's the same answer as yours. I wanted to make a difference."

"But you had a great childhood. You're close with your family. Why feel the need to help kids?"

She picked up a cookie and ripped off a corner. The way she opened her mouth, her tongue sweeping out the slightest bit to taste the chocolate before she popped it into her mouth, had his body aching in an unbearable way. He shifted on his small chair and wondered what the chances were of getting her into bed.

He wasn't a betting man, but he didn't think his odds were too good on this night.

Their eyes connected again, and her hand froze on its way to her mouth. The sexual chemistry between them was insane. She took a shuddering breath, and while she was doing her best to pretend nothing was happening between them, he had no doubt there was magic in the air. She could deny it, but it was there.

"Did you ever think of doing something else?" she asked.

"Nope, not really. I'm a pretty stubborn man, and once something gets locked inside my head, there's really no turning back," he said.

"Is that a warning?" she asked, surprising him with her sass.

"Would you take heed if it was?" he said, his lips turned wide. His cheeks were actually a bit sore from smiling so much.

"I'd take it as a challenge," she answered, surprising him.

"I've never been able to resist a challenge myself," he said.

"I guess we're both pretty stubborn," she said before resuming her small bites of cookie. The way this woman ate was driving him mad.

The two of them chatted as they consumed far too many calories. He found that not only was he attracted to her, but he actually enjoyed her company. That was rarer than people realized.

When you connected with someone, it was foolish to ignore it. And one thing people would never be able to say about Arden was that he was a fool. Yes, when he made up his mind, he went after what he wanted. And yes, he wanted Keera. What he wasn't sure about was exactly what he wanted her for. Was it just sex?

"I have to say I'm a bit worried about your chair," he told her as he shifted. "I'm not sure it's gonna keep holding me. Maybe we should move to the couch."

Her eyes narrowed, and he realized he'd kill to know what was going through her mind.

"Just because my furniture doesn't come from some high-end retailer doesn't make it any less useful," she assured him.

He held up a hand. "Whoa, where did that come from?"

"I don't like snobs," she said.

"How is that comment me being a snob?" he asked.

"You've been extremely wealthy your entire life, so being here in my apartment is the definition of 'slumming it' for you," she told him.

He sat back and looked at her. "Are you a reverse snob?" he asked, liking the shock in her eyes.

"What's that supposed to mean?" she questioned.

"I don't judge you for your life. Why should you judge me for mine?" he asked. This was a conversation he'd had before, but her answers would tell him a lot about her.

"I've known wealthy people, and they think money gives them the right to do whatever they want, whenever they want. It's obscene," she said.

"Just because someone has the money to enjoy some of the finer things in life doesn't define who they are," he pointed out.

"It defines a lot of people," she said.

"Does it define you?" he asked. Her head turned as she looked at him, trying to figure out where he was going with this conversation. He was confusing her, and that was good. It was nice to keep someone off-kilter once in a while.

"I refuse to be defined. I get to choose the path I want to take. And I will never let money rule my life," she assured him.

"Good. Me, either," he told her. He leaned closer, their heads close, but not close enough. She stayed there for a moment before backing away.

"I'm sorry," she finally said. "It's just that wealthy people confuse me. They don't understand how the rest of the world lives, don't understand what it's like to be hungry or worried about how they're going to pay their bills. And they are a little too judgmental about the rest of the population."

"Basically, you're telling me I don't have compassion or common sense," he said with a chuckle.

"No!" she assured him. "I wasn't talking specifically about you . . ." She trailed off when he continued laughing. "You're making me uncomfortable on purpose, aren't you?" she asked before giving in and letting out her own chuckle.

"Maybe a little. But you *are* being quick to judge me without getting to know me," he told her.

They finished their dessert, and Arden took the time to get to know this woman a little more while also letting her see he wasn't the person she'd so quickly assumed he was. Arden could see she was definitely not a woman eager to jump into a quick affair, but she was also skittish when it came to relationships.

He wasn't sure where that left them.

"We've consumed a million calories today, and I think it's now time to call it a night," she told him.

Arden was surprised by the disappointment her words filled him with. But he didn't want her to feel as if he wasn't willing to respect or listen to her. He rose from the table and held out a hand to help her up.

With reluctance, she gave it to him, and he slowly pulled her to her feet. The two of them stood there for a few moments, and though the sexual tension was as thick as fog, he also felt comfortable. He liked being with this woman.

Reaching out, he ran a finger down her cheek, enjoying when her eyes dilated. Damn, he wanted to kiss her. And he knew she'd let him. But somehow he knew it wasn't the right moment. Tonight had been about building trust. He couldn't blow that.

"Good night, Keera," he said, his voice husky.

"Good night," she replied, her voice barely above a whisper.

Though it felt as if his legs were weighed down and he was slogging through the mud, he let her go and walked to the door. It had been a pretty great night. He planned on a lot more just like it.

Chapter Thirteen

Keera had never spent an entire week as sexually and mentally frustrated as she had in the last, very long seven-day period. Arden insisted on picking her up and dropping her off every day. The problem with this arrangement was that every moment she spent with the man was one more moment she was afraid she wouldn't be able to let him go from her life.

Right now there was danger in the air, and Keera was most definitely a woman who liked to research things. She had read more than one article about how dangerous it was to start any sort of relationship with another person while your emotions were running on overdrive.

Add to that her sexual attraction to the man, and the fact that it had been so long since she'd had sex that she couldn't remember the last time, and she was a bomb about to go off. If he brushed her arm or back one more time, she didn't think she could be responsible for what happened next.

"Are you ready to head out?" the man who was constantly in her thoughts asked from her doorway.

Just like always, her belly did a few flip-flops at the sight of him. As he moved into her office, she held her breath, knowing the moment she took in some air, she was going to inhale his scent. She'd swear under oath the man had some secret pheromone he mixed into his cologne.

"Yes, I'm finished," she said, her voice tight enough that Arden looked at her curiously. He'd learned not to question her when she was in a mood like this. He certainly wasn't a foolish man. That much could be said about him.

Max came around her desk to greet her with a lick against her hand as he waited for his treat. Yes, she'd gone out and bought the dog a bag of goodies, and he knew exactly where they were in her office—no matter how many times she hid them, seeing if she could fool the mutt.

This time he went over to her coat tree and pawed a double-lined cooler bag, then gave her a look that seemed to say, *Come on, you can do better than this.* The dog's amusement instantly lightened her mood. She chuckled as she moved over to the bag and opened it, taking out a snack and giving it to Max, who gently took it from her.

"You're such a sweetheart," she told him as she gave him a quick scratch before putting on her jacket and grabbing her purse.

"With you he is. He's still a pain in my butt," Arden said. "I think you're just the animal whisperer. I can't believe that mean alley cat was purring beneath your feet the other day. He drew blood on my ankle the day before. We need to catch him so I can take him to Doc Evan to get a checkup and maybe find a home for him, not that anyone would want that beast."

"Oh, Tom is misunderstood," she told Arden, who grumbled beneath his breath.

"Yeah, so is Max, apparently," he told her.

"Max is a good boy. I can't believe you got him for free," she said. "I remember a girl in school had a German shepherd that she said cost as much as her car."

"Yeah, they are loyal dogs, but that doesn't mean I ever wanted a pet," he told her.

"I'd gladly take him off your hands if the apartment building allowed pets," she said with a sigh.

Max moved closer to her and rubbed his head against her waist. She really did feel as if the animal could understand conversations. It'd be pretty dang cool if he did. And though Arden might grumble and moan about the dog, she had noticed he was softening with the animal. He'd even started petting the dog at times when he didn't realize what he was doing. She had a feeling that he and Max weren't ever going to part.

"You can have him. I'll talk to the apartment management," Arden said, but she noticed how he looked at the dog and winced as if instantly regretting his words.

"You should be very glad I know you don't mean that or you'd be losing a pet and then crying about it when you're all by yourself," she told him.

"I don't stand around crying," Arden assured her.

"Mm-hmm," she mumbled. He uttered something else and then held open the back door for Max to jump in before opening her door. She'd learned to wait for him to do it. It seemed to offend him if she opened a door by herself. She refused to admit that this was another thing she liked about the man. His ego was big enough without her needing to stroke it for him.

When they missed the turn to her apartment, Keera looked at him quizzically. "Where are we going?" He turned his head and grinned.

"Our second date," he said, his eyes gleaming.

"When did we have a first date?" she asked before thinking of correcting him—the two of them definitely weren't dating. It was hard enough to even think straight when he gave her that blinding smile with those twinkling eyes, let alone try to put him in his place. Besides, Keera thought, his place was pretty much wherever he wanted it to be.

"Dinner last week," he told her.

"It ended with a break-in at my apartment, not a kiss. Therefore, that wasn't a date," she said before she could even think about the impact of her words.

Arden's smile faded as he stopped at a light, his eyes burning so hot Keera felt her skin heat up about fifty degrees. She knew she should quickly try to take back her words, but she couldn't even breathe with him looking at her like that, let alone try to force words out.

"I'll make sure this date ends a hell of a lot better," he promised.

A car honked behind them, and Keera let out her breath in a rush when Arden was forced to face forward. She quickly unrolled her window, her skin on fire, a slight sheen of sweat coating her forehead.

She wasn't sure she was going to last the night with this man, not if he continued to look at her that way. For the past two weeks, something had been building within her, something she had tried to squelch, and had failed horribly at doing.

She was pretty sure where the two of them were headed, and she knew without a doubt that it was a mistake, but she couldn't seem to talk herself out of it. She wanted to feel his lips on hers, wanted to know if this was all in her imagination or if there really was a sexual spark that would light them both on fire.

She could try to lie to herself all she wanted, but it seemed it was impossible to lie to Arden, because he could see right through the boulders she was lining her path with. He wasn't a man to be discouraged when there was something he wanted. And much to her horror and delight, it appeared that she was something he wanted—at least for now.

Keera wondered if she could be okay with all of this, if she could have a casual fling with this magnetic man without letting her heart or emotions get involved. Part of her was confident she could do just that. The rest of her knew that was a load of hogwash. She might keep herself closely guarded, but there was a part of her that was screaming to be set free.

Was Arden the person who was going to do that? And if he somehow cracked this wall she'd so carefully surrounded herself with, would she survive the impact of it tumbling down?

Keera didn't know the answers to these questions, but it appeared as if she wasn't going to have time to analyze it. It appeared as if the storm that had been building between the two of them was coming to its peak. Maybe neither of them would survive. Or maybe she'd finally be set free.

Chapter Fourteen

Sweat beaded on Arden's palms as he pulled up his vehicle to the gate at the end of his driveway. Normally he left it open, not wanting to bother with waiting on it to open or close. But knowing he was bringing Keera back to his place, and knowing no one had been caught yet for stalking her, he was more concerned about her safety than about a mere convenience for himself.

"Where are we?" she asked.

"My house," he said.

"Is this a good idea?" she asked, and he wanted to tell her, *Probably not.*

"It's a great idea," he told her instead. He turned away before he could try to analyze what she was thinking. He didn't want anything to stop him from driving forward, from the sight of her in his home.

Of course, he knew she'd been expecting him to take her to a restaurant. When she hadn't protested him taking her on a date, he'd been elated. When she'd made the comment about it not being a date because he hadn't kissed her, he'd been desperate to get her alone.

He'd been aroused from the moment he'd first met her. But the more time he spent with her, the more he realized that there was so much more to this woman than merely a pretty face and smoking-hot body.

She was beautiful, funny, sassy, brilliant, and had a heart she was dying to share with the world. Something had happened to her that made her afraid of doing just that, and Arden realized he could easily look into her history, find out what it was that had made her so afraid. With most people that's exactly what he would have done.

But with Keera, he had stopped himself. He didn't want to invade her privacy. He needed to make her trust him enough that she would voluntarily share her story. There was a piece of her that was so vulnerable, it broke his heart. But the strength of her also impressed him.

She wasn't a victim, not by any means, and she didn't want to play one. That fact alone made him respect her. If he added to all of that the rest of her assets, he wondered if he was ever going to let this woman out of his life.

He was beginning to think the answer to that was a big fat whopping *no*. Instead of that filling him with terror, it filled him with peace. Maybe after this night together, after he hopefully got a few more answers, he'd have to go see his mom. His sister was still visiting, since her husband, Ace, had been called away for something, and she said she couldn't stand sleeping in her bed without him there.

"Does any of your family live with you?" she asked.

"Trying to figure out if we'll be alone?" he asked with a waggle of his brows.

"It's a pretty big place," she said, her cheeks turning a little pink.

"I live alone, but my sister could drop in at any minute. She's staying with Mom and Dad right now 'cause her husband, Ace, is out of town for work."

"What does he do?" she asked.

"He's military, and damn good at it," he told her. "And as much as the thought of my baby sister being in any relationship is terrifying, I have to admit I respect the hell out of my brother-in-law. He loves my sister with a passion that's consuming and more than obvious, so he's earned my respect."

"I bet it wasn't easy for him with four big brothers towering over him," she said.

Arden laughed. "Ace isn't easily intimidated, which is the only kind of man Dakota would ever be with. And while he might have a tough exterior and put his ass on the line to save others, he still has zero insecurities over worshipping his wife and giving her the respect she deserves. That's made all of us like him and his brothers."

"What's your sister like?" she asked, making him smile even more.

"Ah, Dakota is amazing, and stubborn, and absolutely determined to do anything her brothers can do. We'd all gladly die for her, but now she has a husband who'd walk over a lava flow to get to her, even if it was only to tell her one last time how much he loved her before he was pulled under. That kind of devotion can't be faked. That kind of love was the only kind Dakota would have ever accepted," he said.

"Wow, you're more of a romantic than I would've thought," she told him.

He thought about that for a couple of seconds. "That's the only way to love," he admitted. "Somewhere along the path I've been on, I've realized my own goals have changed. I don't want to just get by. After seeing how happy my sister is, then watching how devoted my brother Kian is to his beautiful wife, I want more."

Arden looked at Keera as she nervously chewed her bottom lip. Was she the one he'd find he couldn't live without? He honestly didn't know. But one thing he knew beyond a shadow of a doubt was that he was intrigued enough to find out if he'd be willing to let her go—or willing to walk through fire for her.

He pulled into his garage and turned off the engine. His heart thudded as he stepped from the car. He hadn't brought a woman to his place in years. He hadn't had this house very long, but even the place before this had been his sacred area, and he hadn't wanted it tainted with the memory of some one-night stand.

But Keera Thompson certainly wasn't a one-night stand. And his goal in bringing her to his place wasn't to get her into bed. He wouldn't fight that if it were to happen, it just wasn't his goal. He wanted to see how it made him feel to have her inside his walls. He was about to find out.

He opened her car door, and she was silent as her hand drifted to Max's head. She might not realize it, but anytime she was nervous, scared, sad—anything, really—she reached for the dog. And Max seemed to always know when she needed him, because he would walk extra close to her, lean his head against her, comfort her. The two had bonded in a way Arden had never bonded with an animal.

Arden did like the mutt, though he wasn't actually admitting that to his smug brother or to Keera, but he liked having him around. He might grumble and moan at Arden, but he was also brilliant and useful, and . . . okay, he was damn likable.

The second he opened the door into his house, the smell of garlic and parsley, onions and oregano, and other enticing flavors hit their noses. Arden's stomach growled its appreciation of such delectable scents, knowing wherever those scents led, food was available for consumption.

"Oh, you got dinner from Bianchi's, didn't you?" Keera asked, not even noticing anything about his house as she followed her nose.

Arden was almost disappointed she was seemingly unimpressed with his place, but then again, since she had called him a snob, he realized that maybe he should be grateful she wasn't thinking too much about it. And admittedly, the aroma coming from his kitchen was ridiculously enticing. He'd give her the tour later.

They rounded the corner to his kitchen, and Angela, his tiny wisp of a housekeeper, or more aptly, the woman who ensured he didn't live in a pigsty and had food in his refrigerator, stepped away from the counter to greet them.

"I was hoping to get out of your hair before you got home," Angela said, grinning at both of them.

"Then you wouldn't have gotten to meet Keera," Arden told her.

"I've been looking forward to it," Angela said. "A new person can't move into this town without everyone knowing about it."

Arden noticed how Keera tensed at Angela's words. She really didn't like to be the center of attention. He wasn't sure if it was because she had something to hide or if she was just a private person. If it was the latter, he could completely understand.

"I like your town. It's very nice to meet you," Keera said after a second too long.

Angela was a sweet woman who had moved to town a year before. She had a little girl who was full of energy, and this job had been perfect for her, as Arden was more than flexible with the hours.

"I'm sorry you've been having so much trouble at the school and now at your home," Angela said.

"We'll get to the bottom of it," Keera assured the woman.

"I have no doubt about that. I've gotten to know the Forbes family quite well, and once they start something, they don't stop," Angela said with a laugh.

"That's for sure," Arden agreed.

Max was making laps around the kitchen island, the delicious aromas a little too much for the dog to take.

Angela laughed and told them, "I'll get out of your way so you can enjoy a nice meal. It looks like Max is ready for dinner."

"Yeah, he can have his dog food," Arden grumbled.

"Don't be such a bully. He can share with me," Keera said. "Isn't that right, Max?"

The dog immediately moved to Keera's side with his head against her, his favorite position. Arden couldn't believe he was growing jealous of a dog. But he wouldn't mind his head resting against her, especially if they were naked.

He ripped his gaze away from Keera before those thoughts could go any further. For one thing, he needed to feed her, and for another, he didn't want her to think he'd brought her to his place just to get her into his bed—though he'd do a happy dance if she wanted to go there.

"Have a nice evening," Arden told Angela.

She left, and it was just the three of them. Arden moved over to the stove where everything was sitting on warmers. The table was set, so Arden pulled out a salad bowl and began mixing the precut ingredients.

"Can I help with anything?" Keera asked.

"Nope. You're a guest. I want you to sit back and enjoy," he told her.

Arden liked having Keera in his kitchen. It was nice, and so damn domestic. He could picture the two of them coming home together after a fulfilling day at work, preparing a meal, sitting down and eating, then rushing to the bedroom . . .

He had to stop himself again from allowing his thoughts to go off in that direction. But it wasn't an easy thing to do. Keera was on his mind all the time now, and with her in his house, it was making it even worse. There was just so much to this woman that he wanted to know, and the only way to do that was to get her to let down her guard.

When the salad was put together, he fed Max, then told him to go lie down, which the dog did, surprisingly. Keera seemed a little disappointed to have the mutt leave her side. Maybe Max was a good defense for her. He wanted to assure her they didn't need a chaperone. He could behave if he had to.

"Let's sit," he told her.

She followed him to the table, and he poured them each a glass of wine. She took a sip and sighed as the flavors hit her tongue, and just like that, Arden was thinking of the bedroom again. It appeared Keera wasn't able to do anything that didn't turn him on.

"Want me to dish you up?" Arden asked.

Keera laughed, the sound instantly warming him. "I think I'm capable of doing that much at least," she assured him. He pulled the lids off the dishes, and Keera sighed again.

"I'm going to get fat if I keep eating this food," she said as she took a nice helping of ravioli.

"Nah, you run around too much for that," he assured her.

"I need to start taking time to go to the gym again. My last apartment complex had a nice workout room. This one doesn't," she complained.

"I have a great setup here. Feel free to use it anytime," he offered. He wouldn't mind her in his gym, not one little bit, preferably in one of those sexy little workout bras and a pair of barely there shorts.

"Thanks, but I like the noise of a gym, and the motivation of watching others and seeing how they change through the months," she told him.

"I've never paid attention to things like that," he admitted.

"I'm always watching people. Some people say that humans are so predictable, but I disagree. I see miracles all the time, and I've seen how a strong will can supersede expectations. There's nothing more motivating than a Cinderella story for me. I like to see someone beat the odds."

"I like to see the same thing," he told her. "We had a kid a few years ago who went through some pretty hard knocks in life. His father had been an abusive alcoholic, and he could have chosen a wrong path. But instead, he worked hard, studied even more, trained twice as much as the other kids, and decided he wasn't going to allow his circumstances to define who he was," Arden said.

"What happened with him?" Keera asked.

They took their time with their food, neither of them in a hurry as they enjoyed each other's conversation. Yes, he really could get used to this.

"He got a football scholarship to University of Oregon. He's on the dean's list and on his way to becoming an attorney," Arden proudly said. He didn't admit that he'd also provided an anonymous scholarship for the kid.

"That's great," Keera said, her eyes lighting up. "That's why I love my job so much. Those success stories make the hard days worth it."

"I agree. I knew from the moment I stepped into my first course at Stanford that I would teach. It was just who I decided to be."

"Wow, Stanford. Nice school," she said.

"After growing up in rainy Washington, I wanted some heat," he told her. "I should have chosen Hawaii, though. But then I might not have come back."

"Yeah, that would be a tough one. But I have to admit I couldn't live on an island. I would feel too trapped. Going on vacation to an isle is one thing, but not being able to jump in my car and go anywhere I want is unacceptable."

"I've never thought about it that way. You can always hop on a jet," he told her.

"Not if an EMP strike hits and all the planes are grounded. Then you're trapped in a small place. You'd have to live off coffee and pineapple," she said.

"As long as I had coffee, I'd survive," he said. "Imagine the world without a good cup of java." He shuddered to even think such a horrible thought.

"That would be the ultimate punishment for me," she told him, seeming just as horrified at the idea.

The conversation was light as they finished their meal. By the end of it, Arden knew one thing for sure—he wasn't letting her go.

Chapter Fifteen

Keera realized she was growing much too comfortable around Arden. The more time she spent with him, the more relaxed she became. At that thought, she nearly panicked. Getting comfortable with someone, or even with her own life, was a dangerous thing to do. She'd been there before, thought everything was fine. Then her rose-colored glasses had been yanked off her in the most painful way imaginable.

Rising from the table, Keera took her dishes to the sink, then helped Arden gather the rest, though he tried to protest. She ignored him.

"You had this meal put together, even if you didn't do it on your own. The least I can do is clean up," she told him.

"I like cleaning. It gives me a moment to unwind after a long day," he said.

"I'm surprised. You don't seem like the kind of man who does his own dishes," she told him.

"Ouch," he said with a laugh. "You act as if I'm a snob."

"If the shoe fits . . . ," she said, but she softened the words with a smile.

He stood next to her as they rinsed the dishes and placed them in the washer.

"I should get back home," she said when there was a shift in the air. The house was so quiet, and their dinner had been too relaxed and intimate. The only thing on her mind now was to make a quick escape.

But he'd driven her there, so she wasn't going to be able to simply run out the door.

"Are you in a hurry to leave?" he asked. The tone of his voice made her look up. His eyes were lit with heat and questions she in no way knew how to answer.

"Something will happen if I don't go," she said with honesty.

Those words made his eyes darken, which made her stomach clench with need. One hunger had been sated, but another one had been aroused, and it didn't seem there was anything she could do to stop it.

Twisting away from the counter, Keera's body was in motion, but her feet weren't. She let out a cry when she nearly fell to the floor as pain ripped through her ankle. Arden was immediately at her side, gripping her to keep her upright.

"Are you okay?" he asked, his voice low and hungry, but some of the fire was dampened by her careless injury.

Wincing, she pushed back from him and gripped the counter. "I'm okay," she told him, though when she tried to put weight on her foot, it sent a throb up her leg. It was probably nothing, just going to be sore for a couple of hours.

"Let me carry you to the couch so I can see what you've done," he said. He didn't try to grab her again, though. She tried putting weight on the foot again, and pain shot up her leg. She wasn't moving on her own right now.

She was trying desperately not to look at Arden, because all she could see in his eyes was their two bodies entwined together in a sweaty mass of pleasure. But even looking away from the intensity of his gaze, she was still left seeing the sexy sweep of his dark hair, the slight stubble sprinkling his firm jaw, the width of his shoulders, the narrowing of his hips. She was panting, and it wasn't from pain.

"Just give me a second. I'll be okay," she said. She knew if his hands came into contact with her body again she wouldn't be able to make a wise decision—the only decision she should make.

"This is ridiculous," he said in a huff as he reached out to her, taking the choice out of her hands. With no effort whatsoever, he pulled her off the ground, and Keera found herself pressed against his chest as he began walking.

She could feel the heat radiating off him, see the pulse thumping in the side of his neck, smell his delicious aroma that was a pure aphrodisiac to her already heightened senses.

Giving in to the desire of his touch, Keera leaned her head against the soft cotton of his shirt, hoping the living room wasn't too close by. She closed her eyes and allowed her senses to take over, telling her mind it was time to shut off.

It had been so long since she'd allowed herself to be held, so long since she'd let go of the rigid control she took pride in. At this moment, she didn't understand why it was so important for her to never lose control. There were many people who could do so without regret or consequence.

They made it to the living room, but Arden simply stopped, not releasing her. Keera opened her eyes and leaned back, gazing into his intense expression.

"You are so damn beautiful," he told her, a low growl reverberating through him.

Her heart thumped as she reached up and ran her fingers across his jaw, which tensed beneath her touch.

"Kiss me," she whispered. Those hadn't been the words she'd planned on saying. But somehow that's all she was able to muster.

Maybe this had been inevitable from the moment their eyes had first connected, and maybe she was just weak. All she knew with absolute certainty was that if she didn't act on the invitation in his eyes, she'd go home regretting it for the rest of her life.

She assured herself that Arden was in no way a danger for her. This wasn't a relationship that could go anywhere. They weren't soul mates, weren't even compatible. So it was safe to have her needs met by him. It would be mutually beneficial to both of them.

She told herself all of this, but as fire leaped in his eyes and his head began to lower, somewhere deep inside her, she knew she was lying to herself.

"Are you sure?" he asked, his hot breath brushing across her lips.

"Yes, kiss me," she told him, her hands wrapping behind his head as she wound her fingers in his thick hair.

Arden didn't ask again. His head lowered, his lips consuming hers with so much heat and passion she was sure he'd thought of this moment as much as she had. No more words needed to be said as his hands gripped her body while his mouth devoured her.

She had no need for oxygen as he fed the flames of desire within her. Without being aware of her actions, she moved her hands across the large expanse of his shoulders and began undoing the buttons of his shirt. He wrenched his lips from hers, his eyes dark and hungry.

"What do you want, Keera?" He growled.

There was no more hesitation. She was done thinking—at least for now. "I want you, Arden, just you," she said, not recognizing her own voice.

He trembled beneath her, then they were moving. Keera saw nothing as he quickly made his way down wide hallways decorated with priceless items. She was too focused on the feel of his body next to hers, the touch of his fingers against her thighs, his lips only millimeters away.

They reached the bedroom, and Arden lay her down, stepping back and caressing her from head to toe with only his eyes. She nearly came from that look alone. He reached up and finished undoing his shirt, shrugging it off, while never taking his gaze from her.

She watched in utter fascination as he revealed himself to her one beautiful inch at a time. He was even more striking than she had pictured—his chest solid, his stomach taut, with the perfect amount of ripples.

His pants fell down, and moisture surged between her thighs at the thickness of his erection. He was utter perfection, and there wasn't a single part of her that wanted to back out of what was about to happen.

She licked her lips, and he groaned, snapping her eyes back to his face. His jaw was clenched as he began removing her clothes. And Keera wiggled the best she could to help him. Her fingers shook as she gave up and let him finish. She decided to simply hold on and enjoy.

"You're so unbelievably beautiful," he said, the awe in his voice making her believe him.

"I was going to say the same about you," she admitted.

Arden reached over to his nightstand and pulled out several condoms, making her stomach tingle again. She had no doubt this was a man who could go and go and go. She had a feeling neither of them would sleep this night.

Arden hovered over her, his heated skin covering hers as he leaned down, his lips taking hers again, stopping all words. He ravished her completely before turning them so they were on their sides, his hands moving up and down her back as he crushed her breasts to his hard chest.

Keera squirmed in his embrace, feeling the need to be closer to him. She couldn't touch him enough, couldn't bank this fire. But Arden had other plans. He shifted her again, pushing her onto her back as he began trailing his mouth down her neck, licking, sucking, and nipping on her sensitive skin, making her cry out his name, the only word she seemed capable of saying.

He teased her breasts, his large palms cupping them as his tongue circled her nipples until they were throbbing peaks that he lapped at, making her back arch off the bed. Any pain she'd felt earlier in her ankle was now an afterthought as pure pleasure rushed through her.

"Please, Arden, please . . . ," she begged. She was on fire, her body aching. She was empty, knowing that only he could complete her. The heat burned her as she spread her thighs, needing him to plunge inside.

As he continued sucking her breasts, she felt an orgasm building, felt her core clench. He hadn't even touched her there yet, and she was coming undone. She wasn't sure she'd be able to handle much more. She didn't have time to think such thoughts, though, because he ran his tongue down the center of her breasts as his fingers trailed along her sides.

He pushed her legs farther apart, his hot breath rushing over her wet flesh before he leaned into her, his lips whispering across the top of her quivering core. She pushed her hips up, needing him to stop teasing her.

The first swipe of his tongue along her folds made her scream out his name as she wiggled beneath him. He spread her open and found that sweet spot, closing his lips around her as his tongue caressed her in the most beautiful way. He sucked hard, and Keera let go, her body exploding in utter bliss.

Tremor after tremor shook through her as Arden continued sucking her sensitive flesh, his tongue laving against her, making her orgasm go on and on. She twisted beneath him, but still he didn't stop, his moans vibrating against her. He felt every pulse, sucking her in perfect rhythm, knowing how to give her the ultimate pleasure.

As the orgasm finally diminished, Keera's body went lax beneath him, exhaustion running through her. She had never felt something so intense. She realized she might never feel it like that again.

Arden's tongue swept across her core again, making Keera tense. "No more. I can't take more," she told him.

"Oh, my poor Keera, yes, you can," he assured her before his tongue lapped at her again and again. Then he shoved two fingers deep inside her wet core, and unbelievably, she felt a sharp tug of pleasure so intense it nearly sent her into another orgasm.

She groaned as he found a perfect rhythm, pumping in and out of her as his magical tongue danced on her heated flesh.

"Please, Arden, please," she begged.

"What do you want, Keera?" he asked, his fingers still pumping slowly in and out of her heat as he crawled up her body, his tongue circling her nipples before he was leaning over her, his mouth inches from her own, his hardness pressing into her thighs.

"I want you inside me," she said.

"I am," he told her, his fingers finding places within her that continued to stoke the flames of her desire.

"I want you buried in me, not just your fingers," she cried as she arched her hips.

He pulled his fingers from her, and she whimpered at the loss, but then he was between her thighs, his thickness resting against her opening. He leaned down and captured her mouth again, the taste of her pleasure on his tongue.

She pushed against him, and he barely slipped inside, drawing out her torture for what felt like years. "Please," she cried out when he released her lips.

He captured them again at the same time as he thrust into her. He buried himself deep, completely taking her breath away. He stopped as he allowed her body to adjust to his beautiful perfection.

His mouth gentled on hers as his tongue traced her lips. His fingers squeezed her hips, and she felt a shudder pass through him. She realized it was taking everything within him to hold back.

"Take me hard . . . now," she demanded.

His eyes flashed to hers, and another tremor ran across her flesh. Then he buried his head against her neck, biting down as he began moving, hard and fast. She wrapped her legs around his waist and held on, her fingernails digging into his back as she cried out his name.

It didn't take much longer for Keera to let go again, this orgasm even more powerful than the last as they came together, her body squeezing him, their cries mingling in the air. He continued pumping inside her until there was nothing left for either of them to give. Then he collapsed against her, and she kept herself wrapped tightly around him.

She was so tired, but felt sated and powerful at the same time. She'd brought the ultimate pleasure to this strong man. And he'd given her something unlike anything she'd felt before. It was beautiful, and she refused to regret it.

With what seemed like enormous effort, Arden turned them so he was on his back with her draped over him. He'd managed to keep them connected as he did this, and she felt him twitch inside her, causing heat to stir again.

She opened her eyes as he pushed up, shocking her. How could either of them feel the need for this to go on? Then she looked over and saw the condoms, and she smiled. She'd known this night would be eternal.

With great effort, she pulled up, feeling empty the second he wasn't inside her. He frowned. But Keera moved down his body, pulling the condom off him and tossing it aside. They could clean up the mess later.

She leaned down and took his thickness deep inside her mouth, humming her pleasure as his fingers curled into her hair and he let out a cry of encouragement. And this was just the beginning of their night. Keera was no longer in a hurry to go anywhere.

Chapter Sixteen

Keera had been more than grateful that student conferences had been going on for the past couple of days at school. Arden had been too busy to continuously check up on her. She refused to regret their night together, and her body was still sore from the workout of being in bed with Arden all night. And still, she was more than happy she'd done it.

She did know there was no way it could happen again. She'd had a hard enough time leaving his bed. If she made that night a recurring thing, she might not ever be able to let him go—even when he wanted her gone.

One thing she'd learned about Arden in the past few weeks was that he was loyal to a fault. And during this investigation, he considered her his responsibility. When this was all finished, he'd be free of her, the adrenaline of it would wane, and they would realize they had nothing in common.

Sure, they were both in the education system, but that was it. He was from an esteemed family, idolized in his community, and knew exactly who he was and where he was going. She couldn't say the same about herself. This couldn't work for them. If she could just get her body to accept the logic of it, she'd be hurting a whole lot less.

And the one thing she really didn't want to admit, not even to herself, was the fact that she would disgrace his family. She didn't think he'd ever admit that to her, but she knew the truth. Her heart hurt as she pushed those thoughts away.

With her Saturday morning just beginning, Keera had too much time on her hands to think. And no matter how many times she told herself to push Arden from her mind, she couldn't seem to do it. Even out of the bedroom, he was thoughtful, intelligent, humorous, and so much more. Most of all, he was dangerous—to her hormones and her heart.

Shaking those thoughts away, Keera reminded herself that she'd been alone for a long time. After the disaster of her last failed relationship, she had decided a bit of loneliness was much better than the possible repercussions of having a partner.

Leaving her apartment complex, she began moving toward her car when she saw a shadow dart from the bushes in the corner of the lot. She halted, turning just in time to see someone duck behind a thick tree. She froze.

Her adrenaline surging, Keera tried to decide what to do first. Should she run to her car, dial 911, or go back inside? Normally she wouldn't be so hesitant, but she didn't know for sure someone was actually out there in a malevolent way. She'd only caught them from the corner of her eye, and maybe they were just jogging.

She gazed at the area, seeing no additional movement. Before she could decide what to do next, the purr of an expensive motor could be heard coming into her lot. She turned again to find a sleek black sports car stopping next to her perfectly acceptable Toyota hybrid.

The door opened and Arden climbed out, looking as if he wouldn't fit inside the thing. He began striding her way, and Max popped his head out the open back window and let out a greeting as his tongue dropped from his smiling mouth.

The smile Arden wore instantly made Keera's knees shake. It seemed all the lectures in the world she could give herself wouldn't do any good, because the second she was in his presence, any thoughts of distance quickly fell out the window.

"Good morning," he said, stopping a mere two feet from her. Keera felt slightly tongue-tied and had to shake it off before responding.

"Why are you here so early on a Saturday?" she asked, distracted as she looked at the bushes again.

"We haven't had a chance to visit in the last couple days, and I missed you," he told her. His words made the fluttering in her stomach amp up to a whole new level. It also made her knees clench together as her core began to throb. With just the sound of his voice, the smell of his unique scent, his smile, that sparkle in his eyes—with just his presence, she was nearly a blubbering mess.

His smile dimmed as he looked at her.

"What's the matter?"

"I thought I saw someone suspicious over in those shrubs right before you got here," she blurted.

The smile evaporated as Arden tensed and he scanned the shrubbery. He took her arm and pulled her toward his car, where he was closer to Max. His tension made her more nervous, which hadn't been what she'd been intending.

"What did they look like?" he asked, his eyes continuously scanning the area.

"I didn't see much, and it was probably nothing. I just think all of this is making me jumpier than I've ever been before," she admitted.

"I'd rather you're overcautious than not careful enough," he said.

He was beginning to relax when he saw nothing. But then a sharp bang echoed through the air, and Keera nearly had a heart attack. Before she could even think of responding to what had sounded like a gunshot, Arden grabbed her and had her underneath him on the ground in less than two seconds.

Though she was in danger, it was the last thing on her mind as his weight pressed into her, his scent instantly enveloping her. Every thought she had about distance and walls flew out the window.

That's how vulnerable Keera was to this man. It wasn't something she was at all proud of. If she could think clearly, she'd push him away, make that call to the police she should have already made, and then stay as far from Arden Forbes as humanly possible.

As Arden looked out, a junker car ground its gears as it passed down her street, and another loud pop exploded as a thick cloud of black smoke polluted the air. Both Arden and Keera relaxed as they realized no one was firing at them.

But with Arden relaxing, his weight rested more fully into her, and Keera was very aware he was lying on top of her, in the middle of the morning in a parking lot where her neighbors could clearly see them if they so much as looked out their windows, let alone walked outside.

Keera was new to this town, and she really didn't want to get the kind of reputation she'd get if anyone found her in such a compromising situation with one of the Forbes men.

She meant to push Arden away, but every point where their bodies touched, the most pleasurable burn was happening, and it made it nearly impossible to want him to move, even knowing her reputation was on the line.

"I think we're safe now," she said, her voice too husky.

His eyes burned into hers as he shifted, slowly enough for her to feel the impact of their bodies being thrown together, his hardness pressing into her thigh. She was disappointed when he pushed himself to his knees, then stood and reached out to help her to her feet.

Her lips were tingling, and she was more than aware that she wouldn't have fought him had he leaned down and kissed her. She'd forgotten how beautiful it was to have another person's mouth against hers until she'd kissed him.

"I guess we're both a little jumpy," she told him, trying to cover up her nervousness. "I'm hoping the neighbors didn't see that."

"Sorry. I hope I didn't hurt you," he said as he reached across the short distance between them and ran his hands over her arms, causing her skin to burn.

She pulled back, not needing him to realize the power he held over her. She blamed it on the fact that she was lonelier than she'd realized. She could almost convince herself she wasn't so attracted to him, that she was just hungry for any human's touch. But even as she thought it, she knew there had been opportunities before, but none of them had tempted her like Arden could.

He captured her gaze again, his eyes burning against her skin as he looked her over. "I can't let anything happen to you," he said, stepping a bit closer and placing his hand against her shoulder.

She shuddered as she looked at his mouth, her own lips parched. Even gazing at this man heated her body to inferno temperatures. He was so much more dangerous than she'd first thought.

"I'm fine. I'm sure what's been happening at the school has nothing to do with me as a person," she said.

"We can agree to disagree about that," Arden told her.

She knew she wasn't going to win an argument with the man, so she decided it was best to call it a loss and escape as quickly as possible. But with her emotions aflutter, she couldn't even remember what it was she'd been planning before Arden had shown up.

"I better get going," she told him, trying to make herself step away.

"Yes, let's get out of here," he said, opening his passenger door.

She crossed her arms over her chest, hating that her heart was still beating out of control. She tried to give him her sternest look.

"I don't remember saying I'd go anywhere with you." Her voice was a bit firmer. When he looked at her, his lips turning up in the most beautiful smile, she knew she was sunk. This man most certainly had a way of getting what he wanted—and apparently what he wanted right now was her.

Chapter Seventeen

Keera sat with Arden at a picnic table in the park, people milling about them, some playing Frisbee, kids laughing in the playground, teenagers making out behind trees. It was a beautiful, sunny afternoon, and she was enjoying herself. And that was the problem.

Somehow the man had managed to not only change her mind about going out with him for the day, but she was enjoying herself as they spent time together. Being with Arden was becoming an obsession, and most likely it was too late for her to stop it.

It had been so long since she'd even had a friendship that she felt lost in this town where everyone knew their neighbors, and felt even more lost with this handsome man who had made it his mission to save her. How was she supposed to turn him down, though, when he wasn't a man who accepted defeat?

If Arden weren't so sweet, such a Prince Charming, out to save the kids, the community, and her, then this would be a different story. But he was that one-in-a-million guy who people talked about. He was that person romance authors wrote books about. He was damn near irresistible, even to a stronger woman than she considered herself.

A breeze blew past them, carrying Arden's scent to her, making her close her eyes and for just a moment imagine she was just a normal woman, out with an ordinary man, and everything would be fine. There was no evil in the world, and past trauma didn't exist.

For just a blessed, beautiful few seconds, she felt the weight of her sorrows lift, float away in the breeze, and she felt true joy.

Arden looked up, catching her gaze, smiling. She noticed that he was very aware of who was around them, of any possible areas where someone could sneak up from, but he didn't allow that to overrun him. He still knew how to relax, knew how to keep her calm. He knew how to have fun.

"Keera," Arden said, snapping Keera out of her thoughts as she focused on him.

"Yes?" She couldn't remember what they'd been talking about that had sent her into her own head.

"You were telling me about your family," he reminded her.

Ah, yes, of course he wanted to know what kind of people she came from. That's why she'd mentally retreated. Maybe there was a part of her that wanted to tell him exactly who she was because she knew he'd find out and run far and fast from her. But there was another part—an even bigger part, it seemed—that wanted to keep him in the dark.

"I'd rather hear more about yours," she said, forcing a laugh that sounded fake even to her own ears.

"I've told you about Kian, Owen, Dakota, and you've met Declan. You have to meet my parents to truly appreciate them," he said. "Plus, with the way the school gossip channels run, I'm sure you know enough about my family to write a thesis on us," he added with a laugh. "Quit hedging unless you want to be at this park until midnight."

She had no doubt he'd stay true to his word and not let her get away until she gave him something. The thing was, she was finding she wanted to share a piece of her past with him, wanted to let out some of these emotions that seemed to be drowning her lately.

"My dad isn't a good man," she began. She was almost shocked when she said those six little words. If Arden had reacted with disgust or there was judgment in his eyes, maybe she wouldn't have been able to continue, but he sat back and waited.

"Do you see him much?" he asked.

"No, I haven't seen him in years," she admitted.

"Is that his choice or yours?"

She hesitated, thinking about it for a while. "When I was younger, he got in a lot of trouble." She was surprised to find she was giving Arden this much information. Now that he had her name and knew her father was a criminal, it wouldn't take much for him to put all the pieces together. It didn't normally take people long. She'd thought about changing her name, but what good would that do? If someone wanted information, they were going to find it.

"So he got in trouble, and then he left?" Arden asked. He seemed more horrified by this fact than anything else. Maybe it was because Arden was the type of guy who could never walk away from his family. There were men out there who didn't. Logically she knew this even if emotionally she didn't believe it.

"Yes, he ran," she admitted. "But he did call once out of the blue a couple years later. It wasn't because he missed me. It was because he wanted something."

"What could he possibly think he'd get from you after leaving you at such a tender age?" Arden asked, showing his open disgust.

"What it was doesn't matter. I had changed a lot already at that point. My mother was useless, so drugged out she didn't even know if it was night or day, and I was determined to live somewhat normally. For a while I tried keeping things together, but eventually I couldn't handle it anymore, and I left, too."

"How old were you?" Arden asked.

"When I left home?" she clarified.

"Yes," he answered. She could see how desperately he was trying to keep his tone neutral. She could also see he was horrified on her behalf. She saw that reaction a lot, actually, but after it all sank in, most people would shy away from her. Once they knew she was the daughter of an infamous drug lord, they didn't come back. "He's had several new families since then, new identities," she said matter-of-factly.

"Who is he?" Arden asked.

"It really doesn't matter. He moved on with his life, and I've moved on with mine."

"You're taking this a lot better than most would," Arden said. He reached for her, but she was too vulnerable to be touched by him right now, when sharing this particular story. Arden was too much of an upstanding citizen to date someone like her, to even be friends with her.

"He was busted with so much cocaine, he could've supplied a small country. They thought I was involved with it. I was fifteen at the time. I was seventeen when I ran away from home."

"Keera . . . ," he began. She didn't want his sympathy. For some reason that would hurt her more than if he told her she was worthless. Maybe it was because she wasn't a victim anymore, and maybe it was because she thought of herself as stronger than she actually was. Whatever it was, she just needed to not have Arden look at her differently. She'd rather he permanently removed himself from her life than look at her like she was nothing more than a white-trash druggie who had no right to be influencing the children of his town.

"I grew up in a world of wealth and privilege. Neither of my parents gave a crap about my brother or me. Holidays were spent apart, summers apart. We never had a nanny too long, so no relationships were forged with anyone, but I didn't know any of that was wrong. I had all of the best clothes, the newest gadgets, anything I could ever want," she said, trying to make it sound like that had been great.

"And you were utterly alone," Arden said, not as a question. He was the first one to come to that conclusion. She hadn't told too many people this story, but the ones who did know thought she was bragging or this was a golden time in her life. They had no idea how wrong they were.

"Both of my parents had affairs all the time. They never tried to hide it. When my father got busted, he ran, but he was never alone. My mother wasn't sad to lose him; she was terrified of losing her lifestyle. But we all did. The government seized everything, right down to my Rolex watch and Gucci boots," she said with a bitter laugh. She hadn't cared about the material things, but she had cared that they'd gone from at least having food on the table to literally barely having a ramshackle roof over their heads and sharing the floor with mice.

"How did you make it to college?" he asked.

Here again was another question she was never asked.

She smiled, this time allowing him to take her hand. She knew it was dangerous to do, but she was beginning to trust this man.

"I was a good student, a really good student, so I got scholarships, and I have a lot of student loans," she said. Now she was afraid he'd think she was after him for his money. Nothing she could say here was helping her feel better about herself.

"Not many would rise above. I'm impressed," he told her. She so desperately wanted to trust him.

"It is what it is," she said with a shrug.

She hadn't told him who her father was, but a few key words on the computer and he'd know. Maybe it was better this was out in the open. If she was going to get fired from her job, she'd rather have it happen now, before she was too attached to this town, too attached to Arden. She feared it might already be too late for that, but she'd prefer that it happened sooner rather than later.

Keera stopped speaking and waited for Arden to comment on what he'd just learned. She was, on the one hand, afraid of the goodbye, and on the other, it felt as if a weight had been lifted.

Though the waiting was only taking seconds, it felt like a lifetime. Keera was afraid to look up, afraid to see disgust in his eyes. Everything within her was screaming for her to stand up, to leave this park, to leave this town. But Keera wasn't that seventeen-year-old scared girl anymore.

She refused to run. She might start over, but she wouldn't cower. That's what her father had done, and that's what her brother had done.

"Keera," he said softly. She didn't meet his gaze. "Please look at me," he said, his tone not changing. She'd appear a coward if she didn't do what he'd asked, so with great effort she squared her shoulders and looked up, making sure to meet his gaze, defiance in her own. All she saw in his eyes was kindness.

"You live here now, and you're no longer alone," he said, shocking her.

"Arden . . . ," she began. She didn't know what she really wanted to say, but it was most likely a warning that it was in his best interest to stay far away from her.

"I don't say things I don't mean. You'll never be alone again," he told her, conviction ringing in his tone, making her almost believe what he was saying.

"I prefer to be alone," she said. At one time she'd actually meant that. "It's less complicated."

He squeezed her hand, and Keera realized she wasn't interested in letting him go at this moment.

"That's what we say to ourselves when it doesn't seem like we have any other choice," Arden said. She wondered if he was right. She wondered if it was one more layer of her protecting herself to think she was better off without anyone.

"How would you know?" she asked. "You're surrounded with family and friends. Everyone wants to be with you."

"You should remember from those years you thought you had everything," he began. "You can be surrounded by people, but that doesn't mean you aren't lonely."

His words stunned her. He smiled as he shook his head, and she was quiet as she waited for him to continue.

"Don't take that the wrong way. I have incredible parents, wonderful siblings, and I do love this community, but we all go through journeys, and times in our lives where we feel"—he paused, as if searching for the right words—"where we feel we aren't good enough or where we compare ourselves to others and find that we come up short."

"You felt as if you weren't good enough?" she asked, obviously stunned.

"Hey, that shouldn't be such a shock," he said, flicking his finger under her chin and smiling.

"But why would you ever think you're not good enough?" she pushed.

"Trust me, I'm confident in myself," he told her before letting out a sigh. "But I grew up a middle child in a family of five siblings. I also decided from a young age I had a passion for teaching, which is far less heroic than becoming a doctor," he told her with a laugh, "or a fireman . . ." He trailed off as he shrugged.

"Do you think your siblings are better than you?" she asked.

"No," he told her quickly. "It's not that at all. I'm just saying that all of us have moments of feeling . . . too ordinary."

Silence greeted those words before Keera smiled. She didn't think he was playing her; she felt he was actually giving her a piece of his vulnerability, but she also had a difficult time imagining him ever feeling as if he was coming up wanting in any situation.

"Well, you are kinda average," she told him when the moment had become too personal.

"I'll show you average," he warned, a sparkle entering his eyes.

And just that quickly, he allowed her past to go back to where it belonged, and her worries faded as he jumped from the table, then proceeded to chase her through the park, allowing her to think she'd gotten away before swooping her up in his arms.

Yes, she was in trouble when it came to Arden Forbes. She was in big, big trouble.

Chapter Eighteen

"There's activity at Keera's apartment," Declan said over the phone.

"What sort of activity?" Arden asked as he grabbed his keys and called Max, who was already on his heels as he heard the tension in Arden's voice.

"The cops were called," Declan told him.

Arden was in his car and speeding down his driveway within seconds. He was more than grateful Keera didn't live far from him. He'd been with her all day at school, and she'd insisted she was fine, that nothing out of the ordinary had happened in a while and she didn't need to be coddled. He'd hated leaving her alone, but he had to respect her wishes.

Besides, he was desperately trying to figure out what his feelings toward this woman were. He knew something was happening between them, and he also knew he was falling for her. But she had been guarded for a very long time, and he wasn't sure he could get through to her, wasn't sure she could open up to anyone after what she'd been through.

He was fighting on whether to look up her story. She'd shared with him, and he felt immensely pleased that she'd opened up to him as much as she had, but he wanted her to give him more, to give it all to him.

He didn't know if she was capable of doing that. It was a real test of trust, and he needed to give her more time. But right now, all he cared about was getting to her, ensuring her safety. Then he could work on her trust more fully when someone wasn't trying their best to destroy her.

Maybe this was about her past, though, and he was being a fool to not find out all he could to ensure her safety. And even though Arden wasn't checking into her past, he was more than sure Declan had. If there was something Arden needed to know to keep her safe, he was sure his brother would tell him.

They got to the apartment building, where two cop cars were sitting, their lights off, their cabs empty. "Let's get to Keera," Arden told Max, who practically pulled Arden from the vehicle. The dog was just as worried about her as he was.

Keera was standing outside her door, speaking to two officers. Arden heard someone inside the small unit and knew there were probably two more checking out whatever was wrong.

"What happened?" Arden asked, knowing the two men speaking with her.

Arden had to respect them, because even though the men knew Arden, they looked to Keera to make sure it was okay for them to share the information. She nodded at the men, who appeared relieved. It sucked in a small town to have to keep something from someone they knew would want to help.

"Ms. Thompson's apartment was broken into. The perps were caught by one of the neighbors, who called it in, but they managed to flee the scene," Officer Nicolson said.

"Did they get a description?" Arden asked. He wanted in that apartment right now.

"Unfortunately, both perps wore ski masks. The neighbor said they were somewhere around six feet tall, lanky, and strong as hell. The neighbor got pushed into the wall as they rushed past him."

"Oh my," Keera said. She must have just beaten him there, and this was news to her as well as him. "Are the neighbors okay?"

"Your neighbors are fine, ma'am," Officer Nicolson assured her.

Arden respected that Keera was more concerned with her neighbors' safety than what could be missing from her apartment. But then again, she'd already lost everything once in her life, so she knew she could replace items. It truly was people who mattered, not objects.

"I wonder if this could be one of the same men who were at the school," Keera said.

"That's what I'm afraid of," Arden told her.

"Do you have any idea what the perps might be trying to find?" the officer asked. "I don't believe in coincidence, and with your office and now your home broken into, it's not a leap saying you're in danger." Arden was glad the officer wasn't sugarcoating this.

"I have nothing of value," she told the officer. Her shoulders drooped, and Arden saw the confusion in her eyes. He moved closer, wrapping his arm around her.

Max was clearly agitated as he whipped his head from her to the open door. He wanted to protect Keera, but he also wanted in that apartment.

"It's okay, Max. Wait," Arden said. He was shocked when the dog looked at him with understanding, then sat at Keera's other side, resting his head against her. Her hand immediately went to the back of Max's ears, and she rubbed, the worry in her eyes dimming. The neighbor who'd called in the report stepped from his apartment, a nice shiner forming on his right eye.

"Oh, Mr. Davis," Keera said, sympathy and guilt in her eyes.

"I'm okay, Keera. Some young punks can't hurt an old man like me," he said, his chest puffing out.

"What happened?" she asked.

"I already told the officers. But I was coming home from the grocery store and saw your door cracked open. After all the odd occurrences around here, I wasn't going to take any chances, so I pushed open the door and called out your name. Two men dressed in black rushed me. I wasn't going to back down, but they bowled me over, sending me against the wall. I fell and caught my eye on the doorknob," he said with a bit of irritation directed at himself.

"You shouldn't have tried to stop them," Keera told him. "But I'm so grateful to have someone like you living next door to me. Thank you." She squeezed his hand, and Arden noticed the tremor she was trying to hide.

"That's what I should be doing. You're a young lady living here on your own. We look out for each other," he assured her.

Keera got tears in her eyes, and she looked down as she pulled herself together. She really didn't like showing weakness. Sometimes it was a person's vulnerabilities that endeared them most to others, though. Maybe it was Arden's job to show her there could be a lot of strength in letting go of what you thought was weakness.

"You're clear to come in now," said one of the officers who'd been inside her apartment.

Keera's body tensed, but Arden was pleased when she allowed him to take her hand as she stepped forward. His gut clenched when he saw her place, and then he felt white-hot fury.

Keera gasped, but was otherwise silent as the two of them stopped only a few feet inside. The place had been wrecked. It appeared as if the people coming in had wanted to cause as much damage as possible. Her curtains were torn down, her plants tumbled over, and the soil ground into the carpet. The couch was turned upside down, with the cushions cut and foam scattered from the kitchen to the living room. She didn't possess many knickknacks, but what few there were lay smashed against the linoleum of the kitchen floor. Containers were spilled, and the faucet had been left on, water coating the floor.

"Why?" she said, her voice a low whisper. "Why would anyone do this to another person?"

Arden didn't have an answer. He couldn't comprehend someone doing this to another, couldn't imagine what would cause someone so much anger to be able to do this.

He squeezed her fingers instead of giving her a senseless answer that would mean nothing. The officers were quiet as they allowed her to go back to her bedroom, where her bed was destroyed. It looked as if an ax had been taken to it. This looked to be more than simple destruction. This appeared to be a hate crime.

"I have nothing for them to take," Keera said, standing in her room, looking so lost that Arden couldn't take it. He pulled her into his arms and held her while she shook.

"Do you have somewhere you can go, Ms. Thompson? With this much destruction, we don't feel it's safe for you to be here," Officer Nicolson said.

She shook her head against his chest, and Arden felt the warm moisture of her tears. Keera was a strong woman, and he knew she was keeping her face buried because she didn't want any of them to see what she deemed as weakness. He ran his fingers through her hair and held her.

She was silent for several moments, then she raised a hand and wiped her face before she sniffled and a shudder passed through her. Then he felt her shoulders firm up and knew she was preparing to put on a brave front. He needed to give her the time to fall apart, but she had to do that when she was ready. When she stepped back from him, her eyes were red, but there was determination in them.

"I don't have somewhere to go, but I'd hope they're done now. They have to have seen there's nothing here," she said, her voice still carrying a note of distress, though she was trying her best to cover it.

Officer Nicolson was about to argue with her when Arden stepped in. "I'll make sure she's safe," he assured the cop, who nodded. It was well known in this town that Arden was a man of his word, and he wouldn't say it if he didn't mean it.

The officer gave her a card, told her to call anytime, then they left after ensuring she'd leave the place after gathering only what she needed.

They made sure to let her know it was an active crime scene, and the less she could taint it, the better the chances they'd find evidence.

Keera didn't move for a long time, and Max stayed right by her side. Though Arden wanted her out of this apartment as soon as humanly possible, he also knew not to push her. She needed patience and understanding more than she needed anything else.

"I can't leave," she finally said. She moved as if to sit on the bed, then looked at it and instead stepped to her closet, where her clothes had been ripped from their hangers. Her dresser had also been tossed, the drawers lying broken on the ground.

"Just grab what you must have, and we'll figure the rest out later," Arden told her.

"I can't . . . I don't know what to do," she said, another tear slipping.

Arden moved over to her, placed his hands on her shoulders, and waited until she was looking him in the eyes. He waited a few more moments before speaking because he wanted to make sure she understood he was serious, that it was okay to lean on another person.

"Sometimes in life, the thing that makes us the strongest is to lean on those we know can help carry our burdens. You accepting help from someone who cares about you doesn't make you weak, doesn't make you a victim, it makes you smart and strong. I'm involved now, Keera, and I won't walk away from you. Let me help you."

He raised a hand and caressed her cheek, wiping away the tear. Max whimpered beside her as if to offer his support as well. Her hand found that safe spot on Max's head as she stared back at Arden, fear and hope mixed in her expression.

"I'm afraid to count on anyone but myself," she admitted.

"It's okay to be scared. As long as you allow someone in," he told her.

One more tear fell before she brushed it away and looked at him with determination. "I don't know how to accept help."

"Then, let me show you," he said.

He looked at the room, and he didn't see anything that could be salvaged. She looked, as well, and seemed to come to the same conclusion.

"There's a hotel in town," she said. She didn't appear happy with that choice. He knew on a principal's salary it wouldn't take her long to run out of funds, especially when she had to replace all that had been lost.

"Do you have rental insurance?" he asked, knowing most people didn't carry it.

"Yes, thankfully, but that will take a while to kick in," she said.

"Well, there's a start. Why don't we get out of here?" he offered.

She glanced around again and then nodded. They made their way out of the apartment, and he led her to his car. She tried to protest, but he promised her they'd come back the next day to get her car. She was too upset to be driving. She relented because she knew he was right. When they passed the hotel, she began to protest, but Arden assured her it was going to be okay.

There was no way he was leaving her alone again, not with someone coming after her. He was taking her where he could guarantee her safety. He was bringing her home. Only then would they both be able to sleep.

The only thing Arden was unsure about now is if he was going to be able to ever let her leave again. In a short time, she'd managed to dig her way into his heart, and he didn't feel the slightest need to push her back out.

Chapter Nineteen

Keera knew the moment Arden passed the hotel that he was bringing her to his house. She also knew she should protest, tell him there was no way she could stay at his place. If the neighbors hadn't already caught the two of them the other day in the parking lot, then her moving into his place was sure to spread gossip across town.

But she was afraid. She might not want to admit her fear, but someone had broken into her office, and then they'd broken into her home, destroying everything in it. She wasn't sure she'd be able to so much as salvage her underwear. She didn't know what she was going to do.

Yes, she had money in her savings account, but if she bought an entirely new wardrobe, she'd be left with little. Keera didn't need a lot in life. She'd learned young that anything you had could be taken from you without notice. But a person did need the basics to get by. And she was a high school principal and had worked hard for years to have a wardrobe she was proud of.

And just like that, it had all been taken from her in the blink of an eye. She felt like that fifteen-year-old girl again, being told that nothing was hers, that it had all been obtained illegally. She hadn't been able to understand then what had been happening.

Sadly enough, she couldn't understand now, either. Because this was such a senseless crime. She had nothing of value—no reason for someone to come into her private space and destroy it. She might not be the best person in the world, but she wasn't cruel, she didn't inspire vendettas in others. It had to be because of her past.

That scared her enough to allow Arden to bring her home. She in no way wanted to put him in danger, but his words ran through her mind, and she knew it was time to lean on someone. She'd get strong again, she assured herself, but maybe she could allow him to carry the weight of her burdens for this one night.

"I won't argue for now because I don't have it in me," she told Arden when he pulled into his garage. "But I can't stay here long," she warned.

Arden just smiled at her in that knowing way that tended to infuriate her. She had no doubt whatsoever that Arden wasn't a man used to hearing the word *no*. He was a man of action, and once he set his mind on something, he was determined to carry it out. The thing he didn't quite understand about her yet, though, was that she was the same as he was in that sense. She could certainly be just as stubborn.

As the two of them walked into his house, Arden was close behind her. With Max knowing the danger was gone, he trotted ahead, going to his food bowl and getting a bite to eat.

With Arden so close to her, and Max not there for a distraction, Keera's nerves jumped. She moved away from him, walking into the living room and gazing out the window at his monstrous backyard. He truly lived in a beautiful area, with far more home than a single guy needed.

Of course, Keera had no doubt he wouldn't be alone in the place long. He might want to take his time to settle down, but eventually he'd want to marry someone, want to start a family. The person he chose would need to be respected, would need to be good enough to carry the Forbes name. That person would never be her.

Keera shook her head as she fought more tears. It wasn't that she didn't believe in herself. It wasn't that she felt one human being was better than any other just because of their social status. It was just that she lived in the real world, and a family like the Forbeses was well known. One of them couldn't get married without the tabloids looking for juicy details.

They'd have a field day with her story, and she'd be the cause of horrific embarrassment for Arden and the rest of his family. She had far too much respect for this man to put him in a position where he'd have to choose between her and his reputation. She now understood that would tear at him.

She'd begun to share her story with him, but she'd in no way finished it. When she did give him the rest, he'd be grateful he hadn't gotten more serious with her than a fantastic night in bed. Men like the Forbeses could certainly get around, and it didn't matter that much who they slept with—it only mattered who they put a ring on.

Arden gave her time to gather herself, and it was just one more thing she appreciated about the man. He made her feel safe, protected, and secure. He made her feel cared about—and most important, he made her feel as if she wasn't alone, as if she truly did have someone she could turn to.

These thoughts about him were dangerous on so many levels. But it didn't matter if she tried to stop them because it was how she felt, and it was too late to turn back. She'd opened herself to him, and no matter what she did to try to stop it, she was going to hurt when he wasn't a part of her life. Keera had no doubt she'd have to eventually move from this town. It would simply be too painful for her to stay, to watch all this slip so easily from her fingers.

"I called my brother Kian. His wife is about your size, so I asked them to bring over some clothes until we can get to the store," Arden said.

That drew Keera's attention. "You didn't need to do that," she told him, embarrassed. She didn't want to feel like a charity case.

"That's what we do here. Last year, one of the students from a very large family had an electrical fire. They lost everything two weeks before

Christmas. The town came together that night and took care of their immediate needs," Arden said, smiling at the memory.

"I'm not surprised, from what I've learned of this town already," she said.

"Those kids also had the best Christmas they could've ever imagined. It was going to take a while for the insurance to kick in and get their house rebuilt, but an anonymous donor came through, and the people of this town gathered, working night and day." His smile grew. "Have you ever watched that show where they build a house in a week?"

She nodded. "It seems impossible."

"Well, I guarantee it can happen. The family was woken Christmas morning from the house they'd been staying in, a place far too small for a family of eight. They were driven home to find a new house, fully furnished with a living room so packed with gifts, the kids might still be opening them." She was amazed when she saw a sparkle in his eyes. He blinked and turned, and when he looked at her again, he'd pulled himself together.

"I'm sure you were a big part of this," she said, her admiration for him growing even more.

"A lot of people were," he said noncommittally. "The point is that the family was a good family, the mother a nurse at the hospital, the father an owner of an accounting firm. They were proud people who have always worked hard, with good children who have been taught well. But sometimes in life we get knocked down, and it doesn't hurt to accept help. They were more than grateful, and gracious as they accepted the town's gift. They have also paid it forward a dozen times since. We're a community that doesn't leave each other out in the cold."

Keera couldn't keep her tears back any longer. She had been there such a short time, and he already considered her part of their town. She wasn't sure she'd be brave enough to walk away—even if it was what was best for this man. Maybe she truly was as selfish as her father had called her the last time they'd spoken.

Chapter Twenty

Being in Arden's house for the past few days had messed with Keera's senses. She wasn't sure what she wanted more—to be left alone, or to have him ravish her for all she was worth. Okay, if she were being honest with herself, she knew what she wanted, but that didn't change what she *should* want.

He was being a perfect gentleman, though, making sure she was fed, letting her have the evenings to herself, allowing her to do her own thing. And it was driving her insane.

"Good morning." The extraperky voice startled Keera as she sat up in bed, gripping the covers tightly to her chest as she gazed at Arden, who was leaning in her doorway, holding a steaming mug of coffee and wearing the sexiest damn smile she'd ever seen.

"Go away," she muttered. She wasn't normally a morning person, but for some reason she was even more grumpy than usual.

"I can't do that. It's a gorgeous day. The sun is shining, the birds are chirping, and you've been locked up inside for too long," he told her. He didn't move forward, just looked perfectly at ease right where he was.

Her eyes narrowed as she scanned his beautiful body. He looked good no matter what he wore, but with the pair of jeans she was sure had been painted on, and a snug black T-shirt, he was drool-worthy. Even his normally mussed hair looked extra nice this morning. She was sure she looked like an utter wreck, and that wasn't helping to improve her mood.

"I see you've dressed up for the day," she said a bit too cattily.

"I look good and you know it," he said with a wink.

"Do you own anything other than skintight black shirts?" she muttered.

He laughed, and she felt her cheeks grow warm.

"Liking the view?" he asked, not a shred of modesty in him.

"I've seen better," she told him. Though, honestly, she hadn't. The last thing this man needed was his ego stroked. He laughed again.

"I haven't," he said, his eyes scanning her from head to toe, making her feel as if the blankets were nonexistent. She tightened her fingers around the comforter and squeezed her thighs together as heat invaded her body. He could turn her to mush with nothing more than a look. If he ever touched her again, she might just combust.

"You look like you've been up awhile. Do you have plans?" she asked.

"I've been awake long enough. I wanted to let you rest, since it seems you've been tossing and turning most nights," he told her. She hated the concern she saw in his eyes. It made it more difficult to be snotty. "Now get up and meet me in the living room."

Keera's body sagged as she sank back into her pillows. She should ignore him, letting him know she'd do things on her own terms. But soon, curiosity won out. What had him so chipper and ready to face the day? Trying not to rush as she showered and dressed, Keera still felt a need to get out there to see Arden.

When she did come out to the living room, Arden wasn't there. But it only took her a few seconds to allow the smells emanating from the kitchen to lead her there. She found him cooking a nice breakfast, humming as he flipped eggs.

"Where's Angela?" she asked.

"It's her day off. I can cook," he told her.

"You've already proven that," she told him. He'd made her a few meals. She definitely owed him one or two at some point.

"Dig in," he said as he handed her a plate. Keera wasn't so stubborn that she was going to turn down a good breakfast.

The two of them dished up, then sat at the table, Keera taking a few long swallows of her coffee before scooping up her food. She'd definitely have to switch to his brand of coffee when she went home. It was rich and dark, and she had been spoiled by it.

He was quiet as he ate, letting her wake up. Though it had only been a few days she'd been staying with him, it seemed as if they were already learning each other's habits. He knew it took her a few minutes to feel human in the morning. He did like to push her, but he also knew when to back off.

"Thanks for breakfast. It's wonderful," she told him.

"Not a problem. I like cooking for you. Much better than cooking for one," he said.

"It's easier, faster, and cheaper to cook for one," she pointed out.

He looked at her and smiled. "But not as satisfying."

"I'll have to agree," she said. "It kind of takes the joy out of the food prep when there's no one to tell you how wonderful it is."

"I fully agree," he said.

"Have you heard anything back from the police yet?" she asked. She hated bringing up the case when the morning was going so well, but unfortunately, her life revolved around the mysteries at both the school and her apartment—at least for now.

"There's nothing new," he told her.

Keera finished her breakfast and lifted her leg up on the chair, wrapping her arm around her knee and squeezing. Her fingers wandered down her shin, and she found herself playing with the necklace she'd turned into an anklet, feeling comfort touching the cold metal.

"You seem to wear that often," he said as he eyed the gold heart.

She felt a pang in her chest. "My brother gave this to me," she said, fighting the urge to cry. "It was only a couple days before he . . . died. Wearing it makes me feel as if he's not really gone, but I worry I'll lose it."

He reached for her, his fingers resting on top of her hand, making her still as she gazed at him.

"I hope I can help you get the answers you need so badly," he told her. Her reply got stuck in her throat as she grew lost in his eyes.

"You've done more for me than anyone else," she said. "It means a lot."

"I'm not doing anything more than anyone else would do," he said, looking away.

"Why do you do that?" she asked.

He looked at her again, confusion in his expression. "Do what?"

"You tend to downplay when you go above and beyond what most people do," she told him.

"I don't do that. But I think if you're searching for affirmation or credit for helping another person, then you're doing it for the wrong reason," he told her.

"I agree with that," she said. "But that doesn't mean you can't also gracefully accept a thank-you."

His lips turned up, and then he chuckled. She was confused.

"Ah, I've just gotten the principal voice," he said as he continued chuckling.

"You did not," she said, pushing his hand away as she sat back and crossed her arms.

"It's okay," he told her. "I find the principal voice pretty damn sexy."

And just like that, the teasing faded, and warmth infused her. She gazed at him, wondering if they were going to be able to stay in this house much longer without combusting. When the silence stretched on too long, and the heat rose too many degrees, Arden finally rose, allowing her to take a breath.

"We need to get out of here for a while. Grab a coat. We'll go on a hike," he said as he walked away from the table.

They tended to go on a lot of hikes. Maybe that was good. It was better than sitting in his house lusting after a man who clearly thought one time with her was plenty. With a sigh, she rose from the table and went to her room.

It was just one more day in a seemingly endless amount of time where she didn't know which way was up and which was down. For as organized a person as she was, the feeling wasn't a good one.

But at least this was a new adventure in life. Maybe, just maybe, it would be one that didn't end with her utter devastation. She could always hope.

Chapter Twenty-One

Sitting in her office, Keera was finishing up her work when there was a tap on her door. She smiled when Ethan walked in. He wore a scowl, which wasn't necessarily unusual, but it also meant this was most likely going to be an unpleasant conversation. With her nerves already tied up, she almost wished her phone would ring so she could get out of this conversation.

"I'm surprised to find you alone," Ethan said as he grumpily sat down in the chair in front of her desk.

"I don't normally have company in here," she told him.

"Yeah, but your watchdog is always hovering these days," he grumbled.

"Max?" she asked, confused. She often did bring Max in with her when Arden was doing something with the kids. She said it was to help him, but the reality was that she really liked the dog. Now that Ethan had mentioned it, she wished Max was with her.

"I was referring to Arden," he said as if she were a small child who needed everything spelled out for her.

"Arden's been protective, since it appears someone has a vendetta against me," she told him.

"Your office was broken into once. That doesn't mean you're in jeopardy," he said with a roll of his eyes.

"And my apartment," she reminded him.

His eyes rounded as he sat up in his chair. "When was your apartment broken into?"

"It was a week ago. I came home, and two people had broken in, trashed my place, then hurt my neighbor as they escaped. They still haven't been caught," she said with a frustrated sigh.

"Why didn't you call me immediately?" he said, then his eyes narrowed. "Because you called Arden." The last sentence wasn't a question.

"For one thing, you just got back yesterday from out of town. And for another, I didn't call him, but I think his brother did, because he was at my place fast," she admitted. "But I was grateful he was there because the cops didn't want me staying there, and I had nowhere else to go."

Ethan's eyes narrowed more as his mouth gaped open. "What do you mean you had nowhere else to go?" Before she could answer, he fired off another sentence. "Are you staying with Arden?"

Color heated her cheeks as she looked at her desk. This was the reason she didn't want people to know she was at Arden's. They were going to make the same assumption she knew Ethan was. It mortified her. Even in this day and age, someone in her position, at the head of a school, could certainly be branded with a scarlet letter *A*.

"Please keep your voice down," she begged. "I don't need my personal business broadcast throughout the school. You know how rumors fly in a small town."

"I thought we were friends. I don't understand why you'd keep something like this from me," he told her. Now he seemed hurt on top of being irritated. Keera wasn't trying to exclude anyone, but Arden had pointed out that the fewer people who knew, the easier it would be to catch whoever was at fault.

"I'm sorry, Ethan. I should have spoken to you right away. You've been nothing but good to me, and if this has to do with the school instead of just me, you should certainly be in on it."

On top of everything else she was feeling, the last thing she wanted was a load of guilt. But Ethan seemed to be more concerned with how he was feeling than her safety. That should bother her, but at the moment she was far more concerned with assuaging this man's feelings.

"Arden hasn't shared a damn thing with me about how this investigation's going. I think he forgets I'm the vice principal of this school, and that I've worked here a long time. I have a right to know what's happening."

There was so much accusation in Ethan's eyes. Though Keera knew she didn't owe anyone details of her personal life, she did feel that she owed Ethan information that could pertain to the school. He had been there much longer than she had, even longer than Arden.

"Are you and Arden a couple now?" Ethan asked. He'd calmed his voice, but she couldn't tell what he thought about the possibility of her dating Arden.

"No," she said too quickly, then forced herself to calm. "He's just a friend, and he wants to get to the bottom of this." There was no way Ethan needed to know her personal business or what she and Arden had done together.

"I could be helping you," Ethan insisted. "Just because Arden has his family's money doesn't make him better than me."

Keera wondered what had happened between Ethan and the Forbes family to make the man so bitter. Maybe it was just a matter of envy. She'd seen that a lot when her family had been wealthy. A lot of people thought money would solve all their problems. She knew firsthand how untrue that actually was.

"I appreciate you offering, Ethan, I truly do. I'm just trying to get this solved so I don't need help from anyone," she told him. "It's very difficult for me to accept."

"Apparently it's not too hard, since you're staying with Arden," he said, a smirk on his lips as if he knew what that entailed and exactly how she was thanking Arden for his generosity.

Fury rushed through Keera, and she had to push it back down. She expected those who didn't know her to think these types of things, but she'd thought she and Ethan had respect for each other. Apparently not.

"I might be temporarily staying with Arden, but I assure you, what I do when I'm outside of these school walls is no one's business," she told him, her shoulders coming back, fire in her eyes. She took pride in the fact that he looked away first. He should feel ashamed for making snap judgments against her.

"He's not the guy you think he is. He has a lot of people fooled," Ethan told her, still refusing to look her in the eyes.

Keera didn't know how to react to this. She didn't know Arden, not that well. Everything she'd seen of him spoke of a good man, but that didn't necessarily mean anything. Ethan had known Arden and his entire family for a long time. But with the way Ethan had been acting over the last few weeks, his opinion wasn't valued.

"How long until you go back home?" he asked when she didn't respond to his last words. He seemed to be backpedaling. He even looked up and gave her a semblance of a smile.

"I don't know. The people destroyed nearly everything in my place. I was able to salvage some clothes, but all the furniture was ruined, along with the flooring. They couldn't have been there more than twenty minutes, but the amount of destruction they caused was equivalent to that of a tornado."

"I'm sorry," he said, seeming to mean the words. "I would've been there for you had I known."

"I appreciate that more than you can imagine," Keera told him. "There's not a lot of people in this world we can count on, so it's always nice to have someone like you in my life."

Keera realized as she said the words, making the man smile, that she wasn't sure she really wanted him to be a part of her life anymore—at least not outside of work. He was just so bitter, and he was now making her uncomfortable.

He stood and walked toward her office door. Maybe he could feel the tension in the room, or maybe he'd come in and said what he needed to, and now he was making his escape. She wasn't sure, but she did know she had no desire to stop him.

"Next time, make sure I'm the first phone call you make," he told her as he paused at her door.

Keera's shoulders tensed again as he looked at her. She wanted to tell him that wasn't going to happen, but what were the chances of anything more occurring? Pretty slim, in reality. It had been very quiet for the past week, so maybe the culprits had found whatever it was they were looking for and they were done with her.

"I will," she said. The lie felt bitter on her tongue.

Ethan's chest puffed out as he smiled for a moment too long before exiting her office. It took several moments for Keera's heart rate to lower and her skin to stop prickling. Ethan wasn't a bad man, but there was something about him that irked her now. Maybe it was because he was so antagonistic toward Arden, someone she cared about.

Keera wasn't sure what it was. She'd learned long ago to take her time in trusting another person. That's why she didn't quite understand her newfound trust in Arden.

That wasn't true. If she was being honest, she'd have to admit she couldn't deny Arden was someone she could turn to in a time of need. She wasn't sure how long that would be the case, but right now he was the first person she thought of when everything was going wrong.

What was more frightening than that, was the fact that she thought of Arden when everything was going right, too. As a matter of fact, she was constantly thinking about Arden and his dang dog. The two of them had wedged themselves inside her wall of protection. She didn't want to put the wall back up.

Chapter Twenty-Two

Keera was getting ready to settle down with a good book. She had the house to herself, which should have been much more pleasant than it was, but she was lonely. When the front door swung open, it caused her to jump as she turned to find four women walking inside.

"Good evening," a cheerful voice called.

Angela was back wearing a grin, looking absolutely stunning. She was accompanied by Roxie, who was married to Arden's brother Kian, and two other women she recognized only from pictures throughout Arden's home.

"Hello," Keera said, unsure what was happening. They were carrying what appeared to be a dress wrapped in plastic, and a couple of bags. They all looked as if they were ready for a night on the town.

"Keera, this is Roxie, Dakota, and Eden," Angela said. "We've come to take you away from this place—just for tonight."

"I have a bunch of work to do," Keera said, automatically taking a step back. Most of her things had been destroyed, and there was no way she could match these women. Even before her clothes had been ruined, she hadn't owned anything like what they were wearing. She was far more a business-casual type of dresser.

"It's Saturday night. Work can wait," Roxie said. "I'll be the first to say you're now living in Edmonds, and we like to know our neighbors. Since you're running the high school, and you and Arden have become such good . . . friends," she added, after a wiggle of her brows and a long enough pause to make Keera squirm, "it's time we hang out."

"I'd love to do that. How about coffee tomorrow?" Keera asked, thinking that was an acceptable compromise.

"Not a chance. I have a sitter tonight, and my husband's waiting. We're going out," Dakota said as she moved forward. "We brought you a killer dress. There's no excuse."

"Oh, well . . ." Keera really didn't know what else she could say without coming across as rude. And as she gazed at the bag, she felt a deep yearning to get dressed up. She'd heard the saying about all work and no play being a bad thing, but work was what sustained her, so she didn't put much stock into it.

"We brought everything you'll need, so we're going to do a rush job getting you ready. Of course, you have flawless skin and luxurious hair, so it won't take much to make you shine," Eden told her.

"I can't believe you've been so thoughtful," Keera said, feeling a sting in her eyes. She blinked them rapidly, in no way wanting to break down in front of these strong women.

"We take care of each other in this town," Dakota said. "And just 'cause I moved away doesn't mean I don't still consider this home," she assured her.

"Before I came here I had no support at all. Now, I truly do feel like this is home," Angela said with a smile. "It won't take you long to feel as if you're right where you belong."

Keera didn't feel as if there was anything going on between Arden and Angela, but she was sort of surprised by it. The woman was absolutely stunning, with her dark hair, dark eyes, and olive complexion. She was shocked she had been working in Arden's home for a while now with nothing happening. But maybe there had just never been a connection.

Or maybe it was just that she read far too many romance books where the maid and homeowner fell in love. Come to think of it, Ruth

Cardello's *Maid for the Billionaire* had been a story like that, and it had been smoking hot. Keera shook her head, getting romance-book stories out of her head. She was already having too many thoughts of Arden and didn't need to make it worse.

"Do you guys go around doing this for everyone?" Keera asked as they handed over the dress.

"Can you imagine how fun that would be?" Eden asked. "We could be fairy godmothers with Prada and Jimmy Choo." She laughed.

"We can stand here and talk all night, but I'd much rather see you getting all hot so I can see Arden's eyes bulge when you arrive," Dakota said with evil glee. "I love watching my brothers take the fall."

Keera held up a hand to stop that train of thought. "Arden and I are just friends," she said, her voice a bit too high. She was trying to convince herself of this as much as these four women.

All four of them chuckled. "Mm-hmm, that's what I thought, too, about Kian," Roxie said. "I had no intention of going there again with him. But the funny thing about love is that we don't always get to choose it. As a matter of fact, we rarely get to choose. One day we're moseying along, thinking we're perfectly content, and *bam*, out of the blue we're shot with an arrow, and no matter how much we try to fight it, we can't."

"Sometimes we also mistake lust for love," Keera pointed out.

"There's nothing wrong with lust," Eden said with a sigh. "I could definitely use some of that right about now."

Dakota laughed as she patted her friend on the arm. "Owen's in town," she said with a wink.

"Yeah, that ship sailed a long time ago," Eden said. But there was something in her eyes that spoke of pain, and Keera knew that was a story worth hearing. Maybe if she got to know these women more, they'd let her in on the details.

"My brothers are a lot of bark, and no bite," Dakota said as she rubbed Eden's shoulder.

"They are good guys," Angela said with a slight blush that intrigued Keera. She really hadn't thought there was anything between her and Arden, but that blush meant something. What was it?

"Most of them are," Eden said, but the words were softened by a smile.

"You know Arden needs to make sure you're safe," Angela said. "When this all began, he was a mess."

"He's a good guy and has been wonderful to me," Keera said, not wanting any of them to think she didn't appreciate what he'd done for her. "He really takes 'helping thy neighbor' seriously."

"Yeah, I think it's a little past helping his neighbor, or wanting to keep you safe," Angela said with a wink, confusing Keera even more.

"Well, I . . . uh . . ." Keera just closed her mouth. She was going to deny it, but the two of them had already combusted once together. But then again, maybe that had waned for him, because he hadn't touched her since she'd moved into his place.

"Just enjoy a sexy man wanting you," Roxie suggested.

Keera felt her cheeks heat. She didn't think he wanted her anymore, but she wasn't going to say that. For one, she didn't want him to want her. Well, maybe she did, but she didn't *want* to feel that way.

"I'll go change. You've convinced me to go out. However," she said, holding up a hand when they all grinned, "it's not for a date with Arden."

She turned with her dress and a bag they'd handed her. She shut the door to the bedroom she was using and nearly cried again when she saw the beautiful undergarments they'd purchased. Normally, to receive such items would make her uncomfortable, but she was literally starting over from scratch, and everything she'd been given in the past week and a half was a blessing.

But to receive such gorgeous items was a real treat. She really should tell them they shouldn't have gone to so much trouble, but that would take the value of the gesture away, and she didn't want to do that. She was very much appreciative of what they were doing for her.

When she looked in the mirror after putting on the formfitting gown, she felt like a princess going to the ball—a modern-day princess. There were no big, poufy skirts with this dress. However, it was the most elegant, stunning thing she'd ever worn, and that was saying a lot, considering she'd grown up with money. But she'd just been a kid then. She was all woman now, with the curves to make her feel positively sexy in the dress they'd picked for her.

When she walked out, they were standing around the kitchen island, hair irons plugged in and makeup set up. She was a little nervous in her four-inch heels, and taking smaller steps so the slit up the side of the dress wasn't quite so revealing.

"Oh, Keera, that dress is utter perfection on you," Roxie said with a sigh. "The color, the cut, the sexy dip in the back. Perfect, absolutely perfect."

"Yes, yes, yes," Dakota agreed as she moved over and pulled Keera up to the counter where a stool was waiting. "Sit." Keera was practically shoved into the chair as her hair band was pulled out and Dakota started curling her long strands.

"Let's just add the finishing touches," Eden told her.

Keera couldn't ever remember being made up before. But she felt like a rock star about to go out onstage as the women fussed with her hair and makeup. She hoped they weren't making her look like she should be on a street corner instead of hanging with them. Even as she had the thought, though, she wasn't worried. These women were far too classy to do something like that.

When they were finished, they stood back, grinning. Angela pulled out a mirror and told her to take a look. Keera wasn't able to speak as she gazed at her reflection. They'd curled her hair so it fell in soft waves across her bare shoulders and down to the middle of her back. They'd highlighted her eyes, and insisted she wear a darker shade of pink than she was used to. She barely resembled the woman she was on a daily basis.

"This is . . . wow . . . ," Keera said, unable to come up with the proper words. Would Arden think this was all for him? Would the townspeople? She began to worry, but then pushed those thoughts away. This was about her, and her alone. It was okay to want to look in a mirror and feel beautiful every once in a while. It was okay to do it every single day, if a person wanted. How you felt about yourself on the outside reflected how you felt on the inside, and it also impacted how you treated others. The more secure you were with yourself, the happier you'd be.

"Stunning is the word you're looking for," Dakota said.

"Sexy as sin," Eden added.

"A vision," Angela told her.

"Thank you," Keera said, the two little words seeming inadequate.

"Not a problem," Roxie told her. "Let's get you to the ball before midnight. We don't want any pumpkins tonight." She waved her imaginary wand in the air, and Keera appreciated the laugh that eased the tension she was feeling at stepping out of the house all dolled up.

As they stepped from the house, a large SUV waited, a driver immediately moving to open the back door. "None of us wanted to be the designated tonight," Dakota said as she led the way.

"Good thinking," Keera said.

"To a beautiful night," Roxie said after pouring them each a glass of wine. They clinked glasses and took a sip, and Keera sat back, wondering how this had become her life.

"And to the wee hours of the morning," Dakota added with a wink that had Keera's cheeks turning red again.

She couldn't deny there was a part of her hoping to get a reaction out of Arden. She wasn't sure when her thinking had begun to change, or when she'd started wishing he'd come visit her bed again, but tonight, that's exactly what she hoped for.

Maybe one more time would be enough . . . Yeah, she was very aware that was a lie she was telling herself to make her think this train of thought was okay. Still, she refused to analyze it too much. She was letting go, for tonight at the very least. And she was going to have a wonderful time. She hoped Arden was a part of that.

Chapter Twenty-Three

There were very few times in Arden's life where his breath was actually taken from him. But as he waited in the lobby of the hotel where he was meeting his family and Keera, he wasn't prepared for the vision that walked in.

Yes, she was stunning every single time he saw her, but when she stepped through the doors, a smile on her pink lips, the blue dress clinging to every delicious curve of her body, and her hair cascading down her back, he literally lost his breath.

He didn't see any other person in the vast lobby, didn't even remember his own name. His body, which was already tense, went rigid as he gazed at her, so blown away he couldn't command his feet to move. He had a moment to stare before she turned, before she saw him.

The smile she wore slowly faded as her eyes dilated, and she let out a whoosh of air. The hunger between the two of them was tangible. It felt as if they could swim through it, it was so thick and humid.

He'd brought her into his home, and though it killed him to do so, he hadn't touched her, had tried to be respectful, and not make her feel she was pressured or obligated in any way to him. He'd been waiting for her to make a move on him. He didn't think he'd be able to wait any longer—not with how incredibly turned on he was at just the sight of her walking.

The five women approached, and Arden stood before them, dumbfounded as he tried to open his mouth, tried to express what a vision she was. A giggle from his sister and a punch in the arm shook him out of his paralysis.

"There aren't words to describe how stunning you are," he said. Her tongue came out and moistened her lips, and he almost dropped to his knees to beg for mercy.

"Thanks," she told him as she licked those kissable lips again. "You look amazing."

Arden couldn't even remember what he'd thrown on, but it didn't matter. For the first time in his life, he felt unworthy to have a woman on his arm. Just as soon as he had that thought, he smiled, brushing it aside. Hell, they were going to be the belles of the ball. He held out his arm and grinned.

"I'd like to escort inside the most beautiful woman I've ever seen," he told her. Arden felt his pants tighten as her cheeks reddened. This was going to be one hell of a night. He wondered how quickly he could escape his friends and family and get her out of that dress that was going to give him wet dreams for years to come.

"Ah, aren't you being the perfect gentleman," Dakota said with a chuckle.

"There are five of us here. We're waiting for more compliments," Roxie said with a laugh.

Though it took a lot of effort, Arden ripped his gaze from Keera to look at the other ladies. "Of course, you are all a vision," he said with a bow. They laughed, knowing he had eyes for only one woman. The four women turned and began walking toward the elevators.

Keera put her arm in his, and he felt as if he'd just been knighted. She'd given him her trust with that small gesture.

"Seriously, Keera, you are stunning every day," he told her, in no hurry to leave this spot right here, where he felt as if the rest of the world had disappeared. "But with your hair down and that dress . . ."

He paused again as he inhaled her sweet scent that was playing havoc with his hormones. "With that dress, you will stop traffic."

She blushed again but didn't look away. There was as much heat in her eyes as he was sure was in his own. Yes, tonight he wasn't going to play the gentleman. Tonight he was going to give them what they both needed. He realized he'd been waiting for her, but he hadn't realized she was too shy to ever make a move. She wanted him as much as he wanted her, even if she was scared. He just had to prove to her she had nothing to fear.

He began moving them to the elevators, and the girls were long gone. Good. He wanted a few more minutes alone with this woman. Though when they stepped inside, several other people crowded in with them. It didn't matter. He'd made his own bubble around the two of them, and no one could pop it.

As a few more people crammed themselves inside at the last minute, Arden and Keera were pushed to the corner, her body pressed against his. His already hard body pulsed painfully as he inhaled her sweet scent, closing his eyes for just a moment to picture her rubbing a dab between her luscious breasts, maybe a line down the inside of her thigh. A groan escaped him, and she looked at him curiously. He shifted, which only brought him that much more tightly against her.

"How set are you on this evening?" he asked, his voice barely above a whisper. Even he could hear the urgency in his voice.

"Why?" she asked. Though she felt his heat, felt the passion between them, she had no idea how close he was to picking her up and finding the nearest closet. Her innocence was turning him on that much more.

"No reason," he said. There was no way he could take her away from here when she had taken the time to dress up. It would be a shame to the rest of the people there to not see the glorious package she was.

The doors to the elevator opened, and Arden wasn't sure if he was grateful or not. His sanity might be saved by escaping the tight confines, but he in no way wanted to let this woman go. He was becoming quite possessive when it came to her. He couldn't remember ever having felt that way toward a woman. He knew there had never been anyone he hadn't been willing to let go.

When they stepped into the upscale lounge, soft piano music was playing, and the lights were dim. It was a nice place, and he was sure he could find some little alcove to whisk her away to. He saw his family all the time and didn't need to tonight. He actually looked around to find potential hiding places.

"Wow, this is stunning," she said as she looked around. He followed the direction of her gaze and tried to see it through her eyes. He'd gotten so used to the finer things in life, he sometimes didn't appreciate the beauty. He had a feeling that being with this woman would help change that for him.

The place had a classy elegance about it, with low-hung chandeliers and cloth-covered tables with vases in the middle holding fresh-cut flowers. Candles burned throughout the room, giving a flickering of light as well as a delicious aroma. The hardwood floors were polished to perfection, and the vaulted ceilings showed exposed beams. It was a beautiful place, and he wished it was just the two of them. He would pull her onto the dance floor before the night was over, he assured himself.

In the corner a band was setting up. *Good.* He loved piano music, but it was more for ambience. Arden wanted this woman in his arms, and he knew this band, knew they played a lot of slow songs. He could wait a little while. The anticipation of this night with her, of touching her, flirting with her, looking into her eyes and watching them burn, was all worth the wait.

By the time they finally got home, they'd detonate. Arden had a feeling it would always be this way with Keera. She inspired him in so many ways. He was certain he wasn't going to let her go. Now he just had to convince her he was worth keeping, that he was worth trusting. Tonight he'd begin showing her they belonged together.

"My family is waiting on us," he said on a sigh.

"We should go, then," she said, seeming almost as disappointed as him.

He thought about lifting her into his arms and walking out, but he wanted her to know that she meant so much more to him than just a roll in the hay. So with that in mind, he stepped forward, pleased to walk through the room knowing every eye was on his date.

She was truly the one a man would be a fool to let get away. Lucky for him, he'd been the one to find her. She was his now. She'd realize that soon. Arden had never given up on something that mattered to him.

And Keera Thompson mattered a lot.

Chapter Twenty-Four

There were butterflies in Keera's stomach as she walked through the crowded lounge, knowing people were watching the two of them. For those who didn't know who Keera was, they were wondering. Not because she seemed intriguing, but because she was on the arm of Arden Forbes.

But the butterflies weren't because of people watching them. No. The butterflies were because he'd looked at her in a way that made her feel like the only woman on the planet—he'd made her feel beautiful, confident, and worthy of being right where she was.

The look he'd given her when their eyes had connected had made her feel as if she were naked and he were stroking her. She'd been very wrong to think he didn't still desire her. The heat inside her body was at inferno levels, because she had no doubt the two of them would make love tonight.

For a moment she'd been confused when he'd asked if she wanted to leave. Now, feeling his body next to hers, feeling the heat scorching between the two of them, she had no doubt why he'd been in such a hurry. If he asked her to leave again, she'd gladly tell him *yes*.

It had been fun to dress up once she'd gotten over the initial shock of it. And to be out with a group of people, especially as wonderful as they were, was something she was grateful to be doing. But now all her thoughts were on her and Arden getting naked, and that was going to make it very difficult to get through the evening without every single person in the room reading the desire in her eyes.

A shudder passed through her as they neared a large table where the girls were sitting, along with half a dozen other people. She didn't realize it, but she scooted a little closer to Arden, who wrapped his hand behind her back and gave her a reassuring squeeze.

"Are you ready for this?" he asked. She sighed before smiling.

"Yes. Thank you for including me," she told him with sincerity.

"You might not be thanking me when the night is over," he said with a chuckle.

She hoped she was thanking him when the night was over. If it ended the way she anticipated it would, they could thank each other over and over again. That thought made the heat practically scorch her, and she had to clench her thighs.

It was odd how turned on she was. It certainly wasn't something she was used to. This man inspired new feelings inside her each time she was in his presence. Maybe the thing she liked most about him was how he made her feel about herself. Would she be a fool to let him go if he didn't want to be released? Yes, she'd be a fool for herself, but she'd be doing him and his family a favor.

They stepped up to the table, and all eyes turned to them. Everyone wore friendly expressions, and Keera relaxed the tiniest bit as Arden began making introductions.

"Everyone, you know Keera Thompson, who's the high school principal. You are also aware of what's been happening at the school," he said, a frown causing his brows to be drawn in.

"We're so glad you were able to make it tonight," Kian said.

"My brother Kian, and you know his wife, Roxie," Arden said. She smiled at the man who was just as stunning as his brother. It was odd how the siblings were all equally attractive, but only one of them stirred red-hot desire within her. She wondered if any of them had ever had a crush on the same woman, or if a woman had had a crush on more than one of them at a time. Maybe someday she'd be brave enough to ask.

"You also know Angela and Eden. Over here is my bratty sister's husband, Ace Armstrong," Arden continued.

"Hey, I resemble that," Dakota said with a wink.

"Not a chance, darling. You're an angel," Ace said with an even bigger wink. The entire table laughed at that, and Dakota shot them a warning look.

"Ace certainly has his work cut out for him," Arden said before he turned to another guy who was sitting next to Owen. "This is Doc Evan. Call him Doc or Evan, or BT," Arden continued with a laugh.

"BT?" she asked.

"I'm the local vet, and I don't need to explain his lame joke, but let's just say it has to do with fixing animals. Evan is fine," he said with a smile as he rose and shook her hand, then leaned in and gave her a hug.

"Mm-hmm, you can back up," Arden said with a scowl.

"Got any cats or dogs?" Evan asked after giving Arden a look she couldn't quite read. It took a moment to realize Evan was purposely goading Arden. This made her want to play along as she smiled. A guy with a sense of humor was certainly one she could be friends with.

"No, but I want a cat," she said.

"Well, I'm your guy. I'll take good care of you," he said with a chuckle.

"Yeah, I'll take care of her just fine," Arden said. "Go and sit back down."

Kian began laughing, making Arden scowl at him. "Jealousy looks good on you, brother," he said. His wife smiled at Arden as well as she tried to hide her laugh behind her napkin.

"Ha, I have nothing to be jealous of. All day long, all Doc does is play in bull sem—"

"Alrighty, then, let's stop that sentence," Dakota said with a laugh. "Unless you're trying to scare your date away."

Evan laughed. "I love what I do. Bring the kids out to the ranch anytime for a field trip. I can always spot future vets," he offered. Then he smacked Arden in the arm before resuming his seat.

"That sounds like a great idea," Keera said. "I'll put a sign-up sheet on the wall and get it arranged." She loved to get the kids out of the classroom. It stimulated them and showed them what their future was going to be like. She hadn't thought of taking them to a ranch before. She hoped she didn't have to leave this school, because the longer she was in this community—being stalked aside—the more she liked this town.

"I'll be on that field trip," Arden said so low she almost missed it.

She stopped and looked at him, realizing he was a little jealous. It was so strange, she found her lips twitching. She couldn't remember anyone ever being jealous over her. It was pretty amazing.

"You forgot me," a man said from the end of the table. Keera noticed when he spoke that Eden looked down, her hand trembling the slightest bit. She really wanted to know what the story was there. This must be the brother Eden had been speaking of.

"My brother Owen is visiting again. Of course, he's been home so much lately, we haven't missed him at all," Arden said.

"Hey, I'm a very missable guy," Owen said with a crooked smile. "And I'm coming home permanently," he announced, making all eyes turn on him.

"You better not be lying," Dakota said as she stared her brother down.

"I went looking for something I thought I needed. What I realized is I didn't have to leave home to know what that was," he said as he looked at his sister. But then his gaze zeroed in on Eden, whose eyes widened for a moment before they narrowed and her shoulders firmed.

Keera knew that look well. And though Owen smiled her way, thinking it might be just that easy for him to have whatever it was he wanted, Keera could see it wasn't going to be such a breeze for him. She wouldn't mind sitting back and watching to see what happened next.

"Where's Declan?" Arden asked, seeming to realize just then that their oldest brother wasn't there. Keera had noticed right away.

"He'll be here soon," Kian said. "He was dealing with some top-secret thing or other." Kian waved his hand like that was an everyday thing. She loved seeing the dynamic between the siblings, their friends, and their spouses. It was truly fascinating to see such a wealthy family who were so . . . well, normal.

Her family hadn't been anything like the Forbes family.

"Do Mom and Dad know we're all together?" Arden asked.

Kian winced. "I was trying not to scare Keera away, and you know Mom," he said.

"Oh, you're gonna pay for this," Owen said with a laugh.

"Hey, you could have called them," Kian pointed out.

"I didn't arrange the get-together. I'm just an innocent bystander," he said as he leaned back in his chair, his hands behind his head. The man was probably pretty lucky he was on the other side of the table from Eden, 'cause Keera had a feeling if she were near him, she'd be kicking those legs, sending Owen flying backward.

"Sit down. We have wine, and the waiter will be back soon," Roxie said.

Arden pulled out her chair, leaving him on one side of her and Angela on the other.

"How are you liking our school?" Owen asked.

"I love it," she answered honestly. "You have amazing programs already in place, a great group of kids, and I see so much potential in implementing new programs, such as visiting local professions," she added as she smiled at Evan.

"Dang straight," Evan said. "Can't wait."

"I bet," Arden said, but he smiled as he rested his arm behind Keera's chair. She was well aware it was a possessive gesture. What surprised her was how much she liked it. "She's well liked by everyone," he added.

"Wait!" Kian said, grinning even bigger.

"What?" Arden asked. His brother was practically bouncing with glee.

"I just realized Keera's your boss," he said with a chuckle. "Oh, Keera, we're going to have to talk," he added with a wink.

"She's the hottest boss I've ever had," Arden said, not in the least intimidated that she held a higher position than him. Of course, he chose to do what he did in spite of his money, and the title wouldn't matter to him. But there were some men who might actually get offended by this fact, some who might be intimidated. Arden Forbes wasn't one of those men.

Arden's fingers shifted, and she was intensely aware when he began gently rubbing them along the bare skin exposed by her dress. A shiver ran through her, and his touch was making it difficult for her to concentrate on the conversation that continued to go on around her. But still, she didn't want him to stop—not one little bit.

She held a glass of water with one hand and the other rested on her lap. Her own fingers twitched with the need to reach between them and rest them on his thigh, draw the same lazy circles on his leg as he was doing.

But they weren't a couple. She didn't feel like she could reach over and do that. She wished she were a little braver. She wasn't sure what would happen if she did. She was trying to talk herself into doing just that, the privacy of the tablecloth making her a little bolder, when they were interrupted.

"Sorry I'm late."

The deep baritone of Declan right behind her made Keera jump, which caused a couple of people at the table who'd noticed to chuckle.

"Don't worry, he has a way of sneaking up on people," Roxie said with a smile.

"Who does?" Declan asked.

"You, of course," she told him.

"I don't have to sneak," he said with a confident look. "I'm welcome wherever I go."

"Ha," Dakota said. "About as welcome as a fly in a mousetrap."

Ace laughed. "You almost got that one right," he told his wife, confusing Keera.

"My little sister likes to make little idioms, and she constantly messes them up," Arden explained.

"I do not," Dakota defended. But she continued to smile. This seemed like a game they'd all been playing for a long time.

What was more interesting than anything else was Keera noticed instantly how Angela went from relaxed and active in the conversation, to tense and silent as she studied her glass as if it would disappear.

The pieces began to click, and Keera was almost relieved. Now it made sense.

"You didn't save me a chair?" Declan asked as he looked around the group. He wasn't at all offended by this, more amused—if the man could show amusement, that was.

"Take mine. I want to explore the balcony," Keera said mischievously.

Angela turned to stare incredulously at her, and Keera smiled. Yes, she'd made a good call on that one. She rose, and Arden quickly joined her.

"I'd love to show you the balcony," he told her, that fire back in his eyes.

"We'll get another chair before you get back," Evan said as he scooted a bit, as if he was going to have it put next to him.

"You're amusing tonight, Doc," Arden said as he wrapped his arm around Keera.

Keera was now relaxed, but Angela sure wasn't as Declan sat down next to her, his frame much bigger than Keera's, causing his leg to lightly brush up against Angela's. The woman gave Keera one more stern look before she found utter fascination in her glass again.

Arden led her away, and Keera glanced back and smiled. She'd have to get Angela alone soon and ask her what that had been about.

"I like your family," she told him as they made their way toward the patio doors.

"They can be a pain in the butt," he said with a chuckle. "But I can't imagine my life without them."

"You're incredibly lucky," Keera told him.

"I know that. But just wait 'til you meet my mom and dad. You might have some sympathy for me then."

"Are they not very nice?" she asked. She hadn't heard anything negative about them.

"They're amazing," he said with a grin. "And they are snoopy, and protective, and think it's high time their children settled down," he added.

"Ah, you mean they love you," she said, a little envious.

"Yeah, as much as we love them," he admitted.

"My family wasn't like that at all," she said.

"I'm sorry, Keera. I know a lot more families are like yours than mine, but I don't understand it. I can't imagine what it'd be like without each of them in my life. We might kid with each other a lot, and we might have different personalities and different ambitions in life, but at the end of the day, there's nothing we wouldn't do for one another," he said.

"I think we're all defined in a few different ways. We either are taught who we should be, or we change who we're expected to be," she told him. "I decided from a young age I wouldn't be defined by who I was expected to be. You, on the other hand, were raised to be anything you wanted. Sometimes I think it's easier to come from a family like mine because there's no bar set. You can't possibly do worse than those who gave you life," she said, feeling an ache in her chest.

He walked her through the doors, and she was relieved to find no one else out there. It was a cool evening, but Keera didn't mind. He walked her to a back corner and leaned against the rail, then pulled her into his arms.

"You chose right, Keera. You're incredible."

The light was dim, and even through his clothes, his body was hot. She snuggled a little closer to him, feeling safe and warm, feeling desired. This was where she'd wanted to be for the past couple of weeks, but especially on this night.

"Sometimes I feel I have, other times, I . . ." She trailed off. She really wasn't sure how to finish that sentence.

He lifted a hand, brushing her hair back from her face before cupping her cheek in his warm palm. She was lost in his gaze as he looked at her, emotions she didn't understand flashing in his eyes.

Then he didn't say anything else as he lowered his head and finally took her lips in a kiss that made her forget everything but him. That was the power Arden had over her. She could let go of it all when she was in his arms. And when his lips connected with hers, she felt as if she was home.

She tightened her hold around his solid waist and held on as his fingers tangled in her hair, and he kissed her more deeply, leaving their hearts racing, and making them both wish they were somewhere a hell of a lot more private than a lounge balcony with his entire family close by.

When he pulled back, she whimpered, her lips swollen from his kiss, her heart racing, her body on fire. His eyes were dark as they burned straight into her soul.

"Tonight," he said, the word a promise.

Her lips trembled the slightest bit as she gazed back at him, then nodded.

Tonight.

Chapter Twenty-Five

Though Arden had wanted to take Keera home right then and there, she refused, telling him they'd all know exactly why they were leaving. He'd argued that it didn't matter, but she'd won the moment she said her reputation mattered to her. He'd never want her placed in a position where she felt compromised.

So instead of them both being satisfied, he'd brought her back to the table and spent two solid hours of torture next to her while her fingers trailed up and down his thigh beneath the safety of the tablecloth. He was barely able to speak more than a few words here and there between courses.

One thing Arden knew beyond a shadow of a doubt was that Keera was vulnerable, and he had to proceed carefully. He didn't want just this night with her, he wanted forever, but he had to be damn careful with how he presented that.

Arden had zero doubt Keera had feelings for him. She was just so used to putting her own needs and desires at the back of her mind, it would take him time to get her used to embracing what she felt and trusting those emotions, trusting that desire. He could take his time, because he knew in the end, they'd make magic together. She was worth the wait.

Right now, though, he had to sate his hunger. It had been two weeks since they'd made love, and that was far too long. He'd only had her that one night, and it had consumed him, body and soul.

Saying goodbyes as quick as he could manage without rushing Keera or embarrassing her by dragging her caveman-style from the lounge, he let out his first breath of air as they stepped outside and waited for his car to be brought to them. When they got inside, Keera turned and looked at him, her lips parted, her eyes bright.

"If you keep looking at me like that, we won't make it back to the house," he warned, his voice a dangerous growl.

Her eyes widened, but not in fright—in unadulterated excitement. That had his body throbbing even more. He let out a low growl before slamming the car into drive and flooring it. It was only a few miles home, and if he had to count every single line on the road to keep them from crashing, that's what he'd do.

Keera wisely kept on her side of the vehicle, though he could see how she shifted in her seat, how her legs rubbed together as she fought the ache consuming her. They were both burning up from waiting so long to sate this need.

They pulled into his garage, and he wasn't even sure if he managed to get his car into park before slamming open his door and jogging around to her side of the vehicle. He took her hand and pulled her to him, giving her a hard kiss before both of them rushed toward the door.

They didn't make it past the first wall in his house before he pushed her against it, his head lowering, his kiss unrestrained as his lips captured hers, wordlessly stating his intentions. She groaned into his mouth as she reached up, her fingers tangling in his hair as she wiggled against him.

Arden was sure the wall was the only thing keeping the two of them upright. He reached down, cupping her firm ass, squeezing as he lifted her from the ground, and pushing forward, letting her feel how hard he was, how much he needed her. She moaned her approval as her fingers fisted in his hair, pulling him closer.

He reached down lower and cupped her thigh, lifting her leg, incredibly happy with the high slit in the side of her dress. Still, the sound of the material ripping echoed through the hallway as he pushed between her legs. He'd get her a new dress. This one might get shredded.

"There are too many clothes in the way," he said, not recognizing his voice. He spoke against her jaw, then kissed his way to her neck and sucked on the tender skin where her pulse was beating out of control.

"I need you, Arden," she said, her voice scratchy, wanton.

"You have me," he promised. In so many more ways than one. "We need a bed."

He lifted her, his arm beneath the curve of her ass, as he held her leg with the other. She let out a giggle at the position as he began moving down the hallway. He'd been fantasizing about her in his bed again for too long.

He made it to his room, then pressed her against the wall again, unable to go a single step farther without tasting her sweet lips. As she pulled up her other leg, the dress gave out as she wrapped herself around him, her hot core pressed against him.

Dammit! There should be no clothes between them. If he could let go of her for a few seconds, he could remedy that. But even a few seconds was too long in his heightened state.

Keera let out a cry of pleasure as he ran his fingers up her sides, squeezing her luscious breasts. Her nipples pebbled in his palms, and he needed to taste them.

With more effort than he thought he was capable of in that moment, he moved away from the wall, walking to the bed without his lips leaving hers. Only when he felt the mattress against his legs did he lower her, his body immediately aching when she wasn't pressed up against him.

But it was almost worth it to take a step back, to see the flush of her cheeks, the sparkle in her eyes, the tangle of her hair.

"You are the most beautiful woman I've ever laid eyes on," he said, filled with awe.

"Oh, Arden," she said, her arms stretching out to him.

He wanted nothing more than to rip their clothes away and sink deep within her folds. But he also needed to touch and taste every inch of her. He needed to claim her, for her to be his from this night until forever.

He knelt next to the bed, and she whimpered until he took her delicate feet in his large hands and undid the clasps of her sexy-as-hell shoes. He pulled them off and kissed the tops of her feet as he squeezed them. She lay back and moaned.

He ran his hands up her calves, kneading them, appreciating the firmness of her body, how every square inch of her turned him on. He ran his tongue along the inside of her thighs, pushing them apart as he took his time tasting her, appreciating her, building her pleasure to nearly unbearable heights.

He reached the top of her legs, and only a tiny wisp of lace was keeping him from touching her. Easily, he slipped his fingers beneath it and flicked them across her tender flesh, making her scream out his name as her hips arched off the bed.

"You are so damn responsive," he said as he slid his fingers inside her, her core hot and wet and ready.

He needed to see what he was touching, so he pulled from her, making her whimper her displeasure at the loss of his touch. But he reached to her side and found the zipper on the dress, pulling it down, and finally freeing the material.

He tugged the dress away, nearly going insane when he found she wasn't wearing a bra. Her breasts came free, her nipples hard, her chest heaving. With the slightest of tugs, her panties were gone, and there she was before him—beautiful, hot, and waiting.

He leaned back down and ran his tongue across her slick opening. She arched again as her fingers fisted in the blankets. He pushed open her thighs and didn't hold back as he devoured her, running his tongue across every sensitive millimeter of her, circling his lips over her swollen clit and sucking until she begged for mercy.

He flicked his tongue across her flesh again and again, and when he slid his fingers inside her, she screamed, this time her body coming undone as she squeezed him, her orgasm taking her away on a perfect escape.

"More," she groaned, her body still gripping his fingers. "I want you, all of you," she said, her words barely distinguishable.

"Yes, Keera, more," he said.

He climbed up her body, finally getting to taste her ripe nipples, licking and sucking them as she wrapped her legs around his waist and pushed upward, moaning her frustration at the barrier of his clothes preventing them from becoming one.

"Please, take me, please," she said as he sucked hard on her nipple.

"Yes," he agreed. She reluctantly released him, and he tore his clothes away, then grabbed a condom and rolled it on before he was finally lying against her with nothing to keep them apart.

As soon as her legs were wrapped around him, as soon as his thickness was resting against the safety of her hot folds, the urgency that had filled him dimmed. He was right where he needed to be, and it gave him a sense of peace.

He gently rocked his hips, rubbing against the outside of her, against her throbbing flesh, as he savored this moment. He didn't want this night to ever end. Only when she opened her passion-filled eyes did he finally begin to sink inside her, slowly, surely, fully.

"Oh yes, yes, yes," Keera said as her legs clasped him tightly and her fingers clutched the back of his head. "Don't ever stop, Arden, never," she begged.

He knew exactly how she felt. "I'll make love to you all night," he said, knowing he could be happy doing nothing more than lying in her arms day and night.

He moved slowly in and out of her, but soon the need was too great. She squirmed beneath him, and his body throbbed. He needed to give her another release, and take one for himself.

They'd make love all night, but some of this hunger had to abate first or they were both going up in flames. With a fierce cry, he grabbed her hips and slammed inside her, making her eyes snap back open as she looked at him in awed delight.

"Yes!" she encouraged, her fingernails digging into his shoulders as she trembled beneath him. He moved faster, nearly pulling out of her before hammering back down, over and over again, the room filled with cries of their pleasure and the slapping of their skin hitting together.

With a shudder, Keera's body tensed as she leaned against his shoulder, her teeth biting down on him, her core squeezing his erection harder with each contraction.

He let go, pushing deep inside her as his own release overtook him, fire and ice tingling through his body as he swelled within her, throbbing with the force of his release.

When they both stopped shaking, he collapsed on top of her, not willing to pull from her tight body, not willing to let this connection between the two of them end. The first time they'd made love had been amazing; this time it had been otherworldly.

"You're mine, Keera," he said against the soft, damp skin of her neck.

"I'm yours," she said, her voice sated, her body clinging to his just as much as he was holding on to her.

They might have lain that way for seconds, minutes, or hours. Arden didn't know. But soon she began moving her hips—small, gentle thrusts as her lips trailed their way across his neck. Yes, it was time for more. It would always be time for more. She was his, and he would show her exactly what that meant.

Chapter Twenty-Six

Sitting back with a beer, Arden wondered if life got much better than this. Sure, he still had his brother on his ass as he tried figuring out what in the hell was going on with their town. And sure, nothing had been solved. But Arden was having a difficult time caring about that.

He'd fallen in love. It was odd, really. It was something he'd never thought about before. It wasn't that he was anti-love. He just hadn't been in a hurry to seek the perfect soul mate. When Kian had settled down, it had stirred things within Arden, but still, he hadn't been in a hurry.

His parents had always shared a beautiful relationship. Sure, they argued, but never over anything insurmountable. He'd had great role models to look up to. Even with all of that, it didn't matter until you ran into that person you knew you couldn't live your life without.

Arden had found that. And he wasn't willing to let it go. They'd get the situation at the school figured out, and if it did have anything to do with Keera, he'd damn sure find out who was after her, and he'd protect her.

That made him smile, because he loved how strong Keera was. She had far surpassed what most people could live through without a heck of a lot of handouts, and the worst she could say about herself was she had a hard time trusting. He'd give her all the time she needed to see he wasn't like her father. He was with her because he couldn't live without her, because when he looked at her, he saw the person his soul meshed with. He loved her. It truly was that simple and beautiful.

When his phone rang, he thought about ignoring it. But it could be Keera, so he didn't bother with the caller ID before picking it up. He took another sip of beer.

"Arden here," he said as a greeting.

There was a pause on the other end of the line, and still it took a moment for Arden to grow suspicious. It was the sound of heavy breathing that set his teeth to grinding together and made him sit up and pay attention. Whoever was daring to shatter his perfectly great mood would indeed pay the price.

"Is Keera Thompson important to you?" the voice asked.

"Who is this?" Arden demanded.

"Who I am doesn't matter," the person said before Arden could tell the mouthpiece had been covered. He heard the distant sound of coughing coming from the other end of the line, and he waited impatiently. He needed to know who this was.

"What do you want?" Arden asked.

"Some people want her dead and will go to any lengths to make that happen."

"And why is that?" Arden asked.

"Because she's uncovering things that should have remained buried. She will pay the price for that. She has a contract out on her," the person warned.

"If you're going to make threats, I assume you have evidence," Arden said.

"I'm not the one after her. I just happen to know who that person is," the man said. The phone was covered as the coughing started again. If Arden could keep him on the phone long enough, maybe he'd figure out who it was.

"If it's not you, who plans on killing her?" Arden asked, bile rising in his throat as he asked the question. "Give me a name!"

"It's the VP, and this is so much more involved than you could ever comprehend," the man said.

Shock ran through Arden. There wasn't a chance it could be Ethan. No, Arden didn't like the man, had never liked him, but the weasel wasn't capable of going to this much trouble to harass Keera. And besides that, he seemed to genuinely like Keera. What in the world would be the point of him trying to hurt her?

"You have to be mistaken," Arden said.

"If you ignore this, you're responsible for what happens next," the man told him. Arden's gut clenched.

"Can you meet with me?" Arden asked. "I won't give up your identity."

"No. I did what I needed to do. I told you what was going down. Now, it's up to you to keep her safe. She has demons from her past that are knocking at her door, and things have come full circle. Ethan isn't a good man."

"What is he going to do?" Arden asked.

There was a pause. "He hired a hit man, paid that person a lot of money," the man said.

"I need—" The phone line went dead. Arden wasn't getting any further information from this person.

He wanted to think this was a prank call, that the person was doing nothing more than trying to scare Arden. But in his gut he knew the man was speaking the truth. There was something deeper going on here, and Arden didn't know what it was, but he did know that somehow Keera had gotten in the middle of it.

And whoever she'd unknowingly gotten involved with wanted her out of their way. Whoever that was hadn't counted on Arden to be at her side. Yes, Keera was strong, but no one should go through something like this on their own.

It was time for him and Ethan to have a little chat. He needed to give Keera the respect of telling her first, and he wasn't going to do it over the phone. He ran out to his vehicle, grateful he'd only gotten about a quarter of a beer down before the person had called.

He dialed Declan as he made his way to Keera. The only reason he wasn't panicked right now was because she was having an afternoon with his sister and Roxie, and she was just as safe at his brother's house as she would be with him. But still, even knowing that, he pressed his foot down on the accelerator. He needed to get to her, needed to have her at his side where he knew no one could touch her.

He was going to kill Ethan with his bare hands if the man harmed so much as one hair on her head. The little weasel had some major explaining to do, and Arden was going to get to the bottom of it—much sooner rather than later.

Chapter Twenty-Seven

Arden felt like the worst kind of person as Keera stared at him, her face white, her eyes rounded in shock. He'd just delivered the most devastating news he could possibly give to another person, and instead of keeping her safe, he felt as if he was the one hurting her the most.

"Keera, I'm sorry," he said, reaching for her. She backed away, and it killed him not to chase after her, not to comfort her. Declan stood back with Kian while analyzing everything, but still allowing Arden to be the one to tell her.

There was no way Arden would have let Declan tell her. He would have done it in a very black-and-white way that might have sent her over the edge. First her office had been broken into, then she'd been left threatening letters, then her apartment had been trashed, and now she was hearing that someone was actually trying to have her killed.

She was holding up much better than most people would in her situation.

"I think this person is lying," Keera finally said. There were no tears. She sounded upset, but more irritated than frightened.

"I know people, Keera, and my gut tells me this person is telling the truth," Arden told her.

"You don't like Ethan so of course you want to think the worst of him," she said, hurting Arden, though he was trying not to let it.

"This isn't about me liking the man or not. This is about the things that have been happening to you and the school," he said, his tone calm.

"There's no reason for Ethan to want to hurt me. I've never done anything to him. This doesn't make sense. Can't you see that?" she asked, her voice now pleading. Arden looked over to his brothers, silently seeking their advice. They shrugged. Neither of them knew what to say. They were leaving him on his own.

"I know it doesn't make sense to you, as you don't know the man as well as you think you do, but he's a weasel, and I think this is a lot more complicated than you can imagine. I think somehow you've triggered him," Arden said, making her wince.

"You don't even know who this person was who called you. He could be some kid with a voice disguiser who's sitting back getting high, having a hoot. It could be a student who got in trouble. We can't just assume Ethan's guilty. I've never felt he'd do something to hurt me—not once," Keera said.

Her passionate words were making him stop to think. She could be right. He didn't believe she was, but what she said made sense.

"Yes, of course there's a chance the caller wasn't being honest with me, but I'm not willing to risk your safety to find out," Arden said.

She stopped and stared at him, her arms crossed, her breathing heavy. He didn't break eye contact, didn't back down. She might not be worried about her safety, but he damn well was, and he'd protect her whether she was asking for it or not.

"You obviously told Declan about this first since he's here," she said, the words firing at him like bullets. He was glad he had, because she might have convinced him to wait, and he didn't want to wait. He had a good feeling Ethan was guilty. Some people deserved to be innocent until proven guilty—some didn't. "Did you call the cops?"

"No," he told her. "I came straight to you, only calling Declan." He was glad for that as her shoulders eased, that was, until she turned to stare at Declan.

"Did you report this?" she asked. Arden was a bit shocked when he noticed his brother shift on his feet. Keera's schoolteacher voice was even making his tough-as-nails brother feel chastised.

"Not yet, but I intend to," he told her.

"I'm brand new here," Keera said, pleading with both of them to understand. "I seriously don't need to get off on the wrong foot with my VP by accusing him of trying to kill me. Let me talk to him," she said.

Both Arden and Declan were now the ones crossing their arms as they looked at her as they would a pouting child. Arden didn't want to make this situation worse, and he hoped she wouldn't notice.

"I don't think it's a good idea for you to be anywhere near him right now," Arden said, trying not to show his frustration.

"Please," she said, and he felt his resolve shaking. It was difficult for him to deny her something she truly wanted. However, her safety was on the line, and he had to stay firm for her sake.

"How about a compromise?" he asked, ignoring the grumbling coming from the corner where his brothers stood. Declan would understand if he ever allowed himself to fall in love. "We all go to his house and have a chat before we call the cops."

She looked as if she wanted to say *no* to this, but then her shoulders sagged, her eyes so damn sad it broke his heart. "Okay. No cops," she said, the words coming out like a plea, but also firm.

"This isn't a good idea, Arden," Declan said. They both turned to look at him. Kian seemed a lot more amenable to it. Of course, Kian was married and knew what it was like to compromise.

"Well, good or bad idea, it's happening," Arden said.

"At least let me get a warrant," Declan told him.

"That would involve cops," Keera said.

"I can do it without a black-and-white coming," Declan said. "Let's have it in hand just in case." Arden knew when his brother wasn't going to back down. He nodded. Keera sighed, obviously coming to the same conclusion.

"I don't think we'll need it," she said. But that was the last of her argument.

Within an hour, they were leaving the house. Arden was tense as they made their way across town to Ethan's place. They pulled up to the curb, and he could feel tension radiating off Keera.

"He's going to feel like we're attacking him," she said. "Maybe you could wait in the car."

He shook his head. "Max and I come with you. I can ask Declan to hang back."

She sighed, but nodded. They stepped out of the car, and even Max seemed tense as they moved up the walkway that was lined with weeds. The home wasn't in the worst part of town, but it hadn't been maintained. There were more weeds in the yard than grass, and the paint on the side of house was peeling. The windows looked as if they hadn't been washed in years, and there wasn't a car in the cracked driveway.

That didn't mean anything. A lot of people let their houses go to hell, and parked in the garage. He couldn't shake his fear for Keera as he stood on one side of her, Max on the other. She knocked . . . and they waited.

There was no answer. He moved to the side and looked in a window, his body tensing at what he saw. There was garbage strewn about and a ripped couch. It reminded him too much of the scene at Keera's not that long ago.

"He's not here. I think it's time to call this in," he told her. He wouldn't be in such a hurry to leave if Keera wasn't there with him.

"Maybe he's in the back," Keera said, her chin up. She began walking around the house, giving him no choice but to follow. She obviously didn't take her safety too seriously.

They came to the back of the house and looked inside a large patio door, where the mess in the house continued. Keera knocked again, but there wasn't a sound from inside.

She reached for the handle and tugged, and miracle of all miracles, the door cracked open. Max instantly tensed as a low growl rumbled through him, his eyes focused inside.

"Stay there!" Arden told her, his hand covering hers. "Max doesn't get this upset unless something's wrong."

"He might be hurt in there," Keera said, obviously wanting to rush inside.

"We'll find out." He took her hand, pulling her away from the door as he called out for Declan, who was immediately at their side. "Looks like we're going to need that search warrant after all," he told his brother, who looked down at the dog and nodded.

Declan picked up his phone and called the police. This was no longer a compromise he could afford to keep with Keera. Something was in that house that wasn't supposed to be there—and they were about to find out what that was.

Chapter Twenty-Eight

Keera's throat tightened as she stood trembling on Ethan's back lawn. She hated the waiting but understood why it had to be done right.

"What if he's hurt? We need to get in," she said, fighting back her fear for Ethan. It wasn't as if they were best friends, but he'd been the first one in this town to take the time to know her. She felt she owed him her loyalty.

"I'll go in," Declan said a few minutes later. Two squad cars were now there, and the policemen nodded. No one was going to argue with his authority.

He opened the back door, his gun drawn as he disappeared inside the house. It felt like the longest seconds of her life as she waited for him to do a quick search before allowing anyone else to enter.

Max was still growling as he strained to follow Declan. Something was in there that interested the dog. Keera wasn't sure what it was, but she was definitely afraid to find out. She didn't want any of this to be true about Ethan. She didn't want him to be a bad guy.

Declan came back to the door. "Ethan's not here. You can come in now," he said.

Keera didn't wait to see if that included her. She needed to make sure he wasn't lying to her. She didn't take him as the kind of man to do that, but right now it felt as if her world had once again been flipped upside down. And a person could only have that happen so many times before it all became too much.

As soon as Declan allowed him to, Max sprang forward, disappearing down a hallway. They moved quickly after the dog, who entered what looked like a spare room that was sparsely furnished, with a rickety desk with papers strewn about it and a rusty file cabinet.

Max went to the closet and sat, his growl low as he waited for them to open the door.

"Did you check this closet?" Keera asked, terrified she was going to find Ethan's bloody body on the other side of the door.

"No," Declan said. He inched forward, his gun still ready. Then he opened the door, and Keera gasped.

"Looks like we found our drug supplier," Arden said with a low whistle.

"And why he might want to stop Keera from digging any further," Declan said.

"But I wasn't the one who started this. Of course I don't want drugs in the school, but why would he come after me?" Keera asked, unable to look away from the massive amount of cocaine wrapped in plastic.

"I don't know, but I hope you now believe he's after you," Arden said, sympathy in his eyes. Keera took a few steps back, unable to deny the truth any longer, but feeling betrayed by a person who'd claimed to be her friend. The sad thing was, that's how it always happened. She hadn't ever been able to maintain relationships because of exactly what was in front of her.

Her father had been a high-ranking drug dealer, and apparently Ethan was, too. He certainly didn't live like her father, though. Did he know her dad? Is that why he had been so nice to her? Was it a show all along?

Keera was so disappointed; she didn't know what to think or feel.

"I'm sorry," Arden said, wrapping his arms around her. For a single moment she allowed him to take a bit of the burden from her. Ethan was just one more person in a long line of people who had zero qualms about betraying her. It hurt more than she wanted to admit.

"He was a heck of an actor," she said. She pulled back to look at Arden. "I really had no clue it was him bringing drugs into the school. I guess he had the perfect cover-up, though. He knew which lockers were safe, knew the schedule, and normally had the school all to himself. He made a comment my second week there that most principals didn't stay so late. He wasn't happy about my after-hours activities with the kids, either. I guess it was messing with his operation."

She was so disheartened. But at least the drug problem was solved, or getting closer to being solved.

"We still don't know if anyone else is involved," Declan said.

"I was wondering the same thing," Keera admitted. "I don't know if he brought students into this or staff members. I feel like I can't trust anyone."

"Right now, you can't," Declan said, making Keera wince.

"You can trust us," Arden told her, shooting his brother a look. If she wasn't so frustrated right now, she might have found that amusing.

"Sir, you might want to look at this," one of the cops said, holding up a file.

"What is it?" Declan asked. The cop looked from Declan to Keera as he squirmed on his feet. "Spit it out." Declan wasn't the most patient of people.

"Uh . . . well, it has Ms. Thompson's name on it."

Arden tensed next to her. Declan's eyes narrowed as he stepped over to the cop and took the file. He looked at it a moment, and his already steely gaze became even more glacial. He looked at Keera and then his brother.

“This goes deeper than I realized,” he said. Keera felt her insides clench. She didn’t want to read that file, didn’t want to know what it contained. But she also couldn’t bury her head in the sand any longer.

She held out her hand, and Declan gave her the file. She knew when she opened it her life would change again. Her world so often spun out of control, she wondered what it would be like to live a boring, normal life. She would probably never know.

Chapter Twenty-Nine

Keera walked next to Arden as they entered his house. There were so many thoughts spinning in her head. Who had her father truly been? What had he been up to? What did it have to do with Edmonds? How had she ended up in this town?

She had none of those answers. Arden paced the living room as he dealt with his own frustrations, neither of them talking a heck of a lot.

"I could kill that man, Keera. I could put my hands around his neck and kill him," Arden said.

Keera had never had a white knight in her corner, and she found she liked it, found she needed it. She didn't want to need it, but there was something so wonderful about Arden. It honestly terrified her.

"Can I have a few minutes to process this?" she asked as she moved over to the fireplace and sat down on the couch, facing the flames as she gripped the folder.

"Of course," he told her.

She sat there for an endless amount of time, staring at the flames as her fingers rubbed over the top of the folder. She was scared, so scared. Arden stopped pacing as he faced her, his sympathy almost too much for her to bear.

"We can take all night if you need," Arden said. "But the sooner we rip off the bandage and get some answers, the sooner you're free from this."

"I'm afraid to see what's in here," she admitted.

"No matter what's there, I'm right here beside you," Arden assured her.

Keera looked up at this man who'd been so helpful. He'd bent over backward to keep her safe, to help solve issues that seemed to revolve around her. He seemed a little too perfect to be true.

"You've done so much for me, Arden. Thank you," she told him.

"You're welcome," he said.

"You're learning to take gratitude a lot better," she said.

"Someone told me I should just accept it when a person thanks me," he replied.

The light bantering eased the weight that had been pressing down on her chest since the moment she'd been handed the file. She smiled gratefully at Arden before looking back at the folder in her lap.

"Okay, I'm ready to do this," she said as she opened the cover. She didn't let out a breath as she gazed at the papers.

Arden moved closer as she sifted through the file, reading things that made her blood run cold, that made her heart slow, and made her realize the world was in no way a fair place.

She spent about thirty minutes reading and rereading. Arden stayed at her side, but he didn't ask questions, didn't push her, didn't do anything other than be a comforting presence.

"Did you know about this?" she finally asked.

She was looking at the final paper. It had all her former addresses, phone numbers, favorite places to go, people she was acquainted with. This file contained her entire life.

"No, Keera. Please believe me. I had no idea," he said.

"Did Declan know?" she asked.

"I have no idea," he said.

"He's FBI. I find it difficult to believe he didn't know," she said.

"I think he might know some," Arden admitted.

"But he didn't tell you?" she questioned.

"No. I didn't want to be biased by this investigation. I wanted to come to my own conclusions," he said.

"About me?" she asked. She felt so close to falling apart. She truly hoped that wasn't going to happen, but she couldn't guarantee anything at the moment.

"At first, yeah, I wanted to get my own opinion of you. And to be honest, I wasn't sure if you were involved in this or not," he told her.

"And now?" she asked. She was trying not to be hurt. He was just being honest with her.

"Do you need to ask?"

"Yes, I need to ask," she told him. "Especially after seeing this file, especially after figuring out that my life has never been my life like I thought it was. Apparently, I've been a puppet on strings without even knowing," she said, her words breaking at the end.

"You don't have to be strong right now," he told her.

Without allowing her to refuse, he lifted her, setting her on his lap and wrapping his arms around her. They were both quiet as she reluctantly allowed him to carry some of her burden.

"You didn't answer me," she finally said.

His fingers were running through her hair before he leaned back so she could look into his eyes. They were so gentle it scared her. She didn't want to trust this man, didn't want to lean on him.

"I don't think you're capable of doing anything to hurt anyone," he said.

"A few months ago, I could have told you emphatically that I couldn't hurt another person," she told him before looking at the file again. "Now, I don't know what I'm capable of."

"Then let me assure you of who you are," he told her. He leaned in and kissed her. It wasn't a passionate kiss; it was comforting. He was taking some of her worries on himself, trying to ease her confusion and pain.

When he leaned back, she did feel lighter, felt that he'd been successful in removing some of the weight from her shoulders. She just wasn't sure how he managed to do that.

"I knew my father had left us for another family," she said after leaning against him, allowing this new information to process in her muddled brain.

"Yeah, probably more than one family," Arden said.

"Definitely more than one family. But I didn't know these lives would intertwine," she said. "When he left us, I thought that was it."

"Apparently not," Arden said.

"It was Ethan who led me here, wasn't it?" she asked.

"What I don't understand is why. He seemed to like you, then seemed to resent you for getting too close," Arden said.

"Do you swear you didn't know the truth of this before now?" she asked. She didn't trust easily, but she wanted to believe Arden's answer. He again made her look in his eyes.

"I swear I didn't know," he assured her.

She sighed. "Ethan is my stepbrother." Saying the words out loud seemed so unreal. "And apparently my real brother knew about it."

"What does that mean?" he asked.

"I don't know. I can't fathom it. I don't care about him, don't care if he was one of the many kids I'm sure my father had in his household. I probably have a dozen or more stepsiblings. They all mean nothing to me. I just don't understand why this one person wanted to know me, why he brought me here," she said.

"What does he have to do with your brother and his death?" Arden asked.

"There's one person who knows," she said. "I just don't know if I can ask him or trust his answers."

Silence greeted these words. Arden continued rubbing his fingers through her hair as they both got lost in their thoughts.

"There's nothing you can't face," he finally assured her.

"Maybe it's best to just let the past stay where it is," she said.

"That might be the case if your life wasn't in danger," he countered.

It might be time for Keera to face the one person she thought had died in her heart a long time ago. She wasn't sure she could do it. She wasn't sure she wanted to get to the bottom of all of this. She also didn't know if she had any other choice.

"Can we not think about it anymore tonight?" Keera asked after she sank a little bit closer against Arden. She wanted to simply wash it all away.

"I'll do anything you want," Arden said.

"I don't want to think about Ethan, or my father. I don't want to think about stalkers, or safety issues. I want a few hours to let my mind go blank. I just need your arms around me," Keera said.

"I'm so grateful you've come into my life," he said. His eyes shimmered as he looked at her, cupping her cheek as he held her in place with nothing more than his gaze.

"I can't believe you'd say that with all the trouble I've caused," she told him. She added a laugh, but in reality, she didn't find the situation humorous.

His fingers stilled where they rested at the sides of her eyes. "You've done nothing, Keera. What you actually bring to me is indescribable," he told her.

She desperately wanted to believe what he was saying. But she couldn't. She couldn't open up that much to him. Instead, she pressed against him, her hands wrapping around his solid waist.

They had a lot of problems to solve, but as she snuggled closer to him, it just didn't seem to matter anymore. At least for tonight, none of it mattered.

Chapter Thirty

Daniel Thompson was a poor excuse for a father. It wasn't difficult to find out exactly where he was, and it wasn't with the new family he'd begun after bailing on Keera and her brother. And it was so much closer than she would have imagined.

She wasn't going to admit how much it was breaking her heart that he was living so close to her and still hadn't wanted to be a part of her life. The last she'd known was he'd been in Southern California living in a gated mansion. He always lived well, and he had no guilt about it. He hadn't cared that he'd abandoned his family—he'd just gone on to make new ones.

Now he was living in Victoria, Canada, in a mansion on the beach. He was going by a new name and had a wife Keera's age. Keera was unbelievably disgusted as they pulled up to the entrance, and embarrassed beyond reason to have Arden next to her to see this man.

"I don't know what the point of this is," she said, not wanting to enter this place. There was a guard shack with a man gazing at their rental car.

"We need to get answers, and that file raised more questions than anything else," Arden told her.

"He won't let me in," she said. That would be the ultimate embarrassment.

"Oh, he'll let us in," Arden said, his eyes narrowing.

The place looked as if it belonged to a movie star. While Keera and her brother had lost everything because of this man, he'd simply moved on and started a new life several times over. She now realized he'd never suffered. He probably had kept money stashed away, not caring that his former family had nothing left. That's how heartless he was.

Arden pulled forward, taking the choice away from her. He rolled down his window, and the unsmiling guard stepped up to the car. The man was a giant, and he didn't look at all as if he'd let them in.

"State your business," the man said.

"Arden Forbes to see Dale Worth," Arden said with such a note of authority, the man seemed a bit unsure for a moment.

"You're not on the list," the man said.

"Trust me, he's going to want to see me," Arden said with confidence.

"And why is that?" the guard asked.

"Because he can talk to me now as Dale Worth, or he can talk to the FBI as Daniel Thompson," Arden said with that same smile.

The man said nothing, just stepped back from the car and went into his shack, immediately picking up his phone. He never came back out, but the gate suddenly opened in front of them.

"Wow," Keera said. "He didn't even ask who I was."

"I'm sure the guard knows," Arden said. "Your father might be the scum of the earth for what he did, but I guarantee you he knows where you are at all times, and what you look like."

"I don't like the thought of that," Keera said. "It feels like a violation."

"It most definitely is a violation," Arden said. "I'm going to have a real difficult time speaking to this man, but I promise to keep my cool."

"I hope I can do the same," Keera said.

He took her hand and squeezed. Then he pulled up to the house and got out, taking her hand again as soon as she stepped from the car. The front door opened before they had a chance to knock.

It felt far more like walking into a museum than a person's home, and the instant she looked around at his expensive items, it took her back to her youth, making her want to turn around and run.

She'd grown up with this exact wealth, and it had brought nothing but cold. She found herself pulling her hand away from Arden. He had more money than her father. She tried telling herself that Arden was in no way her father, but the money parallel was too close for comfort, and being here now made that so much more obvious.

"You're here to see Mr. Worth?" a woman asked, walking from another room, looking so damn elegant in her pantsuit and perfect hair.

"Yes," Arden said. "How long will it be?"

"Someone will be out shortly to escort you to him," the woman replied.

Now Keera was confused. Was her father such a coward he needed to put on this show? Or maybe Arden was wrong. Maybe the man had no idea it was her there.

They didn't have to wait long before another woman approached, this one in scrubs, though just as beautiful as the first with her coiffed hair and pearl earrings.

"Mr. Forbes, please come this way," the woman said.

"Thank you," Arden replied. He reached for Keera again, but she pulled away. He winced, making her feel guilty, but right now she didn't have it in her.

They followed the woman down several hallways, and the elegance at the front of the place became sparser and more hospital-like as they went through a pair of double doors. The woman took them through another door, and then they were in a large room where she saw a man in a wheelchair looking out a huge window, his back to them.

"What is going on?" Keera asked. "Is that Daniel?" She stopped and cleared her throat. "I mean Dale," she finished, her voice barely above a whisper. Her father had so many aliases it was hard to keep track. She wondered if his birth name was Daniel, or if maybe he'd had a family before hers. She didn't know if she'd get any of those answers.

"Yes, that's Mr. Worth," the woman said. "He's agreed to see you."

As they slowly approached him, she noticed his eyes were shut. She wouldn't have recognized the man if she'd passed him on a sidewalk. His once-perfect dark hair was now gone, his skin was wrinkled, and he had tubes in his nose. Keera looked at Arden, who seemed just as surprised as she was. The information they'd received hadn't said anything like this.

"What's wrong with him?" Keera asked.

The nurse looked down at Daniel, or Dale, as he was now called, with an affectionate smile.

"He has stage-four stomach cancer. He doesn't have much time left," she replied as she brushed a hand down his arm. The woman actually cared about him. Keera wondered why, wondered if her father had been a better man with his staff than he had been with his family, or multiple families.

"Mr. Worth, Arden Forbes," the woman said as she gently shook his arm. "And your daughter."

Keera was stunned when the woman said this. Arden had been right. He knew she was there; his staff knew what she looked like. There were so many emotions running through her she didn't know what to think about any of it. She couldn't process it. She might not ever be able to.

Her father, a man who had once been so strong, so controlling, and so cold, slowly opened his eyes. For a moment his expression filled with confusion, and then his gaze zeroed in on Keera, and she saw the same light in them she'd seen as a child.

He didn't even look at Arden. It might as well have been just the two of them alone in the room.

"I knew you'd come," he said, his voice weak and raspy.

"How?" Keera asked. "How would you even think I could find you?"

There was no greeting, no small talk. Why should there be? She wanted to get out of there as quickly as possible.

"Because I was the one who made the calls to Mr. Forbes. I was the one trying to protect you. It might have taken me too long to realize what I did to you, but I'm hoping that in these last moments it will give you peace knowing I did what was right," he told her.

"How do you even know any of this was going on?" she asked.

"Because I always know where you are, and the moment you took that job in Edmonds, I knew the past was going to come crashing around us both," he told her. "I knew Ethan had led you there."

"He's trying to hurt me, though. Why would he lead me there?" she asked.

Her father began coughing, and she automatically reached out, before pulling her arm back and stumbling away, almost feeling tainted by being too close to this man. Her entire life had been nothing but lies, and she didn't know how to deal with that. She didn't know how to deal with any of this.

"Rachel, my daughter is going to take me for a walk," Dale said.

The nurse nodded, then turned and moved away. Even in his frail state, he wielded so much power. Keera remembered that, remembered how afraid of him everyone had been. Now, he still held power in his knowledge, but the difference was that *she* wasn't afraid anymore.

"Go out the door to the left. We'll take the path that leads to a beautiful view of the ocean. It might be my last time to see it," he said.

"If you're trying to garner sympathy, it's not working," Keera told him. Though she wanted to be cold, even saying those words hurt her. She could never be the type of person to intentionally hurt another—even someone who had once destroyed her.

"I know far too well I can't earn your trust or sympathy," Dale said. "I know it's too late for that. But some sins of the past will haunt us forever, and you should at least know who your enemies are."

"Any enemies I have are because of the life you chose to lead," she told him. Her throat hurt with the pain of holding back her tears. But her father hadn't earned the right to see her sadness. She refused to fall apart in front of the man.

Arden held open the door, and Keera pushed her father through it, easily following the shaded path to the edge of the property. They stopped when they reached a nice alcove. The view truly was spectacular. She decided to focus on that for a moment and let her rapidly beating heart have a break.

When she turned back around, Dale was studying her. She wanted to tell him to look away, that he didn't have the right to look at her, but that was her pettiness coming to the surface, not who she really was.

"Is Ethan Dower really your stepson?" she asked, trying to mask the hurt. "Why does he want to hurt me? Why did he lead me to Edmonds? What is he looking for . . . ?" She trailed off.

"You were never meant to go to Edmonds," Dale said, shaking his head. "But Ethan is a bad person, and the best way to get back at me is to hurt the only child I ever cared about," her father said.

"You never cared about me. You couldn't have walked away as easily as you did if you had," she said. "And I had nothing to do with you, with what you did when I was a child, what you've obviously been doing since you left us behind," she added, a small shake entering her voice.

"It doesn't matter if you have knowledge of it or not. There are people out there who think they can get to me through you. It's okay, though, because I'm taking care of that," he told her.

"I need answers. I don't want amends from you or excuses. I don't want your help. I just want this to stop. When you walked away from me and my brother, you cut ties with us, and that should have been the end of our connection to you," she told him.

"There's never an end when it comes to blood," he said as he shook his head.

"Then tell me," she demanded, reaching for him, but taking her hand back at the last minute. She couldn't touch this man, wasn't sure what it would do to her.

"The doctor has told me my time will come any day now. I might have been the monster who plays in your nightmares, but I am your father," he said before coughing again. He then looked her in the eyes, his vision perfectly clear. "I wanted your face to be the last I saw."

"It won't be. I'm not staying long," she told him. "You won't give me what I want, and I have no desire to reminisce about the past. It wasn't a happy life for me. Tell me something or I'm walking away right now." He smiled at her, and she felt herself growing more tense.

"Ethan was the son of the woman I married after your mother," Dale finally said. Keera watched him, waiting.

"Why does he want to hurt me?" she asked.

"Because he figured out your brother got away with a significant amount of money," Dale said with a laugh. "My son truly was a chip off the old block."

"You say this like you're proud," she said with disgust. "My brother being a thief isn't something to be proud of."

"But you're involved, too," Dale said, gazing at her with far too much knowledge.

"I don't know how many times I need to say this," she snapped. "But I'm not involved and want nothing to do with your disgusting world."

"They won't stop coming after you," he told her.

"They will when I stop them," Arden said, interrupting the conversation.

"I hope you can protect her," Dale said, looking briefly at Arden before turning back to her.

"I can protect myself. I learned how to do it when you abandoned me," she assured him.

"Then I did leave you with something," Dale told her.

"Don't think for one minute you have anything to do with who I am," she told him.

"Don't you want to give an old man a little peace in his dying moments?" Dale asked.

"You won't get peace, not with the way you've lived your life. You'll die alone in this big mansion because love and loyalty mean nothing to you. I don't know why you let us in, because you obviously won't give me anything useful," she said, frustration making her voice more bitter than she'd like.

"Watch out for Ethan," Dale said quietly.

"Why?" she yelled. "What do I have to watch out for?"

He gazed at her a few moments without speaking, and then fiddled with the blankets in his lap. The water bottle that was sitting there fell off and began rolling away.

"Would you mind getting that?" he asked.

Keera sighed, then moved over to grab it. The thunderous explosion behind her made her heart jump into her throat as she whirled around. Arden was staring at Dale with horror before his head whipped around to her.

"I'm so sorry," he said, quickly coming to her and pulling her into his arms, blocking her view of her father.

"What . . . what happened?" she asked, her voice trembling.

"He was fast. I don't know how he was that fast. He pulled the gun from beneath the blanket and shot himself before I could take a single step in his direction. I'm so sorry, Keera, I'm so sorry."

This was the first time she had seen her father in ten years, and he'd just killed himself in front of her. As if she didn't have trauma from before, now it was a thousand times worse.

"Why? Why would he do that?" she asked.

"He lived and died on his terms, not giving a damn about the damage he was causing you," Arden said. "We need to leave." She tried to look at her father again, and Arden cupped her cheek. "Don't look at him. Don't give him that power over you."

The nurse came running out, her eyes round with horror.

"What did you do?" she cried.

"He shot himself. Call the police," Arden told her.

She looked at him in disbelief. "Security is on their way. Don't go anywhere," she said before running back into the house.

"It's okay, Keera, let's move toward the house," he said, wrapping his arm around her and taking her back up the walk.

Security met them, and Arden told them what happened. Keera was in shock. It didn't take long for the camera tapes to be reviewed, clearing them of any wrongdoing. The cops came, and Arden explained it again to them. Keera couldn't speak.

It took a couple of hours before they were able to get away. By the time Arden loaded her into the car, she was finished. Though Edmonds hadn't been her home for very long, it was now her haven, even with all that had happened in the past months. She wanted to go home.

"You'll be okay, Keera. I'll make sure of it," Arden promised.

"No. I don't think I will," she said. Her voice was void of all emotion. She didn't want to depend on anyone right now, but she couldn't deny even to herself that she was grateful to have Arden beside her. Right now, she didn't want to be alone.

She closed her eyes as soon as they were on the road, and she told herself for now that she'd simply take one breath in and one breath out. She wouldn't show how much she was falling apart. Failure was for the weak. She would never be weak again.

Chapter Thirty-One

Arden was at a loss for words. Keera was trying her hardest to pull away from him, to retreat, and he knew she needed time to come to terms with seeing her father again . . . and losing him the way she had.

Yes, she'd lost him years ago, if she had ever truly had him in the first place. But the coward had died how he wanted to. He'd decided he wanted her face to be the last he saw, so he'd left her with nightmares for the rest of her life just so he could have what he wanted in his last moments on this earth.

He had been a selfish man his entire life, and while most would at least try to achieve redemption in their final moments, he'd chosen not to—he'd chosen to be that pathetic, weak, irredeemable man. Arden was scared of what that was going to do to this beautiful woman he'd gotten to know, scared it might be the final straw as far as what she could handle.

He stayed close to her but respected her silence as they drove home. They had no new answers, and she was in more jeopardy now than ever before. Someone thought she was valuable to them. And until he figured out who that person was—and though Ethan was certainly involved, he didn't take Ethan as the mastermind behind it all—Arden wouldn't feel right letting her out of his sight.

"I want to shower," Keera said as soon as they got back to the house.

She didn't make it more than a couple of steps before Max was at her side, his head instantly resting at her side. She reached out as she always did, her fingers weaving through the soft fur behind his ears. Though she was obviously still in pain, Arden could see the instant comfort the dog offered her.

"Yes, of course. Take your time. I called Angela ahead of time, and she'll have food when you're ready."

"I don't think I can eat," she said.

He leaned in and kissed her forehead. She flinched as if even a small touch was painful. That hurt him more than he'd ever admit. It wasn't about him, it was strictly about her right now.

"Take a hot shower and get some clean clothes on and then we'll see how you feel," he told her.

She gave Max one more loving caress, then turned and walked away, going into the spare room. For the past week she'd slept and showered in Arden's room. Again, it hurt that she was trying to separate herself from him. But that's what she needed right now. He could give her the space she thought she wanted, because he knew she'd come back to him. He was nothing like her father, and she would understand that when she wasn't hurting so much.

When she didn't emerge after a half hour, Arden grew worried. He went to her room, and what he found broke his heart into a million pieces. Keera was sitting on the bed, her hair still wet, a pair of sweats and one of his old T-shirts hanging loosely on her as she buried her head in her hands, her body shaking with sobs.

She'd been through a lot in a short time, and he hadn't once seen her fall apart like this. She needed him now far more than she needed space. He quietly walked to her, sat down on the bed, and pulled her into his arms.

An anguished cry escaped her throat as she tensed for only a fraction of a second. Then she clung to him as she let out everything she'd been holding in. He rubbed her back, whispering words of comfort, hoping he was helping her even the slightest bit.

"I'm sorry, Keera, I'm so very sorry. This isn't on you, none of this is on you," he promised.

"It is," she said, her tears strangling her voice. "I shouldn't have gone there. I shouldn't have come to this town," she said.

"No, this is the best place for you. It's where you belong," he assured her.

"But there's something bad here. I didn't know my father's evilness reached so far," she choked out.

"None of that's on you. In spite of him, you've become this amazing woman, this beacon for children going through chaos. Some people would use a life like the one you led as an excuse to be terrible human beings, but you chose to rise, you chose to make other people's lives better. Remember that," he said.

He leaned back so she could see his face, see that he was serious, that he cared about her, appreciated her—so she'd believe him.

"You are kind, talented, smart, and beautiful. Don't allow that man, who doesn't deserve to be called your father, take any of that away," he demanded.

Her tears dried as she gazed at him. He could see the confusion in her face, could see how desperately she wanted to believe him, but he could also see the doubt in her eyes. Being with her father today had taken her so many steps back in her journey of letting him go. Arden should have gone on his own, but he hadn't wanted to take that decision from her. Had he known what would happen . . .

Of course he wouldn't have taken her there had he known. But still, he had to live with that guilt, with knowing the trauma she was going to face because they'd shown up on that man's doorstep.

"I hate him," Keera said. She hiccupped, but the tears didn't begin again. "I hate him for what he did to my brother and me. I hate him for walking away like we meant nothing. And I hate him for being a coward, for taking his life in front of me," she said.

"Feel that anger. Let it flow through you and evaporate. Don't give him this power over you for very long. He doesn't deserve it," Arden told her.

"I won't give him anything else of me," she promised.

"Good. Because you are too good for him," Arden told her.

She leaned forward and kissed him. It was a slow kiss, a sweet kiss. And it felt far too much like a goodbye. It terrified Arden as she pulled back and looked at him, her eyes lost.

"Thank you for being there for me today. It means a lot," she told him.

But her voice had changed. And she untangled herself from his arms and stood, moving over to the window and looking outside at the gloomy night. Her shoulders stayed firm, and she kept her arms crossed as she held herself, protected herself.

He knew she was thinking they couldn't stay together, knew she was trying to let him go. What she didn't know was he wasn't going to allow that to happen. They'd figure this case out, and then he'd show her what she truly meant to him.

They'd have forever, and he'd show her how a father was supposed to be with his children. Though he ached inside, the hope he felt for the two of them warmed his chest.

She was his as much as he was hers. They had forever to figure it all out.

"Let's eat," he said.

"I'm not hungry," she replied.

"Then humor me," he told her. He moved over to her but didn't touch her this time. "Come on."

She stopped fighting him, and they went into the kitchen, where Angela had left the food on warmers. He served them each a small plate, and they took it into the living room instead of sitting at the table. The dimmer lights and view out the windows was better for her peace of mind at this moment.

She had barely touched her food when the house phone rang. She moved liked she was going to get it.

"Let it go to voice mail. It's not important," he said.

"It could have something to do with today," she told him.

He sighed as he stood and grabbed it, not giving the most pleasant of greetings. Then his entire body went still as he looked at Keera. She tensed, knowing that whatever news was coming through the line wasn't going to be something she'd want to hear.

"We will be right there," he said before hanging up.

He looked at Keera, who let out a breath and looked at him with a new resolve.

"Whatever it is, I can take it," she said.

"A person can only deal with so much before they break," he told her. "But there's no way I can keep this from you, though that's exactly what I want to do."

She gave him a semblance of a smile. "I know. You're that guy," she said. He wasn't exactly sure what that meant, but he wasn't going to ask her to explain it right now. "Just tell me. We might as well get all of the bad over with at one time."

"That was Declan. They've found Ethan," he said.

She tensed, before her eyes narrowed.

"Good. Let's go have a chat with him." She'd been so sad at the thought of the man betraying her, but after seeing her father, after learning Ethan had been phony the entire time she'd known him, she now wanted answers.

"He's at the school," he said.

Her brows knit in confusion. "Why wouldn't they take him in?"

"He's in a standoff with the police. He has a gun . . . ," he said, letting that sink in before he continued. "And hostages."

Keera's eyes widened before she closed them and leaned her head back. She only took about three seconds before they flashed back open and she rose to her feet. Arden was humbled by her strength and resolve.

"Let's go have a chat, then, shall we?" she said.

Arden nodded. This time he took her hand and didn't let go as they left the house. Right now, they needed each other—nothing else mattered.

Chapter Thirty-Two

Keera was amazed at what a person could endure and still keep sane, still keep moving. It was odd, really, how the human psyche worked. It was beautiful, if a person was to really think about it.

As she and Arden arrived at the school, she was in disbelief as she saw the police vehicles, the SWAT team van, ambulances, fire engines—all of them with flashing lights—and people milling about the parking lot, a large group in a tent around a table, their heads bent together.

This couldn't all be for *one* person. This couldn't be happening because of her. What had Ethan done? Who did he have? What was going on? They approached, her stomach tied in knots, her body tense. Arden moved next to her as they moved toward the tent.

"Thanks for getting here so quickly," Declan said at their arrival.

"Of course," Arden told him. "What's happening? What's the plan?"

"He's in the basement in a room where there aren't any windows."

"What are his demands?" Arden asked. Keera was glad he was asking the questions, because at this point she couldn't quite think. She was so scared of who might be in there, no longer sure of what the man was capable.

A man turned, someone Keera hadn't seen before. He nodded at her. "Noah Mills," he said before turning to Arden. "I've tried negotiating with him. He was dismissive and wouldn't talk to me. We don't know at this point what he wants." He turned back to Keera. "We're hoping you can help us figure that out since this is your school."

The pressure she felt weighed her shoulders as they slumped. She shook her head. "I thought I knew this man, but I don't know him at all. He's been here so much longer than me. He . . . he . . ." She stopped, took a deep breath. "I thought he loved this school, loved this town. I thought . . . He was my first friend here," she finished. It was such a foolish thing to say, but she was so hurt that one more person in her life had turned out to be so untrustworthy.

"How many kids does he have in there?" Arden asked. Keera needed to know this information, but at the same time, she wasn't sure she wanted to know.

"We know of three," Noah told them. "Their parents said they were working on a project."

"We have to get them out," Keera said. She shook off her fear as she forced herself to calm. She couldn't think of this like it was her fault, couldn't pity herself right now. At this moment what she needed to do was help get those kids to safety. And maybe get Ethan out, too.

She was angry and frustrated with the man, but he had possible answers to what was going on in her life, why people were coming after her. She needed this to end with him alive so she could get those answers.

"I'll talk to him. Let me see if I can reason with him," Keera suggested.

"That's not a good idea," Arden told her. "This situation is sticky, and we only have one shot at this."

"I can do this," she told him, looking him in the eyes. "Obviously, I've done something to this man to make him want me dead. Let me see if I can reason with him, if I can get him to come out and talk to me," she said. "Or if he will trade the hostages for me."

"That won't happen!" Arden thundered.

Her shoulders set. "I'd rather be in there than have those kids inside," she told him.

"We don't trade hostages," Declan said. All the men and women were staring at her now, and she knew that plan was a no-go, but she had to try something.

"Okay. I thought that was a long shot, but at least let me try to get him on the phone," Keera pleaded.

Noah looked to Declan and Arden, which set her teeth to grinding. He didn't need their permission to allow her to do something. No, he didn't know her, but he was about to.

"This is *my* school, as you pointed out. You *will* let me in on this, you *will* let me try to solve this," she demanded. She was relieved when she saw a flash of respect in Noah's eyes. If he respected her, then he wouldn't try to hold her back.

"Okay, we'll let you make the call," Noah said. Keera refused to look at Arden or Declan. This wasn't about them. Right now, this was about Keera and Ethan and those students. She prayed she didn't screw it up.

Noah handed her a phone with a number already in place. All she had to do was hit the "Send" button. She took a deep breath, hoping to keep her voice calm and reasonable, hoping Ethan wasn't high, hoping he had the ability to speak with her.

She hit the button and waited. It picked up after the third ring, but all she heard on the other end was heavy breathing. She listened for a moment, and her heart broke when she heard quiet sobs in the background. The students had to be so terrified, so unsure of why this was happening to them.

"Ethan, it's me, Keera," she said, her voice soft, calm, friendly. "Please talk to me. Please tell me what I can do to make this situation better."

It was quiet for one of the longest moments of Keera's life, but she waited, knowing she needed to give him time to adjust to it being her on the other end of the line. If he was answering the call, then there was still hope he wanted to work things out.

"Why are you here?" he demanded, his voice filled with hate. She wondered if he had assumed she was already dead.

"I'm here for you," she said. "You were here for me from the moment I came into this town. Now let me return the favor."

She wasn't sure if she actually meant those words or not. She'd sell her soul right now if it meant the safe return of the kids locked inside with that man. But a part of her had always wanted to save people. She wondered if that went so far as to protect those who would wish her harm.

"You have no idea who I really am," he snapped. "Or what I'm capable of." The deadly menace in his voice shook her to her very soul.

"I don't think any of us really know anyone. We do our best, but everyone has secrets. Don't let this moment be the one that defines your entire life, Ethan. This is your town, your school, your kids. Please remember that," she pleaded. "Let me be your friend, let me know you."

"I brought you to this town, and you screwed it all up. It could have been great, but you didn't do what you were supposed to do," he yelled. "You can live with this being on your shoulders."

His voice was so cold, so cruel. He wasn't the most pleasant of men on a daily basis, but this was a whole other side of him she hadn't known was possible. She closed her eyes and forced herself to take a couple of deep breaths. She didn't want to take too long, didn't want him to feel as if she wasn't hearing him.

"I'm so sorry. I'll leave," she said. "If that's what will make you happy, I'll leave."

She felt Arden beside her, felt how his body tensed at her words. But she couldn't think about Arden right now. All she could do was try to hold it together long enough to get those kids to safety.

"It's too late for that," he said, and this time some of the menace left his tone as he seemed more resigned to his new fate. "Everyone knows who I am now. It's too late."

This was a broken man, and that made him incredibly dangerous.

"Please let the kids leave, Ethan. You and I can figure this out together, but please let them go," she begged.

His breath huffed in and out, and she knew he was pacing. The sobs would become clearer as he neared the kids, then fade as he stepped to the other side of the room. She couldn't imagine what they were going through, not knowing if they'd ever get out of there, if they'd ever see their families again.

"I can't. It's all over if I don't have them," he told her.

"Ethan, please," she begged.

But he snarled into the phone, and then the line went dead. Keera's hand shook as she gripped the phone tight. She'd failed them. She hadn't even made a dent in the situation, and she could have put the kids in even more jeopardy.

"You did good, Keera, that was great," Declan said, his hand lifting to press against her shoulder.

She looked up at Arden's brother, tears coming down her cheeks that she hadn't even realized were falling.

"No, I failed," she told him.

His eyes were warmer than she'd ever seen them as he shook his head. "No, none of this is on you. He's an evil man who's doing unspeakable things. There's no excuse for that. Don't you take this on," Declan told her.

She was so stunned by this transformation of one of the scariest men she'd ever met. He was normally so hard. But she could see why he did so well at his job. He no longer suspected her of being involved with this, so he considered her a victim now, and obviously he treated those he felt were in need different than the rest of the world.

"It will be okay," he assured her.

"You can't promise that," she told him.

"I don't fail at my job," Declan said. "And I *will* get those kids out of there. You have helped with doing that."

"Thank you," she told him. She didn't believe him, but this wasn't about her, she reminded herself again. And the more time Declan had to spend trying to make her feel better about herself, the less time he was spending on saving those kids. She'd go over all of this in her mind later. But right now, she just wanted to get through each second until she saw her students' faces.

Declan nodded at her; then he and Noah bent their heads back together.

"He's right, you did well," Arden told her.

She just nodded. "Help them," she said. He looked at her as if he wanted to say something but didn't know quite what it was. She understood that, as well.

The SWAT team was on standby, waiting to rush the building, and everyone who wasn't actively planning was quiet as they did their best to keep up hope that none of the children would be harmed.

When the phone she'd been talking on several minutes earlier rang, it nearly made Keera jump out of her skin. Noah picked it up and looked at Keera.

"Are you ready for this?" he asked.

She nodded as she took the phone and answered. Her voice shook the slightest bit, but she took in a breath and tried again.

"Hello, Ethan, thank you for calling back," she told him. "I'm so sorry I've upset you."

"I've been doing a lot of thinking," he said, and the tone of his voice surprised her. He didn't sound like himself, he sounded as if he truly was having a mental breakdown. This situation kept getting more dangerous.

"What have you been thinking about?" she asked, trying to keep it light.

"I realized you coming here wasn't so bad," he told her. "You do tend to mess things up, but we've always had a connection from the moment I saw your picture in your dad's shit. I knew I'd know you one day, and I had to have you here. At first, I was happy about it, but then you messed it up." The way he said this made Keera's stomach turn, bringing bile into her throat. She prayed to keep it down. Now wasn't the time to throw up. She could break down later.

"Yes, we have a connection," she said instead, keeping the wince from her tone.

"But you forgot all about me the minute Arden took an interest in you," he snapped. "And you wouldn't quit digging into things you had no business digging into!"

His words shocked her. She knew he wasn't the biggest fan of Arden, but she didn't understand why he was this bitter about it. He continued speaking before she could think of something to say.

"If Arden hadn't taken an interest in you, none of this would be happening. They would have never found the drugs, never found the link," he said.

"I'm sorry, Ethan. I'm sorry I became friends with Arden." She couldn't look at the man as she said this. Because it was in no way true. "I don't need to be friends with him anymore. It can go back to you and I."

No one said anything as she made this false promise, and she was glad for that. She didn't need to look into their faces to see they were most likely as irritated as she was at having to talk so nicely to this man who didn't deserve it.

"It doesn't matter anymore. You went too far, and now I have to pay the price for it," he said, still not willing to take any of the responsibility on his own shoulders.

"Nothing has gone too far. I'm sorry. I'll make it right," she told him.

The phone went dead again, and Keera's heart sank. He sounded as if he'd made his decision to go ahead with whatever he was going to do.

She hadn't helped at all. She might have even made it worse, reminding him of how angry he was with her, of how upset he was.

"The kids," she gasped.

Noah looked at her and nodded. "We have to send the team in now. He's left us no choice."

Keera felt tears well again. If the SWAT team went in, there was more likely a chance of someone getting hurt or killed. She'd failed, and now the burden of those deaths would be on her shoulders.

"You did your best. It's hard to reason with someone that far gone," Noah said. "You did better than any of us could have."

She appreciated that he was trying to help ease her guilt, but she didn't think anything could at this point.

"If anything happens to the kids," she said, fighting down her hysteria.

"We will bring them home," Noah assured her.

The SWAT team got into position.

But before they could move forward, the front door of the school opened. Keera's body tensed as several snipers aimed their rifles toward the door. It took a moment, and then the three girls who always studied together while waiting for the football team to get out of practice came running through the doors, their sobs echoing through the parking lot as the SWAT team ran to them, quickly shielding them from the door as they escorted them to safety. The girls were quickly questioned, being asked if anyone else was in there. They assured them that only Ethan was left.

"Let him surrender," Keera begged. She owed this man nothing, but she knew if the team went in, Ethan had no chance of coming out alive.

But before the decision could be made, Ethan stepped out the front doors. He held a small gun in his hand, pointing it at the ground as he stood there looking out at the activity in the school parking lot. She wondered if he was aware it was all because of him.

She wasn't close enough to see into his eyes, couldn't tell what he was thinking or feeling. He said nothing as he looked around. No one said anything to him, but all eyes were on the man, on the hand that held the gun, waiting to see if he was going to do a suicide-by-cop, or if he was going to surrender.

When several tense seconds had gone by, a voice called out for Ethan to drop his weapon and move forward with his hands up.

Keera had her answer about what was going to happen next when his lips twitched up in an eerie way as his eyes scanned the crowd. He seemed to be searching for someone. When his eyes met hers, she knew it had been her.

He raised his arm, the gun pointed straight at her. She was so shocked she didn't even think to move. Arden, on the other hand, was much faster.

He quickly pulled her behind him, facing Ethan as another shout called out for Ethan to drop the weapon. Keera couldn't see, but she was very aware of three gunshots going off.

Arden's arms were wrapped around her, and she felt his entire body tense, and fear rushed through her. Had Ethan shot him, trying to get to her?

"We're okay, Keera. We're okay," Arden said. His voice sounded as if it were coming through a tunnel. It took a long while for the words to process in her foggy brain.

They were okay. But activity was moving around them, and she knew one person wasn't. She knew Ethan was dead.

She was dazed as she pulled away from Arden. She couldn't even look at him right now, couldn't look at anyone. She turned instead and looked at the place by the front door where Ethan's still body lay. She took a step in his direction but was stopped.

"Don't go there," Arden told her.

She wanted to shake him off, but she knew if he didn't stop her, others would. A couple of the SWAT team members were already at

Ethan's prone body, kicking the gun away from him and checking his pulse. They knew he was gone, but they still had to check. The guys turned and nodded, and the ambulance workers walked slowly to Ethan and covered him.

This was a crime scene and a lot of work had to be done. This would haunt their school for years to come. Ethan had gotten his glory, and maybe that's exactly what he had intended.

And with Ethan dead, she might never get answers. This nightmare might not ever end. She didn't want to have that thought during this tragic time, but she'd just witnessed the deaths of two people in less than twenty-four hours. She was in shock.

"Take her home, Arden," Declan said. It was odd how all of their voices sounded so far away. "She's going down . . ." was the last thing she heard before blessed darkness took her away.

Chapter Thirty-Three

Keera had snapped back to reality, finding herself cuddled up in Arden's arms. She'd felt foolish she'd allowed the stress to pull her under, but she'd told him she was fine and asked to be let down.

He'd done what she'd requested, but then he'd put his arm around her as he led her to his vehicle and drove her home. They hadn't spoken as they made the short trek to his house, and when he'd tried taking her to his room, she'd told him she wanted to be alone.

He hadn't wanted to give her that, but she'd asked him to respect her enough to listen to her. That had done the trick, and he'd allowed her to go into her room and shut the door. She hadn't slept much that night.

She should have known something was off, should have seen what Ethan was doing, what he was bringing into her school. The guilt weighed heavy on her shoulders. She'd grown complacent in her life with her father out of it. But after growing up with drugs and crime, she should have been the first to know something was off when she'd come to Edmonds.

Maybe she'd just been living in denial for so long, it was the only way she knew how to live. Kicking herself repeatedly wasn't going to help. What she had to do was once again pick up the shattered pieces of her life and try to figure out how to have some sort of normalcy. One thing she knew beyond a shadow of a doubt was that she wasn't going to get it by living in this alternate reality with Arden.

It was time to go home.

Her apartment didn't have much in it, but she'd started over once before, and she could do it again. This time, though, she was older, and much wiser. Or at least she felt she was.

She stepped into Arden's living room after she'd packed her bags with the clothes his family had brought her. She wouldn't walk out without talking to him first.

Arden was standing by the window, his back to her. She stopped and enjoyed the view of him for a few peaceful seconds. He truly had been good to her, and she knew he wasn't going to like her leaving, but Ethan had been killed, and her father was in no way a threat no matter what he had planned.

The problem was, they didn't know who else was involved. But they might never know. Their biggest leads had both died before they could say anything. And there was no way Keera was going to live in fear for the rest of her life.

The worst part of all of it was not knowing the story of her brother's death. She didn't think she'd ever get answers to any of it, and that wasn't something she wanted hanging over her forever. But even if it was, she couldn't impose on Arden indefinitely, not when she knew he wanted more than she was capable of giving.

"You seem to be in deep thought," she said as she approached Arden.

He turned to face her, but she was well aware he'd already known she was there. He would have been a nightmare to play hide-and-seek with because he always seemed to know when someone was around.

"A lot's happened lately, and especially in the past two days. I've been going over it and over it in my mind, trying to see where the connections are," he told her. "You didn't sleep well," he pointed out.

"Yeah, I have circles over my circles now," she said, rubbing at her eyes. She hadn't even bothered with makeup. It was no use at this point, and she didn't have to be anywhere. She'd have to try to fix it before school in two days.

"You're still beautiful," he told her, making her heart beat a little faster. It was so strange how much this man affected her. She would miss that. If she were being honest with herself, she'd miss a lot about him.

"I'm a mess, but I'll live with it," she said with the semblance of a smile.

"This isn't over yet, Keera," he told her, his body tense. "I know you're growing restless, and I know you have a need to get out of here, but I can feel in my gut that this isn't over. You can't be on your own right now."

She sucked in her breath, unable to let it back out again. "I wish you wouldn't say that. I have to keep living, or whoever has tried to scare me other than Ethan is winning in this game they're playing," she told him. "I refuse to be bullied into dancing to a tune for their entertainment."

"It's not about letting them win or lose, it's about being smart. Please just give me a little longer to get this solved. Declan is collecting more leads. We're so damn close."

"Arden," she began with a sigh, and he held up his hand to stop her.

"We just need a little more time," he said.

"I think you believe this is solvable, that there's always an answer. But sometimes in life, bad things happen and we never get to know why. Children die when there's no reason behind it, vehicles fail and crash for no reason, and people get murdered without ever having a killer found. We might just need to accept that our biggest leads are both dead and we don't get to know why there was a file on me and my brother, and why things happened the way they did."

If she resigned herself to thinking this way, then she didn't feel as out of control. If she believed like he did, then she was disappointed every time they didn't get what it was they'd been trying to find.

He opened his mouth to respond when his phone rang. He looked at the caller ID, then looked at her apologetically. "It's my brother. I need to take this."

She waited as he answered the call, then tensed. He was silent as he listened to whatever his brother was telling him, but the tension in the room had gone up by several degrees. Keera didn't want to know what the call was about, didn't think there was any further bad news she could handle.

But even as she had that thought, she realized there really wasn't anything more that could happen to her. There weren't any other people in her life with the power to hurt her, at least not emotionally. Of course, they could kill her, but that was out of her hands.

Arden hung up the phone and turned to her. Tension flowed through his big, beautiful shoulders, but determination shone in his eyes. He stepped toward her, and though Keera wanted to retreat, wanted to protect herself from the feeling his touch would give her, she wouldn't keep running—and that included running from this man. Moving home wasn't a retreat, it was reclaiming what was already hers.

Arden stopped in front of her, reaching out to her, his hands gentle on her shoulders. "I don't want to hear about the call," she told him.

He smiled. "That was Declan, as you probably figured out. It's not a big deal, but we need to go and check something out," he told her.

"I think you're sugarcoating it, because you're pretty tense right now."

He smiled again, the first genuine smile she'd seen on him in a while. They hadn't had a heck of a lot to smile about in the last few days.

"You're beginning to read me as well as I can you," he told her.

"Yeah, I've noticed that," she admitted. Her thoughts and feelings grew so jumbled when he was this close, when he touched her. She didn't like it one bit.

"I love you, Keera," he said, almost seeming as shocked at saying it as she was at hearing the words.

Her heart fluttered at the words as emotions choked her throat. But she couldn't allow these emotions in. She couldn't trust love, not at this point in her life. Her father had told her he loved her, too, and his actions had contradicted his words.

No, Arden had done nothing but be great to her, but they'd also been living in this heightened world since they'd known each other. There was no way for them to know if any of this was real—or if any of it could last.

"I can't stay here anymore," she told him, fighting back tears. "I can't do the love thing again. I just . . . I can't," she said, pleading with him to understand. She didn't want to hurt him. And she'd be doing exactly that if she didn't let him know now that they weren't going to ride off into the sunset together.

She expected anger, or even distance, but Arden simply looked at her and smiled as he lifted his hand to her cheek and gently caressed her.

"I didn't mean to blurt that out. I know this is bad timing, and I know you need time. And I'll give you all of it that you want. Just know I'm not easy to dissuade," he said.

He leaned down and kissed her cheek, making her heart ache that much more. Then he let her go and stepped back. She wanted to run to her room, grab her bag, and scramble out the door. But he was leaving, and she could follow after he was gone and not have to face a big fight over it.

"Angela's on her way here. Please wait until I get back. We don't have to talk tonight. I don't expect you ever to come to my bed unless it's what you want. But I truly am worried for your safety. Please let me check out this lead, and all the rest can be sorted through later."

He didn't ask much from her. She could give him one more night. Maybe she even needed to make love to him one more time—a fitting goodbye. She wasn't sure if that would help or send her further out of control. She didn't know if she'd find out or not.

"Okay," she said. "I'll wait until you get back."

"Thank you."

He and Max turned and walked from the house, and Keera had to fight back tears as she walked to the window and watched him drive away. She'd given him her word that she wouldn't go anywhere, and she had her integrity clearly in place, even if she didn't have much else. So though her heart felt as if it was breaking over and over again, and though she wanted to run far and fast, she didn't.

Keera sat down and waited for Angela. The two of them could wait for Arden to get back. Each time he went out on something like this, Keera was a mess. If he got hurt trying to help her, she wasn't sure she could forgive herself.

Yes, Arden was a grown man and more than capable of making his own choices. But if she had never come to this town, he wouldn't be in danger all the time.

He loved her.

His softly spoken words played on repeat in her head. She tried telling herself they were just words, that they didn't matter. But each time she closed her eyes and heard the echo of his voice saying them, her heart beat a little faster.

She was truly afraid she loved him back. Even if she wasn't sure what that word meant, even if she didn't feel she was capable of loving someone or being loved. Arden had made running away that much harder.

Angela arrived, and they visited for a little while before she insisted on making Keera something to eat. She said if she didn't feed her, she had no doubt Keera would live on nothing more than coffee. Keera couldn't even argue with her, as the woman was 100 percent right.

Keera went into Arden's office and looked over all the notes they had lying out as she tried again to make sense of all that had been happening. Staring at the papers, praying to see something she hadn't seen before, she gave up after a while.

There was a crashing noise from somewhere in the house, which instantly worried Keera.

"Are you okay, Angela?" she called. But there was no answer.

Dread ran up and down Keera's spine. Something was definitely wrong. She crept out of the office, looking both ways before going down the hallway.

She didn't call Angela's name again. There was something inside her telling her all wasn't well. She should be lifting her phone, calling Arden, but she'd been through a tremendous amount of stress lately, and she assured herself she was doing nothing more than overreacting. She was sure the noise she'd heard had been from Angela puttering around in the kitchen.

And though that's exactly what she wanted to believe, she felt herself trembling as she neared the kitchen. She couldn't hear a sound, which didn't bode well for Angela. The woman wasn't known for being quiet while she was cooking. She loved loud music and danced her way through a meal, telling them the food turned out so much better when the cook did a few dances while preparing it.

Telling herself she'd made a promise to face her fears, Keera pushed open the door that led to the kitchen. Then she froze.

She should have paid more attention to her instincts and not just barged into the room. Angela was on the floor, facedown, her eyes closed. Keera wasn't even sure if she was still alive.

Standing over her friend was a man dressed fully in black, not a single thing about him on view, nothing to help identify him. He looked up, giving her no idea what his expression was. But what she did notice was the deadly looking black gun he held in his hand, the one that lifted as he realized she was there.

Keera wanted to help Angela, but she had to get away from this man and make a phone call if either of them had the slightest chance. She didn't let out a single sound as she turned and sprinted away from the kitchen, seeking the best place to hide.

She heard heavy footsteps behind her and knew the man was practically breathing down her neck. She really wished Max was there with her now instead of having gone with Arden. She could use the dog a hell of a lot more.

She turned down a hallway when someone grabbed her hair, stopping her from moving forward. Though she'd fight to the death, Keera had a feeling her time was up, that Arden had been right. She had a feeling she wasn't going to get lucky this time.

Chapter Thirty-Four

Keera hid beneath a desk in Arden's house, for once grateful for the size of the place. She knew she couldn't hide much longer, had to go check on Angela, but she'd barely managed to get away from her potential killer, and she needed a few minutes to clear her head to figure out what to do next.

Would Arden come back in time? Could she save herself and Angela? Or was Angela already dead? This man wanted something from her, even if that was simply to kill her. She should have listened to Arden, shouldn't have buried her head in the sand and thought it would all work out.

But she was apparently no safer in Arden's house than she'd been in her own place. This man had penetrated Arden's fence, and he'd come straight into the house. She wanted to know who he was, what he was doing there.

"Keera, come out, come out, wherever you are," the man called, his voice a taunt. She shivered as she fought back the overwhelming fear.

As her life hung in the balance, she realized on so many levels what a fool she was. She might never get to see Arden again, might not get to apologize to him. He'd shown her so much kindness, and she knew in that moment that he was real, that what he said was real. She knew she loved him, but he might never know that. She feared if she died on this night, he'd forever blame himself.

Instead of hiding, she should be looking for a phone, calling Arden, telling him she loved him and it wasn't his fault. She didn't think there was a chance of him making it back to the house in time.

The man sounded closer as he called out her name again, more anger in his tone instead of the taunting it had been for the past five minutes. He was growing frustrated at not being able to find her.

Then she heard him retreat, and she climbed out from under the desk and quietly snuck into the next room to find Arden's house phone. She heard a noise, like something being dragged, and froze when she heard the heavy breathing of the intruder too close for comfort.

"You have five seconds to come out or your little friend gets her throat slit," the man called.

All the blood in Keera's body went icy cold. He could be lying. Angela might already be dead. But Keera couldn't take that chance, couldn't play with another's life.

With terror clogging her throat, she stepped from the room and made her way down the hallway. The man was standing in the living room, holding Angela in front of him with a knife to her throat. He hadn't been bluffing. Keera could see Angela's chest moving in and out, and for now at least, she was alive.

"Please let her go. It's me you have a problem with," Keera said. He had to have knocked Angela out because she didn't move, didn't open her eyes, didn't try to get away from the man.

Keera prayed Angela would be saved from this, that she'd sleep through the entire event and wake up a little traumatized, but at least okay enough to get home to her child. If Keera thought it would help, she'd tell the man Angela was a mother—to please have mercy on her. But he didn't care. That might make it worse.

"You have something I want," the man said, not releasing Angela.

"Anything I have is yours," Keera assured him. There was nothing worth keeping—nothing other than human life—that wasn't replaceable.

She couldn't see the movement of his mouth, as the mask completely covered his face. She didn't recognize his voice, either, though she was trying to memorize every single detail about the man she could, just in case she somehow made it out of this alive.

"The necklace your brother gave you," he snapped. "You don't wear it, and it hasn't been anywhere you spend time." He was utterly frustrated. It appeared he'd been looking for this item for quite some time. But why? It wasn't of that much value. She was utterly confused.

She also knew exactly where it was, but she had no doubt the moment she gave it to him, he'd be finished with her and Angela. She tried figuring out how to delay this moment, hoping and praying Arden would soon be there.

"It's worth nothing," she told him.

"It's worth so much more than you can imagine. Is it worth her life, though?" he asked. She could hear the lust in his tone, how he wanted to plunge that knife into Angela and then her. He'd killed before. She had zero doubt about it. She also knew he would take her life the moment he was finished with her.

The only thing she could hope for at this point was to save Angela.

"I have it in my room," she said. "Let Angela go and I'll get it for you."

The man shoved Angela away from him, her still body crumpling to the floor. Keera was worried about her friend, but grateful when a slight whimper escaped Angela's mouth. She shifted as if trying to wake up, and Keera knew she had to get this man away from her.

"Let's go," he snapped.

Keera turned, knowing he was on her heels. She also felt a pinch of pain as he jabbed something against her back. She realized he'd put the knife away and was holding his gun again. The knife was terrifying and a horrific way to die, but the gun was so final. She didn't have a chance to fend him off with that weapon.

Stepping into her room, Keera went over to her purse and picked it up. She'd worn the necklace around her ankle for years. It had been the last thing her brother had given her. It had hurt too much to keep it next to her heart, so she'd worn it beneath her socks instead.

"Give it to me!" the man cried, growing more agitated.

"Why do you want a cheap necklace?" she demanded.

"You'll find out," he said.

Keera knew the second he held this necklace in his hands, he'd be done with her. One bullet to her head would solve his problems, making it impossible for her to tell anyone what he'd been after. Not that it would matter for her to tell anyone. It was just a stupid necklace, worth no more than a couple hundred bucks. Sure, that was a lot of money for a lot of people, but it wasn't an amount worth killing over.

His eyes were on her, the gun at his side. Keera made her move. She threw the purse in his face, shocking him. She then took off, planning on going around him. She managed to get out of the room. She was rushing through the living room, heading for the kitchen, when she felt his steely fingers wrap around her arm, halting her midstride. He'd recovered far faster than she would have imagined.

He slammed her head into the wall, and Keera's vision blurred as blackness threatened to take her under. She fought with everything she had not to give in to the darkness, even though that would give her a blessed escape.

She crumpled to the floor as she tried to keep herself awake, alert. She was losing on both counts. But she could see him dump the contents of her bag before he tore open the purse with his knife, crying out with triumph as his fingers wrapped around the thin gold chain with a heart attached to it.

The charm wasn't meant to be opened, but he took his knife and pried it apart, and much to Keera's surprise, a small piece of paper fell out. There was no way for her to see what was on it. The man laughed as if he'd found a priceless treasure.

He put the paper in a plastic bag and sealed it, then tucked it safely in his pocket before he turned his attention back to her as he raised his gun, aiming straight for her head.

"I have no further use for you," he said casually, as if this was just another day on the job. She could almost feel him smiling beneath his mask.

"Can I at least know why I'm going to die?" she asked.

There was no point in begging for her life. But she did believe in an afterlife, so she'd love to have the answer of her death before she went on to whatever came next for her. She wasn't sure she'd earned a ticket into heaven. She hoped so, but she was so far from perfect, it wasn't even funny.

"This is the code to a vault that holds a hell of a lot of money," the man said.

"What are you talking about?" She was so confused.

"Your brother found your dad. He stole a lot of money from him, was going to make sure you were taken care of. He messed with the wrong people, and it cost him his life," the guy told her.

"No, you're wrong," Keera said. She was trying to remember what her brother had said to her when he'd given her the necklace. It had been so long ago, and her brain was already fuzzy from the trauma she'd been through this night.

"I'd love to keep playing with you, but it's time for me to go," the man said. Even though he'd gotten what he'd come for and he could safely disappear, he took pleasure in taunting her in her last moments on this earth. His evilness knew no bounds.

She wished she'd made that call, or even written a quick note to tell Arden how she felt. It was too late now, far too late. She did look into the black material covering the man's eyes. She wouldn't weep, or beg.

She wanted to look down at his hand, wanted to see the moment his finger began pressing that trigger inward, but she wasn't giving him the satisfaction of looking away from his face. She didn't think he had a soul, didn't think it would be difficult for him to kill her, but this was her last moment, and she needed to be strong.

Instead of the bang of the gun, the earsplitting noise of vicious barking erupted in the room. She was gazing at her killer's face and saw instantly how his body tensed as he looked away from her to see Max racing across the room, straight for the man in question.

Arden called out from behind Max, his voice filled with fury. "Drop the gun now!"

Keera had never heard that steely edge to Arden's voice before, and it sent a shiver down her spine. She was so grateful to hear his voice, and Max's deadly growl.

The man in the mask stepped back, his gun wobbling as he tried to figure out where best to aim it. Was it at the dog about to rip his throat out, the man behind her, who Keera was sure was also holding a gun, or at his original target?

The man must be thinking he had one shot here.

A gun went off, the sound intolerably loud. She gazed at the man in front of her, waiting to see him crumple to the ground. But instead, his arm moved quickly as he took another step back, Max flying through the air at him.

The gun went off again, and Max let out a horrific cry. But he didn't stop. He jumped at the man, his teeth tearing into the killer's wrist, trying to stop him from using his weapon.

The man must have a steel resolve, and Max was obviously weak from his injury because the man shook Max off him, blood dripping from his fingers where Max had punctured his hand.

He lifted his gun again, pointed it at Keera. A round went off again, but this time she watched the man in front of her crumple to the ground, the deadly gun finally falling from his fingers.

Blood dripped from Max's shoulder, and tears streamed down Keera's cheeks as he belly-crawled over to her, laying his head in her lap.

"Please don't die," she sobbed, and she ripped off her shirt and placed the material over his wound, trying to help him.

That's when she turned and found Arden on the floor, blood spilling from his shoulder, almost in the same spot as Max's wound. Declan was holding a cloth over his brother's wound as he looked up at Keera.

"They will both be all right," Declan promised.

"You can't guarantee that," she cried, her words barely audible. She needed to go to Arden, needed to tell him how much she loved him, but she couldn't move, couldn't risk Max losing any more blood.

"Please, please don't die," she cried, her pain for both Arden and Max unbearable. "I can't lose either of you. I love you both so much," she said, her words a slur no one could understand.

Max whimpered as his tongue came out and he licked her leg. He was in so much pain, and still he was protecting her, still he was comforting her. She held the shirt tightly over his wound as the paramedics rushed into the room, two of them immediately going to Arden.

"Max needs help, too," she said as two more ran inside. "Please, please help him. He saved us," she begged. If they refused because he was a dog, *she* would pick up the gun and shoot someone.

But she didn't need to worry. They rushed to her side and immediately assessed Max's injury, speaking to each other as they talked into the mics, calling for two beds and Doc Evan. Max was a retired police dog, and he'd earned their respect.

"Thank you," she said, her attention going from Max to Arden and back again. She knew she couldn't leave either of them. She'd tried to guard her heart, and she'd failed miserably. It didn't matter how much she had to beg, she'd drop to her knees and grovel if that's what it would take, because she hadn't realized how alone she'd always been until one man and one dog had come into her life and saved her in more ways than one.

Chapter Thirty-Five

"Get Dr. Spence Whitman here fast!"

Those were the last words Keera remembered hearing after they arrived at the hospital and both Arden and Max had been rushed into rooms to be saved. She had no idea who Spence Whitman was, but she prayed he was the best, prayed this town loved Arden and Max enough to do all it took to save them.

Keera paced the waiting room for the next two hours as she impatiently waited for news. People came and went, and a crowd built up as the gossip chain spread and everyone heard what had happened.

Many tried talking to her, but she didn't want to talk, didn't want to explain anything. Declan didn't let her out of his sight, and her heart grew a soft spot for the hard man. He wasn't nearly as tough or uncaring as he wanted people to think. He also respected her enough to run interference, to tell the story again and again of what had happened so she didn't have to.

Keera wasn't normally a person to cry, but on this day it seemed she couldn't stop crying. So many tears had fallen, she was sure she was dehydrated. None of that mattered. She couldn't lose Arden or Max. The loss of either would be more than she could take.

Until this day, Keera had felt she could handle anything. There was so much she'd seen in her life, and she'd survived it all. But this was different. She'd thought she'd loved before, but now she realized she hadn't known what love was. How could she have known when she'd never been shown before?

It wasn't until she'd received the unconditional love from Arden, and yes, from a dog, that she truly understood what that word meant. Both Arden and Max had come back for her, something no one had ever done before. They hadn't abandoned her, and she now knew they never would. But because they'd been trying to save her, their lives were in jeopardy.

She waited and waited for news.

Finally, the doors opened, and Doc Evan, another large man, and a small woman holding a colored scrub hat in her hands, walked out. Keera's heart stopped as she waited to hear what they had to say.

Arden's parents and siblings surrounded Keera as the doctors approached, and she was so grateful they weren't going to leave her out of hearing the news.

"Hi, Juliana, Lucian." The man greeted Arden's parents before nodding at the rest of the group. He then zeroed his gaze in on Keera. "You must be Keera," he added with a smile. She looked at him blankly for a heartbeat or two.

"Uh . . . y-yes, I am," she finally said.

"He said your name a couple of times before he was put under," the man said. Then he stopped. "I'm sorry. I'm Dr. Spence Whitman, and this is Dr. Sage Whitman." He didn't elaborate, and Keera was too worried to wonder if they were related or possibly married.

"My husband is taking too long," Sage said, looking at Keera before turning to Juliana. "Arden pulled through perfectly. It wasn't an easy surgery, and a bone in his shoulder splintered, and a piece stuck in his heart, but we got it, and he's going to have a full recovery."

"Oh, thank you," Juliana said as she stepped forward and threw her arms around Sage and then Spence. "Thank you," she repeated, tears streaming down her face.

"You did good, bro," Kian said as he shook Spence's hand and then kissed Sage's hand. "When I knew I couldn't get in there, I wanted you."

"I think the hardest part of being a doctor is feeling so helpless as we stand by when it's someone we love on that table," Spence said, completely understanding what his colleague was saying.

"Yes, yes, it is," Kian said with a sigh.

"Keera, he'll be awake soon, and I think it's your face he's going to want to see," Spence said, a kind smile on his lips.

Tears poured down Keera's face. She was so grateful he was alive. "What about Max?" she asked as she turned her eyes to Doc Evan. She was so afraid they weren't talking about the dog because it hadn't ended well for him.

"I'm sorry," Doc Evan said, and Keera's heart sank. She was unbelievably happy to have Arden be okay, but the pain of losing Max overwhelmed her. Her face fell, and Evan grabbed her arm.

"No!" he said, shaking his head. "Max is fine." It took a moment for the words to sink in. "I'm apologizing for not saying something sooner," he assured Keera.

"Max is okay?" she asked, choking on her words. It was ridiculous how difficult talking had become this entire day.

"Yes, he's just fine, and Arden demanded the dog stay in his room before he went under for surgery," Evan said with a laugh. "He made sure to tell us Max is a hero, and a member of the police force, and should be treated as any other patient." The big grin told Keera he agreed.

"Thank you so much," Keera said. She threw her arms around Evan first, squeezing hard before giving a hug to Spence and Sage next. "Thank you," she repeated. Those words weren't enough, but it was almost more than she could manage to say with how tight her throat was.

Declan put his arm around her shoulders and squeezed. The gesture shocked her as she looked up at the big man who had a suspicious sparkle in his eyes. He blinked and it was gone, and she wondered if she'd imagined it.

"My brother is lucky to have you," he said. "So is Max."

Keera tried her best to pull herself together as she wrapped an arm around Declan and squeezed. He was so large her arm barely fit around the back of him so her hand could rest on his side.

"I'm the lucky one. They saved me, and I don't just mean tonight," she said.

Declan nodded, and Keera faced the doctors again.

"I want to see them both. I need to," she said. "But shouldn't his family go in first?"

Spence looked to Lucian and Juliana, who took Keera's hands and smiled. "You are a good girl," Juliana said as she leaned in and kissed Keera's cheek. The gesture was so motherly it sent more tears pouring from her eyes. No wonder Arden was such a wonderful man. He'd been raised by these parents who knew how to be parents, and he'd had siblings who would die for each other. She couldn't imagine what that would have been like.

She then felt another first in her life as a bit of jealousy crept in. She wanted his family, wanted to be loved like he was loved. She had to remind herself how strong she was because of the life she'd led. She could be thankful for that.

Before Keera could say anything, Juliana squeezed her hand again and continued speaking. "I have a feeling you're going to be family before too long. My son needs to see you. Go in and take care of him. We'll be right behind you."

Keera wasn't about to argue any further. She needed to be with Arden and Max. She wasn't going to feel better until she saw with her own eyes that they were both okay.

"Thank you," Keera told her.

"This way," Spence said as he held out his hand.

She took a step toward what she hoped was her future.

Chapter Thirty-Six

Arden wasn't sure if he was still dreaming when he opened his eyes, but if he was, he wouldn't mind staying in dreamland a little longer. Keera was sitting at his side, her soft fingers gently running over the top of his head, her cheeks red, her eyes worried.

He shut his eyes, then slowly opened them again, and this time, she was looking straight in his, and her lips wobbled as her fingers stilled and she leaned down, pressing her lips against his before she straightened up and gave him the smallest hint of a smile.

"You are exactly who I needed beside me," he told her. His shoulder no longer hurt, and he was thankful for the drugs they'd pumped into him, but he wanted to reach for her and found his hand not cooperating. She seemed to read his mind, and she leaned down, her hand running along his lower arm before her fingers wove through his.

"I'm here, I'm right here," she said, a love unlike anything he'd seen before shining in her eyes. He knew without her saying a word that they were going to be okay. They'd made it through this mess, and though he had a strong feeling it was nowhere near over, it didn't matter anymore, because the two of them were going to be together, and as long as they were, they'd be able to conquer anything.

"Are you okay, Keera? Did he hurt you in any way?" he asked. She definitely appeared as if she'd been crying for a long period of time, but she was in civilian clothes and didn't appear harmed. There were no bruises on her. Just the thought of that man hitting her sent Arden's heart rate monitor to beeping.

"I'm fine," she said. "I promise. You and Max got there and saved me," she said.

He let out a breath of relief, and his heart rate slowly began to lower just as a nurse ran into the room.

"We're good here," he told her. "Go away." Normally he was never rude, but he wanted to be alone with Keera right now.

The nurse wasn't offended, just checked his monitor real quick then exited.

"How's Max?" he asked. He was terrified to hear the answer. He'd been irritated with the dog from the moment his brother had dumped Max on him, but seeing how brave and loyal Max was to Keera had made him fall in love with the mutt without him even realizing it.

"He's right beside you, a hero like his partner," she said with a smile while she shifted out of the way.

He could see Max sleeping peacefully in the bed next to him. He'd demanded they do exactly that, but hadn't hoped they'd come through for him. He owed Spence a freaking trip somewhere for all he and the rest of the staff had done for him and Max.

"The last thing I saw before I was shot was Max lunging for the guy," Arden said. "I thought I'd lose him for sure."

"Me too," she told him. "He was shot, but they worked on him here. He's going to be okay. You both are," she said, before pausing and taking a deep breath. "We're all going to be okay."

"With you here beside me, I know we will," he said.

"I'm sorry I've held back from you, sorry I haven't trusted you sooner," she said.

He so desperately wanted to reach for her. It killed him that he couldn't.

She seemed to understand and gently lifted his hand, placing his palm on her cheek. He sighed his relief at feeling her soft skin beneath his fingertips.

"I love you," he said. "And you never have to apologize for feeling anything. You've gone through so much in your life, it amazes me who you are."

"I love you, Arden. I didn't even know what love was until you and Max. Now I know. And I love you so much I can't imagine losing you," she told him.

His heart filled with happiness. He'd known from the moment he'd looked into her eyes she'd realize they were meant to be together, but there was nothing like hearing her say it. Others had said they loved him before. His parents told him all the time, and so did his siblings.

But hearing the words from this woman who never spoke of love, who hadn't been properly loved before, meant so much to him. He wished he had the correct words to express it to her. But it was okay, because they had a lifetime to figure that out.

"You're going to be surrounded by love for the rest of your life," he assured her.

"Is that so?" she asked, more tears falling as she smiled at him.

"Yes, that's so."

There was no way he was proposing to her when he couldn't drop down on his knees so she'd know how much he worshipped her, but it was okay. She now trusted in his love for her, and in her love for him.

Max let out a whimper, and they both turned to see he'd woken up and was lying in the bed beside them, looking pathetic at being left out of this conversation. Keera laughed, and the sound was absolutely magical. She then tugged on Max's bed, bringing him closer, and locking her between them.

It was perfect. They were perfect. Keera kept one hand clasped in Arden's, and the other on Max's head. Their family was just beginning, and no matter where they were, as long as they were together, they'd be okay.

Epilogue

"Keera, we've found it," Arden said.

Keera looked up, finding Arden and Declan standing in the doorway, solemn expressions on their faces. She was curled up on the couch, Max at her side, his head in her lap, his favorite position.

"Are you sure?" she asked.

It had been three months since Ethan's death, and Arden's and Max's shooting. It had been three beautiful months, where she'd grown to love and trust so fully she couldn't imagine her life without Arden and his family in it.

But the weight of what had happened had been hanging on her shoulders that entire time, and she wanted more answers. She needed to be able to let go of her past, to have a fresh slate so she and Arden could marry and live their lives as normally as possible.

She was no longer afraid of shaming his family. His parents had accepted her with open arms, and even if she had felt inadequate, it was impossible to not feel loved as they embraced her, treating her as if she'd always been a part of their family.

"We're absolutely sure," Arden told her.

"What do we do now?" she asked.

"We see what people were so willing to kill for," Declan said.

Keera rose, making Max grumble. She apologized and gave him an extra scratch before she began moving toward Arden. She was ready to face whatever it was she needed to face as long as she had her man and dog by her side. Before she could say anything else, the front door crashed open. Both Arden and Declan turned, drawing their guns. Even after months of peace, it appeared they were all still jumpy.

"There's a forest fire," Owen shouted as he rounded the corner, not concerned with seeing two of his brothers armed.

"What are you talking about?" Arden asked.

"Where you two were earlier," Owen said, somewhat out of breath.

"Wait, near the vault?" Declan asked, his body tense.

"Yeah, we've all been called in," Owen told him. "But it's quickly getting out of control. This isn't a natural disaster. Someone set it."

Keera felt her blood run cold. "It's not over for me, is it?" she asked.

All three brothers turned to look at her before Arden holstered the weapon he must have forgotten he'd been holding, and quickly strode to her side.

"I don't think this has to do with you," he assured her.

"How can you say that? Since I've come here so much bad has happened," she told him.

"No, you've brought nothing but light to my world," he assured her. "I think this goes deeper than any of us could possibly know. But we will figure it out."

Declan looked at her, determination in his gaze. "Yes, we will, and you have nothing to worry about."

There was so much more to Declan than he allowed the world to see. She was grateful he'd chosen her as one of the people he let in.

"We can talk about the merits of who and what later. We need all hands on deck," Owen said. "I'm barely back a couple of months and someone's trying to burn down my town. Let's go."

When they stepped outside, they could see the haze in the distance where smoke was rising. This wasn't a small fire, and it wasn't going to be easily contained. It appeared as if the mysteries were continuing to unravel.

Keera looked at Arden as he gazed out at the horizon, his brows knit, worry in his eyes. Instead of tensing, she relaxed. They might not have all the answers they needed, but that didn't matter. As long as she was beside Arden, she was safe; she was where she needed to be.

"Go be a hero," she told him.

He looked down at her, so much love shining in his eyes it took her breath away. Then he leaned in and kissed her, still causing butterflies to dance in her belly.

"Hey, I'm the hero," Owen insisted as he tugged on his brother. "I'm the fireman."

"Every story needs its hero. I guess it's your turn," Arden said with a chuckle. He gave Keera another quick kiss, then the three brothers raced away.

Maybe the vault would burn and she'd never see what was inside it. Right now, she didn't even care. She had the love of her life, and she was free—free to live however she wanted. She'd gotten her happily ever after, even if she hadn't been seeking it.

ABOUT THE AUTHOR

Photo © John Evanston

Melody Anne is a *New York Times* and *USA Today* bestselling author whose popular series include Billionaire Bachelors, Surrender, Baby for the Billionaire, and Billionaire Aviators, along with a young adult series and other romance novels. She loves to write about strong, powerful businessmen and the corporate world.

Since finding her true calling, she has been an Amazon top 100 bestselling author for three years in a row. When not writing, Melody spends time with family, friends, and her many pets. A country girl at heart, she loves her small town and is involved in many community projects.